THE SPINNER SAGAS

THE TELLING

KJ MOULLEN

This book is dedicated to my family.

Mom, Dad, & Aunt Jan, thank you for believing in me & giving me that gentle shove that I needed.

Thank you to my husband & kids for sticking with me on this crazy journey we call life.

ACKNOWLEDGMENTS

Thank you to all who have contributed

Josh and Kim Pugh, Connie Cordoza, Dawn Warner, Gil Russell, Howard Smith, James Garwood, Jan Crosser-Cooke, Karen Durant, Larry Coker (El Cee), Melissa and Sandy White, Ashlin Stephens, Kavita Ganness, Lesley Garwood, Michele Roberts, Pattie Serbus, Raelyn Powers, Stacey Jones, Travis Trachta, Josh Canterbury with JCM Photography, & Lindsay Saenz with Vintage Teal Photography

CHAPTER 1

"Blaine! Blaine! Where are you?" The girl quickly turned toward the old A-frame home. Then she turned her attention back toward the babbling creek. "Blaine!" The voice came once again ripping through the serenity of the forest.

"Coming, Mom!" she shouted. Then with a heavy sigh she made her way back toward the house. Each step she took was painfully slow. As she got closer she could see her mom standing on the back porch. She was impatiently surveying the yard and surrounding forest. Her gaze then shifted quickly down to the watch on her wrist. Blaine cleared the forest and picked up her pace.

"Do you know what time it is young lady?" her mother demanded as Blaine climbed the steps to the porch. Before Blaine had a chance to answer the question, her mother continued, "You are going to miss the bus. Then I'll have to drive you to school and that's going to make me late for work. What were you doing out there anyway? Never mind. Come on, let's get a move on."

Her mother turned toward the door and pulled it open, motioning Blaine to enter. Blaine caught her mother's gaze and they locked eyes, "Sorry, mom," Blaine whispered apologetically.

Her mom's face quickly softened. "I know. I just want you to start being more responsible. You are old enough now that I shouldn't have to be holding your hand every step of the way."

"I'll try," Blaine mumbled hanging her head.

Her mom brushed a lock of dark hair away from Blaine's face and smiled. "Go get your things, the bus should be here any minute."

"Okay, mom." Blaine walked over to the hall table and picked up her backpack, which had been carelessly dumped the day before. She looked in the mirror with a sigh. She grabbed a hair clip that desperately hung at the bottom of her shirt, twisted her hair back, and secured it with the clip. She then wiped her sleeve across her mouth and went out the door.

She had just made it to the end of her grandmother's drive-way as the school bus approached and came to a screeching stop. The door swung open beckoning her to enter the dusty bus. As she made her way down the aisle, she scanned the blank faces of her classmates silently hoping to find an empty seat. Today she was in luck. She spotted one vacant seat. She sat down thankful to be spared the torture of mindless small talk with someone she really didn't care to get to know. The bus started with a jump and headed down the dirt road to the main highway.

Blaine stared out the window lost in her own thoughts of how antisocial she could be. It wasn't that she didn't consider getting to know others. Considering how frequently she and her mom moved, it just seemed to be such a waste of time. She was deep in contemplation when a flash that nearly blinded her interrupted her thoughts. Quickly turning toward the source, she saw a brilliant light and the figure of a man coming from the light's core. He seemed to emerge from the center for an instant. Then as quickly as he had appeared, he was gone. Blaine blinked in disbelief. She glanced around the bus to see if anyone else had seen the light and strange figure. But no one else seemed to have noticed. They were all still engrossed in their own conversations. Blaine sighed and sunk into her seat. *Okay, maybe mom is right. I do daydream too much. I'm starting to hallucinate.*

The bus droned on. Blaine closed her eyes, silently going over in her head what she had seen. By the time the bus reached the school, she convinced herself she had imagined the whole thing.

The bus unloaded in front of the high school. Blaine exchanged pleasantries with some passing students as she made her way to the front entrance. She then headed to the nearest bathroom. She pushed open the door. The room was crowded with girls primping and chattering. Blaine sighed and entered the buzzing room. She made her way to the sink, set her backpack down, turned the faucet on, and splashed water on her face. She patted her face dry with a paper towel. She then bent down and searched through her backpack for a moment. Pulling out her hairbrush, she turned toward the mirrored wall that was the main attraction for all the girls that entered the restroom. Blaine ran the brush through her hair trying to tune out the annoyance of giggles and gossip that came from the chattering circle of girls.

"Are those contacts?" She heard a voice say.

"What?" Blaine turned toward the girl who had approached unnoticed. "What did you say?" Blaine inquired again.

"Are those green contacts?" The girl standing next to Blaine asked again. The girl continued looking into the mirror as she spoke seemingly mesmerized by her own reflection.

"No, they are my natural eye color," Blaine replied, displaying a cautious smile.

"Cool, I've never seen eyes as green as yours. Your name's Blaine, right?"

"Yeah." Blaine answered, pausing a moment a bit embarrassed because she couldn't recall who this girl was. "I'm sorry; I don't know your name."

"I'm Jessica. We have chemistry together. You know, fourth period?"

"Oh, sure." Blaine quickly took the cue that she should know Jessica, but still didn't recognize her. "Sorry, being new ... so many faces and all."

"No problem." I've been the new kid on the block before." Jessica flashed a brilliant smile. "Do you live over at Sunset Court?"

"No, I live off Chestnut Road."

"Oh, did your parents buy land over there? There are some really cool hiking trails in that area." Jessica pulled out her lip gloss and began applying it.

"No, my mom and I live with my grandma."

"Cool." Jessica finished the final touches to her lips. She turned toward Blaine, and said, "Hey I got to go. But I'll see you around."

"Sure," answered Blaine, forcing a smile. Jessica grabbed her backpack and walked out of the bathroom. Blaine absently stuffed her brush into her backpack and then headed to her first period classroom.

Blaine's first class was at the far end of the campus. She quickly made her way down the main hall that opened into the commons area. As she crossed the crowded area she glanced out the glass doors at the front of the school. She stopped dead in her tracks. The man she had seen from the bus was standing in front of the doors. She felt he was looking directly at her. Again, he seemed to be engulfed in light. She really couldn't see his face, but she knew it was the same figure from earlier. She could feel him. Blaine's attention was diverted when a student accidentally bumped into her. She had only glanced away for a moment but when she looked back at the doors, the figure was gone.

An overwhelming sense of urgency and anxiety swept over

her. Her heart beat quickly. She took a deep breath as she glanced once more at the front door. She wanted to run. Why or where, she didn't know. It just seemed right. Feeling very confused, she made her way to her first class.

The day seemed to drag on. Blaine played the events of the morning in her head over and over again. She tried to convince herself that they were no big deal. Yet she had never felt anything like this before. As unsettling as it was, the experience made her feel more alive than she had ever felt in her life. The feeling both scared her and intrigued her. She tried to convince herself that what she saw was someone standing in the path of the sun. Why, then, couldn't she shake the feeling that there was more?

The last bell finally sounded. Blaine grabbed her backpack, hesitating a moment to decide if she needed anything from her locker. She didn't, so she headed down the hallway toward the buses. Both sides of the long corridor were lined with brightly painted lockers. The hallway was unusually quiet. As she passed fellow students she looked at their faces. They seem to be somewhat distorted. She realized that she was moving slower than everyone around her. She could see lips moving in conversation yet no sound reached her ears. Everything around her became blurred. She tried to run to the end of the hall, but her legs felt as if they had turned to lead. The walls became transparent and trees seem to emerge from nowhere. Blaine focused on the opening of the hallway that led to the commons. She tried to gather up every ounce of strength to keep her legs moving. As she approached the door to the commons she saw the walls give way, revealing a river landscape. Soon nothing of the school remained. The sensation of falling was so strong it caused her whole body to jump. Suddenly, she was back in the hallway.

Everything was back to normal. The chattering of passing teens once again filled the air. Normally an annoyance, the clamor was actually comforting, reassuring her she was safe. Eyes wide and a bit panicky, she quickly made her way down the hall into the commons and out the front door.

Blaine scanned the front yard of the school. The usual end-of-day drama unfolded before her. Blaine sat down on a bench and buried her face in her hands. Her mind was reeling. She remembered hearing that hallucinations could mean the presence of a brain tumor. She pulled her hands away from her face just in time to see her bus making its slow descent into the parking lot. She stood and headed toward the line of noisy teens waiting to load the past-its-prime, yellow-painted contraption.

CHAPTER 2

The ride home served to settle Blaine's nerves. She stepped off the bus feeling a bit more composed. She walked slowly down the familiar driveway. She felt more at ease with every step. Her grandmother met her on the front porch.

"Hi, hon. how was your day?" Her Grandma's face beamed warmly.

"Okay, I guess," Blaine mumbled as she brushed past her grandmother and walked to the door. Her grandma followed her into the house.

"Now that wasn't very convincing. You want to come into the kitchen and have some milk and cookies and tell me what happened?"

"Grandma, I'm not a child anymore. I'm sixteen," Blaine groaned. She rolled her eyes for effect.

"Okay, how about a Dr. Pepper and some cookies?" That brought a smile to Blaine's lips. She dropped her backpack in the entryway and headed toward the kitchen.

The afternoon sun filtered through the kitchen window creating a warm veil across the table where Blaine sat down.

She looked up at her grandmother as she crossed the kitchen with a plate of cookies in one hand and a soda in the other.

"So, what's got you so down, child?" Blaine's grandma questioned again.

Blaine hesitated a moment then proceeded. "I think there's something wrong with me."

"Now why would you say a thing like that?"

"There have been weird things happening to me."

"Oh?" Her grandmother commented as she took a drink of milk from her glass.

"Yeah, I was walking down the hallway this afternoon when everything became distorted. Then it seemed like the walls disappeared and, out of nowhere, I was near a river. It was kind of scary but it didn't last too long. I've also been seeing this strange burst of light. I think maybe I have a tumor or something." Blaine looked over at her grandmother. The color seemed to have drained from her face. "Grandma, you okay?"

"Yeah, just a little hot flash. I'm sure it's not a brain tumor or anything like that. When your mom gets home, tell her. She can make an appointment with the doctor just to ease your mind." She reached across the table and squeezed Blaine's hand warmly. "It'll be just fine."

Blaine finished her cookies. "I'm going to go upstairs and do some homework."

"Okay dear. I'll call you when dinner is ready."

Blaine pushed away from the table and walked over to where her grandmother sat. She bent down and gave her a kiss on the cheek. "I love you, Grams."

"I love you, too."

Blaine recovered her backpack from the entryway and headed upstairs. As she slowly climbed the stairs she realized how drained she felt. Maybe she would rest her eyes for a little while.

Sleep sounded very enticing at this moment. She reached the top of the stairs. With each step she took, she felt more exhausted. She entered her bedroom and closed the door behind her. She flopped onto her bed, and in minutes was fast asleep.

She had that falling sensation again. It stopped abruptly. The scene shifted to her running in a forest. She seemed to know every twist and turn of the path she was on. The forest seemed to be different than any she had ever seen before. The colors were deeper and richer. Everything seemed to be covered with a brilliant sheen. As she kept running she felt as though her feet were not touching the ground. A sense of urgency suddenly overcame her, paralyzing every fiber of her body. Pain followed. Tears began pouring down her cheeks. She was now having difficulty breathing as sharp pains shot through her lungs. With every breath she took she felt as though her soul was being ripped from her body.

Blaine awoke with a jolt. She sat straight up in bed. Drenched in sweat, she struggled to catch her breath. When she realized she was in the safety of her room she let out a sigh of relief.

"Just a dream." She spoke to herself hoping the sound of her voice would calm her heart and keep it from pounding out of her chest. The bedroom had grown dark with shadows. The last beacon of sunlight was now a mere glimmer across the horizon. She could hear muffled voices coming from downstairs. She lay on her bed a moment longer, collecting herself. Her legs felt shaky as she stood up. She felt like she really had been running through a forest.

She walked to the door. As she opened it she could now make out the voices coming from downstairs. It was her mother and grandmother. Blaine started down the stairs but stopped halfway. She heard her name mentioned but couldn't make out the rest. She continued down the stairs and sat on the last step so she could hear the conversation without being noticed.

"You knew this time would come sooner or later," Her grandma's voice came across calm and comforting.

"I know, mom. I was just hoping the precautions I took when she was younger were strong enough to protect her. I'm her mother; it is my job to protect her. I honestly thought after all this time they would've given up, plus, I didn't think they possessed the resources anymore to find us."

"How do you know it's them that are reaching out? Maybe it's her ... "

"No, that's not possible. There's just no way! No one knows how to do anything like that without being taught!" Blaine's mom cut her grandmother off quickly.

"Now Sairah, you're not letting Blaine choose. This is too important to keep from her any longer. You're making her choice for her. You're assuming what she wants. Trust her with what she needs to know."

Blaine couldn't believe her ears. What were they talking about? *What choice?* She couldn't sit there any longer without saying something. Standing up, she made her way into the kitchen. "I think you should give me the option to choose, mom."

They both quickly turned toward Blaine and stared at her blankly. Blaine's grandma turned back to Sairah. "Tell her. She deserves to know." Her grandma stood up and walked to Blaine. Kissing her on the forehead, she said softly, "Blaine, I love you. I've always told you how special you are. Just remember how much you are loved."

"Mom?" Blaine turned her attention to her mom. Sairah's radiant beauty, which Blaine had always admired, was now diminished. The concern and stress that showed in her eyes almost made her look old.

"Blaine, honey, come and sit down. We need to talk." Blaine

walked over to the kitchen table and sat down across from her mother. Sairah continued, "I have played this conversation over and over again in my mind trying to find the perfect way of telling you. I hardly know where to start." As Sairah spoke she subconsciously ran her finger around the rim of her coffee mug. "We're not originally from here. When I first came here I was pregnant with you."

Blaine interrupted her mom, "Not from here? What do you mean?"

"Please, Blaine," continued her mother. "Let me finish what I need to tell you. Then I'll try to answer all your questions, okay?" Sairah took a deep breath and continued, "I originally came from a place called Renault. In Renault, time and dimensions are different than here ... People can do things that you would consider ... magical, but in Renault they are everyday occurrences."

Blaine raised her eyebrows with that statement. Questions filled her head, but she sat in silence as Sairah continued.

"I am not going to get into a whole lot of detail. That would just complicate things. What you need to know right now is that there are people from Renault that would like to find me and take me back. I don't want that to happen. That's why we have moved around so much. I've tried to keep so much hidden because I did not want to put you in harm's way. But it would appear I didn't do such a great job. They seem to have located us anyway."

Blaine sat silent for a moment avoiding her mother's gaze. Finally, deciding to lock eyes with her mother, she asked, "Who are they and how did they find us?"

"That's what I'm unsure of. They used to have a network in place that allowed them to communicate; however, I believed it is obsolete." Sairah frowned a bit as if searching for the right words. "There are people that can sense or recognize those of us from Renault. These people are referred to as Tellabouts. Some of them originally came from Renault. Others were ... 'touched.' "

"Tellabouts." Blaine laughed at the word. "That sounds like something from a child's fairytale. What do you mean by 'touched'? Are you talking about psychics and fortunetellers?"

"Yes, sort of. It's all very complicated. Before I left Renault I was lead to believe that all communications with Earth was impossible, but I could never be one hundred percent sure of that. I don't want to tell you all of the details. Knowing too much may do more harm than good. The less you know the better."

"I don't think so!" exclaimed Blaine. "All this affects me just as much as it does you. You can't just tell me we are from somewhere else and that people are looking for us to take you back, and then leave it at that. For all I know you're telling me we are from outer space and the mother ship is hovering somewhere over area 51. Come on mom, this is all very surreal. You're saying people with magical powers are out there tracking you down. I deserve to know everything." Blaine could feel her temper flaring out of control. All of her anger was directed toward her mother. She needed to know more!

"Blaine, calm down. Getting upset isn't going to solve anything."

Blaine took a couple of deep breaths. She looked at her mom. Sairah sat there calm and emotionless as if she were in control of the whole situation.

"If you aren't prepared to share everything, at least answer a few questions. If you came here when you were pregnant with me, Grandma must have been with you, or is she not really my grandma!" It came out more of a statement than a question.

Dismay flashed across Sairah's face. "She is a link, a contact. She knows of our world. She took me in and treated me like her own. She loves you so much. You know that. If not for her, we wouldn't be here today. We owe her everything." She needed Blaine to never question her grandmother's love.

Blaine got up and stood in front of the picture window that overlooked the backyard. The sky was now dark. The light from the kitchen cast an eerie glow on the lawn and surrounding forest. Her mom came up behind her and put her hand on her shoulder. "I know it's a lot to absorb and understand right now."

Blaine's only thought at the moment was to get away from her mom. "I'm going to my room." Blaine turned and stormed up the stairs. She felt very betrayed, angry, and confused. She felt that the life as she knew it was a lie. Her mom's unwillingness to tell her the whole story fueled her anger. She stretched across her bed and stared at the ceiling. So many questions were running through her head.

After a while she heard a light knock on her door. It slowly opened.

"Blaine, may I come in please?" Her mom didn't wait for an answer as she hesitantly walked in. She took a seat on the edge of the bed. "You're not crazy. The things that have been happening to you ... someone is trying to contact you."

Propping her head up with her hand, Blaine raised her eyebrows in a questioning manner. "What do you mean contact me?"

"The things you have been experiencing happened because someone from Renault has been trying to contact someone in this dimension. When that happens, a dimensional disturbance occurs. This disturbance also happens when someone is trying to cross over, but only Sensitives can pick up on that."

Blaine just stared at her blankly. "I bet that man I saw was trying to cross over." Blaine mumbled under her breath.

"What do you mean? What man? You never said anything about a man to your grandmother." Her tone was one of alarm.

"He seemed to have been there each time one of those 'disturbances' happened." Blaine made quotation marks in the air when she said disturbances.

"What did he look like?" Asked her mom as she turned her entire body to face Blaine.

"I'm not really sure. I mean I really didn't see him. It is more as if I felt him. Does that make sense?"

"Yes," Sairah whispered. She closed her eyes. Blaine noticed her mom's breathing had become very shallow and irregular.

"Mom what's wrong? You okay?" Blaine sat up.

Sairah took a deep breath and opened her eyes. For a few seconds, they sat there in silence.

"Mom, please explain what is happening," Blaine pleaded. She needed to know more. "Is someone from Renault trying to contact me?"

As she spoke the word Renault, it seemed to reverberate and grow louder and louder. Then a blast exploded from the room out into the evening.

Blaine and Sairah looked at each other, dumbfounded by what had just happened. Sairah stood up and quickly rushed down the stairs with Blaine close behind. The lights were flickering as a dull murmur resonated throughout the house. When they reached the bottom stair Blaine called out to her grandmother.

"In the kitchen," her grandmother called back. Sairah and Blaine entered the kitchen. Blaine's grandmother was holding on to the kitchen countertop for dear life. "What in the world was that?"

"I don't know for sure," answered Sairah. "It appears to have been the result of Blaine saying the word Renault! To have such power she would have to ... " Sairah's voice trailed off into silence.

"I would have to be what, Mom?" Blaine insisted.

"Nothing! We'll talk about it later," snapped Sairah.

Blaine did not pursue her mother's ill attempt to avoid the question. Her head was already swimming.

Sairah composed herself quickly as always, desperately trying to convince herself that it really was nothing.

The flickering of the lights had ceased and the low-frequency murmur gave way to the silence of the night. Nothing more was said about Renault. Blaine sat down at the kitchen table and watched in utter amazement as her mother and grandmother moved about the kitchen preparing dinner as if nothing had happened.

Blaine sat there, wondering about her mother's past. *From what was it she was so desperately trying to escape?* Her thoughts continued. This new revelation gave possible answers to questions Blaine had pondered as far back as she could remember. She never seemed to fit in at school. Her mother refused to let Blaine take an exit exam at fourteen, which would have allowed her to enroll in college. Blaine's guidance counselor, instead, had to be satisfied with Blaine skipping two grades. Blaine was a senior at sixteen.

Sairah was adamant about not calling attention to herself or Blaine. Was it possible Blaine's aptitude for school was based on far more than she had known? Her mother's words *not from this place* echoed in her mind.

Blaine's thoughts were interrupted when her mother asked her to set the table for dinner. As they ate together a feeling of normalcy lingered for a brief moment. Somehow Blaine knew this feeling would be impossible to maintain. Blaine could feel the winds of change coming. She could see it in the great sorrow reflected in her mother's eyes.

In her mind's eye, she looked back at that evening as a photographic still of another lifetime—a lifetime of normalcy, remembered and cherished, but never again to be experienced.

CHAPTER 3

The early morning light seeped through the cracks in the curtain that had been carelessly drawn the night before. Blaine lay motionless in her bed deep in thought. Sleep hadn't come to her the night before. She played in her head over and over her conversation with her mother. Questions and an overwhelming curiosity now filled her thoughts. She took a deep breath and rolled over trying to avoid the encroaching sunlight that now threatened to invade her solace amid the darkness. She lay there with her eyes closed wishing the daylight away when she heard movement outside her bedroom door. As she strained to listen she heard the doorknob to her room click in protest as it was slowly turned. The door opened and a figure stepped into her room.

"Blaine?" Her mother's voice floated across the room.

"Yeah—what's wrong?"

"Get up and get dressed. We have to go." The urgency in her mom's voice was only too evident.

"Go? Go where?" Blaine questioned.

Sairah crossed the room to Blaine's dresser and started shoving clothes into a backpack. She looked up from her packing. "I will answer your questions later. Now get dressed and wear your hiking boots. We'll make way through the forest."

Blaine quickly got out of bed. She was puzzled not only by her mom's actions, but by her speech. She had only heard her mom speak with this dialect when she was angry or extremely upset. In an effort to lighten the moment, Blaine laughed as she mimicked her mom, "We'll make way."

Sairah looked back at her daughter. A sliver of light shown across her face as their eyes met. Instantly, Blaine knew that this was not the time for humor. It was time to go.

They crept quietly down the stairs. At the foot of the stairs Sairah picked up another bag, slung it over her shoulder, looked back at her daughter, and gave her a shy smile. Holding a finger to her lips, Sairah signed for her not to say a word. Blaine followed her mom in silence out the back door.

They stepped onto the back porch. The sky had taken on a grayish tint as night reluctantly gave way to the light of the rising sun.

This time of day always reminded Blaine of the eternal battle of good versus evil. Her mind wandered to the times she had tried to express her ponderings to her mom. Just recently Blaine had tried to engage her mom in a conversation by asking her if she thought good could exist without evil. As usual her mom told her that she thought too much. "Why can't you think of normal teenage things like boys and makeup?"

She pushed these fleeting thoughts out of her mind as she followed Sairah across the backyard toward the woods. The trees looked very ominous in the dull dawn light. As they approached the beaten path that cut to the forest, Blaine paused. "Mom, wait. What about Grandma?"

"She'll be fine. It is better for her not to know where we're going."

"I don't understand any of this. Why can't we just take the car?"

"Blaine, please trust me. It'll be safer this way. I promise all your questions will be answered later, but for now we have to get away!" Her mother abruptly turned and began briskly walking deeper into the woods. Blaine stood for a moment before she took off running to catch up to her mom.

The sun began to make its presence known with every step they took. The dew on the moss and leaves reflected the morning light. Blaine's mind began to wander. *Maybe they weren't drops of dew at all, but little gems left by some absent-minded fairy. How lucky to have this beautiful forest as a playground.* Blaine smiled to herself. She could almost see the fairies peeking out from behind the underbrush waiting impatiently for the intruders to leave so they could resume their play.

The sound of a breaking twig brought her out of her daydream. Her gaze shifted to her mother. Sairah's hair was pulled back into a tight ponytail. The morning sunlight danced off the red highlights forming a halo effect. She wore a sweatshirt and loose-fitting jeans. Blaine marveled at the perfection of her mother's form. Her movements were graceful and effortless. She made her way through the forest like a jungle cat, seemingly possessing knowledge of every tree and bush. *I, on the other hand,* Blaine thought, *make my way clumsily through the world like a clown wearing oversized shoes.* She was tall for her age, which contributed to her feelings of awkwardness. She viewed herself as a misfit on so many levels. Blaine had decided long ago that she must look like her father because she didn't resemble her mother in any way.

Blaine was still lost in her thoughts when she bumped into her mom. "Why did you stop? What's wrong, mom?"

Sairah was frozen in her tracks. She whispered so softly that

Blaine could hardly hear her. "Blaine, get out of sight," Blaine locked eyes with her mother. Fear flashed across Sairah's face. Blaine felt an uneasy feeling creep into her stomach. Without questioning her mother, she quietly stepped off the path and crouched down under some tall brush. Sairah, moving farther down the path, was soon out of sight.

Blaine remained motionless, straining her ears to hear anything. Suddenly the air seemed to grow heavier with every breath she took. Her senses became heightened. The breeze that earlier was gently blowing through the forest was now pelting her skin with agonizing force. The previously calming sounds of chirping birds and the babbling brook became deafening. The early morning sunlight suddenly became devastatingly bright and felt as though it was piercing her retinas. Blaine covered her ears and squeezed her eyes shut to try to block the invasion of her senses, but to no avail. She crumpled in pain, tears streaming down her cheeks.

Softly sobbing, Blaine lay in the bushes in a fetal position. Even the sound of her own voice brought blurring colors of pain to her whole being. Suddenly, blackness whirled around her, giving way to unconsciousness.

CHAPTER 4

A blossom from a nearby lilac tree fell effortlessly from the branch it once so proudly adorned. It bounced softly off Blaine's cheek. Then it danced gracefully and spun its way down to the ground. As it fell Blaine caught a brief whiff of its sweet aroma. Her lids felt like lead. Drawing from her inner strength, Blaine slowly opened her eyes. The stars shone brightly amid the dark sky, casting their silvery light upon her like a protective shield. She blinked a few times to gain focus and to acclimate to the darkness surrounding her. As her eyes adjusted she noticed an amber light that both engulfed her and kept her warm. She panned from left to right, trying to get some bearing on her surroundings until she located the light source; a fire burning somewhere to the right of her. Its warmth washed over her like a welcomed friend. She tried to turn her head to face the fire, but her muscles would not respond. Her breathing was shallow and labored. A sharp pain shot through her lungs as she attempted a deep breath. Once more darkness overcame her.

Blaine woke up with a jolt. The sky, still dark minus the silvery light of the stars that were now hidden behind a blanket of thick clouds. The fire she had felt before was now reduced to dying embers. With the limited glow, she strained to survey her new surroundings. Using her hands to push herself up into a sitting position, she discovered that she was on a soft blanket, perhaps made of cashmere or angora. Blaine froze as she came to the realization that she was not alone. Someone had placed her on this blanket. She remained motionless for a moment. Then ever so slightly she turned her head toward the remains of the once welcoming fire.

The best she could figure, based on the limited lighting, was that the fire appeared to be about nine feet away from her. A sudden spark of an ember provided just enough light to make out the figure of a man sitting on the far side of the dying fire. Fear overtook her. She once again studied the surrounding area, this time looking for a route of escape.

"It's probably best if you don't run off. I can't protect you out there." A peculiar voice shattered the silence of the night.

Focusing her attention in the direction of the voice, Blaine tried to discern the identity of this man who seemed to be able to read her mind and was claiming to be her protector. She sat motionless, straining to clear her mind of muddled thoughts so as to contemplate her next move. The first thing she noticed was that she couldn't identify where she was in the forest. Suddenly, her thoughts turned to her mother. Overcome by concern, she demanded, "My mother! Where is she?" The figure was not forthcoming. "I know you are still out there. I can feel you, so answer me!" Again, only silence.

"I have not an answer for you, Daughter of Sairah." The voice was emotionless and barely audible.

"Then you *do* know her! I need to know where she is and where we are. Why have you taken me?" Blaine's anger ignited as darkness replaced the dying embers.

"Your questions are many. The night is upon us now, so we must rest ourselves for our journey. The light of day comes quickly so, Daughter of Sairah, sleep now and renew your strength for what lies ahead." She heard him shift slightly, and then silence.

Blaine was confused and scared. *Surely this is a dream*, she thought to herself. Her body felt stiff and tired. The softness of the blanket beckoned her, offering renewal. She decided at this moment she needed rest more than answers. Though she was wary of the stranger she took comfort in knowing he had not yet harmed her. He seemed to know of her mother. He probably knew where she was. Tomorrow she would make him tell her. Curling up on the blanket, exhaustion swept over her and sleep came swiftly.

Dawn was just breaking over the horizon when Blaine was rudely awoken by the rumblings of hunger in the pit of her stomach. Rolling over on her back, she opened her eyes and stared up at the sky. Squinting at first, and then blinking a few times, she couldn't believe what she was seeing. The sky was a pale violet color. *Why wasn't it blue?* Remembering her present circumstances, her thoughts quickly turned to the mysterious man from the night before.

She jumped up and scanned the surrounding forest. The light was still very dim, only allowing her to make out the slightest of shapes. She walked around the ashes of last night's fire to the place the stranger had occupied. There was a backpack sitting next to a neatly folded blanket. There was no sign of the stranger.

"Good, Daughter of Sairah, you have awakened," said a voice that came from behind her.

Blaine jumped with fright and quickly turned toward the voice. She could barely make out the figure of a man walking toward her. As the figure drew near her, every muscle in her body tensed. To her surprise instinct took over, and Blaine found herself assuming a defensive stance. Though she had never had formal training in hand-to-hand combat, she somehow knew she had the skill to defend herself were the stranger to attack.

"I have some loafed bread and berries that I gathered this morning for you. I am positive that your hunger has made a strong presence in you." He set a bowl down on a rock near the fire and made his way over to the blanket where Blaine had slept the night before. As the man sat down she felt her body relax.

"Eat! Dawn is breaking." The stranger's mention of morning once again made Blaine aware of the color of the sky, which was growing brighter by the minute; the violet hue now morphing into a bluish violet. The color reminded her of the flowers on her grandmother's butterfly bush. Mesmerized, Blaine continued staring up at the sky.

The spell was broken with the stranger's urgency. "Eat. We must make way before the dawn is fully upon us." His voice was deep and gentle—almost calming. His dialect seemed foreign to Blaine until she remembered the times her mom used the same odd dialect. She replayed her mother's words: "We'll make way through the forest."

The similarity in speech prompted Blaine to ask once again, "Do you know my mother?" It was clear that her annoyance to his silence got his attention. He turned toward her and the two locked gazes. Now with enough light, she was shocked to realize that the stranger was not a man, but a boy who appeared to be a few years older than she.

"If you wish not to eat, then we should make our journey's way." With that Blaine turned her attention to the bowl containing the bread and berries. She moved to the rock where the bowl was perched and picked it up. At that moment Blaine became aware that movement was now effortless. All previous obstacles and pain had faded. She picked up the bowl and quickly emptied it, which quieted her predawn rumblings.

Now gaining strength with each minute, she was determined to get answers. "Where is my mother?"

"That is a question, as before said, I still remain with no answer, Daughter of Sairah."

"Okay, how about an easy one for you. Where are we? Obviously, were not in Kansas anymore."

"This Kansas I know not. To answer your question of our whereabouts would consume the remainder of the safety of dawn. It is an answer that holds no relevance to our journey." His tone was still emotionless. It was as matter-of-fact as if he were telling the time of day to a passerby.

"That answer holds plenty of relevance to our journey. What makes you think I'm going to just wander off into some strange forest with some guy who has taken me against my will? For all I know you are responsible for my mother's disappearance." She glared at him. Anger reflected in her voice. Her annoyance to his lack of answers grew hotter by the second. "I refuse to go with you until you at least tell me where we are!"

As Blaine's eyes flashed with disdain toward the boy, a flicker of emotion crossed the boy's face. It seemed as though a momentary breach occurred in his near robotic stance. Just as quickly, the wind began to pick up; its vicious strength and fury beat against the trees. As soon as the boy uttered a word that Blaine could not decipher, the wind immediately began to subside.

"Daughter of Sairah, it is not my wish to anger you. We must make our journey's way now. This side of Renault is untamed and deemed unsafe." With that he bent down and folded up the blanket that had been her bed the night before. Walking past her, he gathered up his backpack and his blanket all in one motion. He then made his way out of the clearing.

She sat there dumbfounded for a moment. *Renault!* He had said that as if to explain everything. Now he expected her to blindly follow him into the woods like a lost puppy dog. *What arrogance! Someone needs to keep an eye on him*, she thought to herself. The latter got her reevaluating her previous position. She decided it would be in the best interest of everyone involved to follow him. Turning to catch up to him, she spied a canteen that he carelessly left behind. At that moment, she realized her extreme thirst. She picked up the canteen, opened it, and bringing it to her lips, she found that there were only a few swallows of liquid left. To Blaine's surprise it wasn't water but some kind of sweet nectar. She had never tasted anything like it before. What was more surprising was realizing that those few swallows left her completely satisfied. She slung the canteen over her shoulder and swiftly tracked the boy into the forest.

As soon as she stepped from the clearing into the darkness of the forest, a feeling of panic overcame her. She realized the forest was denser than she had expected and she was unable to find any path.

"This way, Daughter of Sairah." Startling as the voice was, it served to diminish her panic. She turned and noticed the boy leaning against a tree. Even though his voice was laced with impatience, his face remained emotionless. As soon as he was sure that he got Blaine's full attention, he continued his way deeper into the darkness of the forest.

"Hey, that's okay. Go on ahead. Right behind you." Blaine called out sarcastically yet silently relieved not to have to face the dark forest on her own. She certainly didn't trust this boy, but following him blindly into the forest was her only option for the moment.

Blaine knew the sun was beginning to brighten the sky with every step they took. She looked up trying to confirm the color. She was still in disbelief that it was really the violet shade she had seen earlier at the campsite. Most of the time the forest was thick and the treetops blocked the sky. Once in a while there was a break in the giant trees, which allowed the sunlight to find its way into the darkness and flood the forest floor. Its brightness would dance on the leaves, creating a rainbow of brilliant color. With her attention focused on the beauty around her, she tripped and stumbled over an exposed tree root. Luckily, she managed to catch her balance before sprawling out on the forest floor. The commotion caught the boy's attention. He stopped quickly and spun around. After concluding no injury was evident he turned in silence and continued the journey into the forest.

"No—I'm okay, really. Don't worry about me," Blaine called out, her sarcasm falling on deaf ears.

CHAPTER 5

The forest grew denser and footing became very tricky. Blaine, impressed with herself, had no problem keeping up with the boy. She found herself falling behind only when something would catch her eye. The forest buzzed with life. The leaves of certain trees seemed to shimmer with shades of pink, teal, and purple. Of course, that was impossible. It was, she decided, some sort of optical illusion caused by the morning light. Blaine prided herself on the vast knowledge she knew about flowers and plants; however, with every step she took she spotted something else she had never seen before. The temptation to slow her pace to admire the beauty around her caused her to constantly fall behind. She would then pick up her pace and catch up with the boy who forged mechanically ahead of her.

Blaine's watch had stopped so she had no idea how long they had been walking but it seemed like forever. Her desire to stop and rest was overridden by her pride. She was determined that this boy, who obviously thought himself superior to her, would never know she was having difficulty keeping up with his pace. Blaine's thirst, however, was beginning to get the best of her. She wished the empty canteen she carried still contained even a few drops of that miraculous nectar.

"Do you long for a drink?" The boy questioned.

"What?" She heard herself asking even though she had clearly heard his question.

"Water. Are you in need of water?" The tone of his voice still sounded flat. There was no hint of arrogance or sarcasm. This puzzled and troubled Blaine. She had tried baiting him with sarcasm and challenging his arrogance by matching his endurance. She was engaged in a spirited battle of wits, but the boy was not even aware of the game. His perception of the situation was different and somehow surprisingly admirable. She unexpectedly felt her defenses lessen.

Grateful he was aware of her discomfort, she replied, "Yes, I am. Thank you." Puzzled, Blaine watched as the boy kept up his pace ahead of her. "Okay, he was just curious," she mumbled under her breath. He glanced back at her briefly but didn't miss a step. "You've got to be kidding," she snorted and began walking again just keeping him insight but making no effort to catch up with him. The boy walked on a while then suddenly cut off to the right vanishing from her line of sight. She hesitated a moment then picked up her pace in an effort not to lose track of him. She came to the spot where he had disappeared and discovered it was an embankment. She cautiously slid down the heavily treed slope. As she reached the bottom, the trees began to thin out. She stood up and quickly scanned the area looking for the boy.

Blaine's search ceased as she headed straight toward a spectacular view of a river that wound its way through a clearing in the forest. Blue diamonds seemed to dance about the riverbed, creating an illusion of water. Even more spectacular were the riverbanks, which were lined with the most beautiful red wildflowers. They looked as though they had been hand dipped in paint. Surrounding them was a thick pattern of iridescent purple flowers. The magnificent floral mixture created an illusion of a carpet—*a carpet fit for royalty*, Blaine thought to herself.

Standing there surveying the majestic scene, Blaine became aware of the fragrance of honeysuckle and butterscotch. She closed her eyes and took a deep breath. Their scent was intoxicating. As Blaine stood there with her eyes closed taking in deep breaths she began to feel very relaxed. All sense of worry and anxiety were gone. A welcome wave of calmness washed over her.

Then somewhere far away Blaine heard the boy's voice, "They are named Everanders. The fairies of the blossoms use them in their freedom dust. Many oracles use them in meditation and vision travel. They are extremely powerful and therefore much desired. They bloom two days a year and only along this river."

Blaine stood there with her eyes closed for several minutes. The boy's voice now seemed to come from inside her mind. She slowly opened her eyes and stared once again at the carpet of flowers. The purple pattern of flowers was moving.

"Did you say fairies?" She questioned as she walked toward the boy. She felt as if she were in a dream. Even though her head felt very light her mind was alive and lucid. She half laughed. "You probably think that I'm high, don't you?"

A look of puzzlement flashed across the boy's face as he responded, "I do not understand your question and therefore cannot answer you, Daughter of Sairah."

"What I'm saying is, do you think I'm naïve enough to believe in fairies and such?"

As the boy turned his focus back to Blaine she was surprised to see a grin appear across his lips. Then he turned and walked toward the carpet of flowers. He moved closer to the edge of the carpet. Blaine followed him until she stood at his side. Now she could see the flowers were buzzing with life. Hundreds of butterflies lofted over the tops of the blossoms, displaying beautiful brilliant colors on their wings. She stepped closer and watched as these beautiful creatures gracefully danced from blossom to blossom amongst the field of majestic red flowers. Fascinated by their carefully orchestrated dance, Blaine suddenly gasped, dropping to her knees in utter disbelief as a fairy fluttered by her. Even though she tried blinking to clear her vision, she realized the truth: these were not butterflies, but fairies dancing their magical ballet above the blossoms.

She felt the boy's presence next to her. They both remained there in silence. Suddenly several fairies stopped their dance above the flowers and gracefully encircled them.

"They are beautiful," Blaine said whispering so she would not scare them all the way. "I've always daydreamed about fairies but never imagined I would actually see one. Now here they are dancing all around me. They are real."

"They have always been real in this existence," the boy said softly.

Blaine quickly shifted her gaze from the miracle she was witnessing to the boy. "What do you mean by this existence?"

Ignoring her question, the boy walked to the river's edge and pulled out a leather canteen. It was identical to the one Blaine had slung over her shoulder earlier this morning. Kneeling down, he immersed his canteen and filled it with river water. He then began splashing water on his face, which caused his olive skin to glisten in the sun. As he stood Blaine noticed how fluid his motions were. A gentle breeze blew a strand of black hair in his carelessly pulled back ponytail. When she moved toward the water's edge she realized for the first time how tall he was.

Copying what the boy had done, Blaine knelt down and filled her canteen. Bringing the cold and refreshing drink to her lips, she couldn't remember a time when water tasted as wonderful as this.

"We must make way. Our journey together will soon be to an end. My quest shall be fulfilled, but yours will continue. Answers shall be had at that time."

She stared at him hoping he would volunteer more information. She searched the boy's face discovering to her surprise that deep wisdom reflected in his dark eyes. The calmness displayed in his entire face, however, somehow made her feel uneasy.

Blaine dipped her canteen in the river again. As she examined the leather canister more closely she realized that it seemed to have its own cooling system. Like so many things in this strange place this simple canister was much more complex than it seemed. The movement of the fairies once more caught her attention. Blaine tried desperately to think of an explanation for the unbelievable events she was experiencing. "Maybe I fell in the forest and hit my head. I could be in some sort of a coma," Blaine heard herself saying out loud.

Her ponderings were interrupted when she heard the boy say, "We must go, Daughter of Sairah." His tone was softer than usual, but Blaine detected a hint of anxiety.

"I have a name you know," Blaine declared. Again, he didn't respond but she thought she saw another smile. He turned and started upstream. "It's Blaine!" She stated loudly. The boy just kept walking. Blaine sighed in frustration and took her place behind him. They had only traveled a few feet when she bravely inquired, "What is your name?"

To her surprise he turned and started to reply, "They call me ... " Just then, he froze as he brought his finger to his lips. Beckoning her to follow, he darted quickly into the closest cover of trees and tall brush. Blaine didn't hesitate for even a moment. The very instant he had sought cover every hair on her body stood on end. Her stomach flipped and she felt she was about to get sick.

They crouched silently in the underbrush. Blaine tried desperately to keep her breathing steady. She could feel her heart beating rapidly. Suddenly, the distant rhythm of running horses caused the earth to rumble under her feet. She looked at the boy, her eyes wide with terror. "You must not speak or move at all. By the spirit of all greatness—hear me well, Blaine!" Blaine heard him, but realized he never spoke since he made his wishes known without moving his lips. Instead of reacting negatively to the telepathic invasion of her mind, Blaine quietly nodded in complete compliance.

Blaine estimated that there were twenty to thirty horses drawing near, the pounding horse's hoofs creating a thunderous roar. Suddenly, her attention was directed toward the boy as she heard him quietly speak two words, "Atie Besoonie." As soon as the second word left his lips, Blaine noticed that both her sound level and clarity of vision became distorted. Surrounding noise sounded like it was engulfed in some sort of bubble.

Blaine couldn't fully see the riders, but she could sense their menacing evil as they drew close to their hiding place. She held her breath as the majestic black beasts—all draped in purple, green, and yellow silks—flared their nostrils and kicked up loose debris with their polished hoofs while they passed Blaine and the boy. A small dust cloud rose like smoke and surrounded the thundering herd.

Most of the horses and riders continued downstream. A small group, however, stopped in the middle of the field of flowers where only minutes ago fairies had danced about. One of the riders dismounted and began walking around. Blaine wondered if the fragrance of the wildflowers had any effect on him. Somehow, she doubted it. The man appeared to be close to seven feet tall and very muscular. He wore body armor. It was not the medieval armor one would associate with King Arthur.

Instead, it resembled modern police body armor that included an unusual metal mesh. He also wore a protective metal helmet, which revealed only his eyes and mouth.

The dismounted rider took several steps in the direction of their hiding place. His eyes scanned the area as if searching for something; perhaps searching for them. Blaine's distorted vision was suddenly replaced with extreme acuity. Even though the rider was several yards from them she could see his piercing green eyes, which scanned the entire embankment. His eyes followed upstream until they locked onto the brush, Blaine and the boy's sanctuary.

He moved closer. Blaine felt her heart leap into her throat. His glare seemed to pierce her very soul. Her mind was suddenly filled with horrific images of death, torture, and devastating destruction. Blaine was completely repulsed by the pure vibration of evil that was emanating from this man.

"Sir, what is it?" Another rider had dismounted and joined the first rider who now appeared to be staring directly at Blaine and the boy.

"A disturbance; there is something powerful ... " The sound of the first rider's voice cut through the morning air like a knife.

The other rider surveyed the area. Unable to pinpoint any reason for concern and hoping not to offend his commanding officer, he meekly offered an explanation. "Sir, I'm sure it is just those pesky fairies from the flower field."

Observing their dialogue, Blaine was able to confirm that these men were members of some sort of military unit.

"No, it's more than just that. It is like nothing I have ever experienced before; magic, strength, extreme power." As he spoke Blaine detected a hint of fear in his voice and observed a flash of uncertainty in his eyes. Then the uncertainty was quickly replaced by a look of determination.

Perceiving the same reactions as Blaine did about the commanding officer, the second soldier chose to focus on his leader's resolve. "Sir, do you want me to bring the men back to search the area?"

Hearing that request, Blaine's heart dropped. There would be no hiding from such a thorough search. In spite of the magical props the boy possessed, they would eventually be discovered. She looked expectantly in the direction of the boy. His eyes were peacefully shut as if he were asleep.

Gaining composure, the commander turned to his subordinate. "Perhaps you're right. Fairies are known to possess magical abilities, but somehow it seems so powerful. No need to waste more time here."

They both stood there for a moment longer. Turning, the second soldier mounted his horse and rode in the direction the other riders had taken. Alone, the commanding officer looked over his shoulder as he mounted his steed. Uttering a strange word, he raised a hand. Just before riding upstream, a ball of fire appeared, suspended over his palm. He approached the field of flowers and released the fireball. In an instant, the beautiful carpet of vivacious majestic color was transformed into a black smoldering heap of ashes. In a flash, the leader and his horse became mere ominous specks in the distance as they rode off to catch up with the others.

Blaine and the boy remained in their hiding place in silence for what seemed an eternity. "Demos Atillia." The boy's voice shattered the silence and startled Blaine. As the sound rang loudly and echoed in Blaine's ears, she noticed that the bubble that once encased them was now completely gone.

The boy tried to stand up, but Blaine reached up and grabbed his arm to stop him. "Wait! Are you sure they're gone? Is it really safe?"

"You do not feel HIS presence any longer. Correct?"

Blaine realized the boy was right and nodded affirmatively. She no longer felt the overwhelming evil. The boy effortlessly exited their hiding place, but Blaine remained there a few moments longer. She watched the boy walk to the place where the commanding officer last stood. Her mind was filled with questions. *What had just occurred? Who were those riders and why didn't they see us? What kind of magic was that?* She stood up. "I'm going to get some answers once and for all," she spoke out loud. "Okay. Enough is enough! You owe me explanations! And you are going to give them to me, now!" she fumed as she emerged from her hiding place. She stormed up behind him. The boy was down on one knee holding something in his hand. She looked over his shoulder and came to a sudden stop. Gasping, Blaine fell to her knees next to him.

In the boy's hand lay the most beautiful creature Blaine had ever seen. The features of the fairy's face were perfect, appearing as if they had been painted on. Her skin was iridescent and sparkled as if she had been dusted with glitter. Her beauty would outshine that of any supermodel that Blaine had ever seen. Sadness overwhelmed Blaine as she realized the fairy lay motionless in the boy's hands. Her wings were illuminated by light that was dimming with every passing second. Then all at once it was completely gone. Blaine's heart filled with immense sorrow.

"Is she dead?" Blaine asked already knowing the answer to her question. Suddenly a wind whirled around them gently lifting the tiny body and suspending it in the air. There was a small burst of light and the fairy's body turned to dust. The dust lingered in the air for a brief moment, glittering in the sun before it was forever lost in the swirling breeze.

Fighting back tears, Blaine shifted her attention to the field of flowers that previously had buzzed with activity and majestic beauty. Nothing remained but scorched, smoldering earth. She turned to look at the boy. His head was bowed and a single tear rolled down his cheek.

"Why?" Blaine searched her mind and was unable to find words to express what she was feeling.

The boy let out a deep sigh as he turned and locked eyes with hers. They sat there in silence for a moment. Then he spoke, "There are answers to your questions. I am resolute when I say look to your heart, Blaine, Daughter of Sairah. Within, are many answers known to you already." His voice was gentle and kind, but the sadness reflected there brought tears to Blaine's eyes. She continued staring intensely into his eyes seeking comfort and some reasonable explanation for all that had happened. Reflected there was such depth of wisdom that for a moment she no longer saw him as a boy, but as a man—a man who knew the sorrows of many souls. She could feel the weight of the burden he carried. A burden so great it involved an entire civilization, which at the moment lingered in the balance. She did not know why this knowledge was given to her, but in her heart, she knew a great truth had been revealed. All the contempt and suspicion she previously felt faded. It was as if their souls touched as these words were burned into her heart.

"In a person's eyes, you see one soul's world. In it lays the pain of many souls. One of the destined ones. The circle is almost complete."

These words echoed in Blaine's head with such force and certainty that it brought excitement to her heart. At the same time, she wept in the depths of her soul.

CHAPTER 6

As Blaine took her eyes from his, the spell was broken. A feeling of enlightenment seemed to make her no longer question her situation.

"We must continue on our journey. It is not wise to linger where evil has been used," the boy calmly stated.

She nodded in agreement and followed him once again, this time without question. They traveled in silence. The forest seemed to darken and much of its luster had faded. She continued walking while reliving the events of the morning. To have felt the joy at seeing such unbelievable beauty for the first time only to have it extinguished by the horrible act of destruction was almost more than she could bear. She was overcome with regret and anguish as she remembered how she remained hidden in that bubble doing nothing to save those helpless fairies. With a deep sigh, she pushed those thoughts out of her mind, replacing them with the troubling question of how she was going to find her mother.

Blaine decided it was time to break the silence. "How much

further to our destination," she asked, giving pause to the fact she had no idea what that destination was.

"Distance is irrelevant, Daughter of Sairah, for our journey together will end in a short while. However, yours has just begun." His words echoed in the trees as if they were the ones actually speaking.

"Always a riddle. Do you ever give a direct answer to a question?" She asked quietly and matter-of-fact—not really expecting an answer.

"Actually, yes" came his reply.

Blaine paused briefly and let out an exaggerated sigh. "There you go again! This is the type of behavior that does not endear you to me." Even as she spoke she knew she was not that annoyed. While it was true that he was not forthcoming with the answers to her questions, she had to admit he was starting to grow on her. Also, the fact that he kept bringing up about them parting ways soon surprisingly brought a touch of sorrow to her heart.

As they continued on their journey she noticed that the trees were beginning to thin out. Looking beyond the boy, she thought she saw something that made her smile. "Is that a road ahead?" Blaine inquired. The boy simply nodded his reply. *Good*, Blaine thought to herself. The long hike on the uneven and wild terrain was beginning to take a toll on her body. *Traveling a well-beaten path would be a major improvement, but a real road would be absolutely glorious.* Even as she thought this, the boy began to veer off to the left, away from the road.

"Wait! Aren't we going to take the road?" Blaine quickened her pace to come alongside him. Her question was answered as she noticed the boy continuing the journey by moving away from the road. As usual the boy's pace remained consistent and untiring. Blaine plodded next to him, occasionally stumbling over a loose rock or exposed tree root. She would glare at him in protest with no effect; there seemed to be no way to penetrate his stoic façade.

The forest floor began to slope upward in a surprisingly severe angle. The steep climb caused Blaine to occasionally lose her balance. The boy glanced back when she lost her footing, but after he saw she was all right he would continue his climb.

Finally, to Blaine's delight he began to slow his pace. He stopped in front of an old majestic tree. In stature, it looked to be a type of redwood. Up close, it turned out to be a birch. The tree glowed, giving off a purple light. Looking around, Blaine saw that every tree in this area was emanating a different color. Blaine's eyes darted from tree to tree, hypnotized by the iridescent light each tree was emitting into the afternoon shadows.

The boy stood in the shadow of the great tree and softly spoke words that Blaine could not understand. To her amazement the tree began to sway as he spoke. The purple glow became a brilliant light, and the tree's roots dislodged from the earth. It moved to the right of the boy. Blaine was surprised to see that underneath where the tree once stood, there was a carved stairwell leading down into the mountain.

The boy motioned for Blaine to enter the stairwell. She hesitated a moment, but when she saw the look on his face she knew his request was not up for debate. She took a deep breath and stepped into the stairwell. It was made of earth and stone. The boy followed closely behind her. As they descended the crude steps the sunlight that had flooded the entrance was slowly being engulfed by the awaiting darkness that occupied the depths of the stairwell. Blaine turned and looked at the boy. The stairwell was getting darker with each descending step. She must have had a look of panic on her face for the boy spoke softly and reassuringly. "The old tree is the protector of this entrance. He will continue at his post."

"So, what you're saying is it—I mean he—is moving to cover the only way out of this underground death trap."

"Yes." The boy spoke in the tone to which Blaine had become so accustomed.

"Great," she mumbled with disdain under her breath. "How are we supposed to see without light?"

"Daughter of Sairah, you will understand much of this world when you begin to disallow the thoughts of your world to overshadow what your soul already knows." Just as he finished speaking, the entrance became completely sealed.

Blaine stood frozen in the dark. She put her hands out touching both sides of the wall. She felt the roots of the trees entwined in the damp walls of the tunnel. Taking a deep breath, she attempted a step forward. As her foot lifted then made contact with the ground, a warm glow filled the space around her. She took another step and again the area in front of her began to illuminate with light. With every step that she took, the tunnel continued lighting the way ahead of her. She glanced over her shoulder at the boy and was surprised to see he actually had a grin on his face. He gently nodded at her as in approval.

Continuing through the tunnel Blaine discovered the roots that lined the walls were not random but rather formed an intricate pattern. Further investigation disclosed that the light source was actually coming from the dirt and stones on the stairs. As they descended she moved her fingers softly across the walls. They were warm to the touch and no longer damp. She thought she felt a slight vibration. "Are we moving under a roadway of some sort?" She directed her gaze back at the boy.

"No." His tone was quiet and serene.

She smiled to herself as the one-word answer washed over her. *Typical!*

The downward slope had now become more level, giving

way to a path that was smooth and even. If Blaine strained her eyes, she could see a light source breaking through the darkness ahead. They drew closer to the light, which seem to be coming from above. Staring straight ahead Blaine began to pick up her pace. As she focused on the light she was not aware that the pathway had morphed into a staircase leading up until she stumbled and caught herself on the first step. Blaine glanced up and saw the source of the light was coming through a doorway at the top of the stairs. Looking back at the boy she said, "We're going up, I assume."

Sliding past her, the boy nodded and began his ascent up the stairs. Blaine allowed him to take three steps before she fell in line behind him. In the light, she could now see the stairway was made of marble. As she took the first step, her foot landed clumsily on a stair. Suddenly, the feeling of anticipation flowed through her like lightning streaking across the night sky. She could not help but hope that once she reached the top of the stairs and walked into the light her odd journey would not only come to an end, but also offer answers to all her questions.

Continuing her climb, Blaine gazed at the boy ahead of her. Light from the doorway was so bright compared to the stairwell she was only able to see his silhouette. As he reached the top of the stairs he disappeared into the brightness, causing Blaine to pause.

"Come now, Daughter of Sairah. Our journey together is nearing its end," the boy's voice floated down the stairs. Blaine climbed the last few steps. Taking a deep breath, she stepped through the doorway.

CHAPTER 7

It took several moments for Blaine's eyes to adjust to the lighting in the room where she now stood. Once her eyes were acclimated, to her surprise the room was not as bright as it had appeared to be from the darkened stairwell. She quickly surveyed the circular room that they now occupied. She saw the boy standing to the left of her speaking very softly to an older man whose silver hair was pulled back into a ponytail. The room itself displayed little decor. There was, however, a small metal table in the middle of the room. On the table was a beautifully painted vase, which housed a bouquet of sweet smelling flowers.

Continuing her survey of the room, Blaine noticed an archway beyond which she saw a closed door. The floor and walls were lined with polished stone.

Blaine took a few steps toward the center of the room. She could hear the boy and the man in conversation. She briefly studied the interaction between the boy and the man, who was shorter and unassuming with a gentle demeanor. Her gaze then fell upon the bouquet of flowers. She recognized the flowers as the same she had seen by the river. Though the flowers in the vase were still buds, she could tell by their vibrant color they were Everanders. Blaine smiled as she recalled the site of the fairies fluttering happily above the carpet of enchanting blossoms. The joy she felt was fleeting, replaced by an overwhelming sadness as she remembered the fate of the fairies at the hands of such evil. As she reached out and touched one of the buds a small white spark surged from her finger, striking one of the buds. Startled, Blaine quickly withdrew her hand and took a step back. "Static electricity," Blaine said out loud. "Very strange!"

Her attention was drawn back to the bud touched by the spark. Her mouth dropped in amazement as she observed the bud was growing larger and larger. It then began to glow. The glow soon encompassed all the buds in the vase and they too emitted the same soft light. The buds slowly began to open one by one becoming a bouquet of beautifully mature Everanders.

Blaine was unaware that the boy and the man had ceased their conversation and had turned their attention to what Blaine was observing. Stepping closer to the table to admire the true beauty of the miracle that had just happened before her very eyes, she noticed movement coming from the center of the flowers. *Probably bees*, Blaine thought to herself. She carefully reached out to softly touch one of the flowers. As she did a small fairy emerged from the petals. Then in turn each flower among its petals revealed the presence of a fairy.

Blaine gasped in surprise and delight as the fairies danced above the bouquet. "Amazing," Blaine whispered out loud.

"Yes, my dear. It truly is." A voice that Blaine didn't recognized caused her to turn her attention to the other end of the room where the boy and the man had previously stood. She was startled to find that they now stood on either side of her. "The 'touch of life' is a most rare and amazing thing." The man spoke reverently. The boy remained silent by her side.

"The 'touch of life?'" Blaine directed her puzzled gaze toward the man.

"Yes, the ability to take energy from one living thing and create life for another. It is a rare gift not seen in these lands for thousands of years."

Blaine shot a quick, questioning glance toward the boy. In that instance she noticed his face no longer displayed its usual stoic expression. A look of surprise was clearly evident. Then before he regained his composure Blaine was sure she saw a flash of fear in his eyes. She said nothing and diverted her attention back to the fairies that were continuing their beautiful dance around the flowers to music only they could hear. Watching them gracefully dance, Blaine was haunted by the fear she had seen in the boy's eyes. Through all they had experienced together on their journey she never saw him express fear. This dominated her thoughts more so than the idea that they believed she had just created life. She, however, believed the fairies had been hiding in the bouquet all along. The belief that anyone possessed a 'touch of life' was just absurd.

Blaine's ruminations were interrupted by the boy's gentle voice. "Daughter of Sairah, Blaine, I take my leave from you now." As he spoke he slowly bent his head downward. "When our paths shall cross again I cannot say. Go safely and listen to those voices of your heart. They will guide you." He turned and walked towards the closed door.

"Wait!" Blaine shouted. "You are not going to just leave me with a perfect stranger?" She quickly glanced at the man standing next to her. "No offense." The boy continued through the door, which seemed to have opened by itself. He never looked back.

The man and Blaine stood in silence for a moment or two. "Well, this is awkward," Blaine said quietly.

The man chuckled, "Yes, I suppose it is." He walked over

to the flowers and held out his hand. One of the fairies landed gracefully in his palm. Blaine drew closer to him so she could observe the fairy more closely. "Fascinating creatures, aren't they?" The man's voice was soft and warm. "It's very interesting that you created them." He spoke while remaining focused on the tiny creature that now perched in his hand.

"*I* created?" Blaine replied, laughing. "I'm having a hard time wrapping my head around that whole 'touch of life' story."

The man didn't answer at first. Slowly, he moved his hand to allow the fairy to fly away. Then he turned and faced Blaine, "I know that the events of the last few days have been very difficult to 'wrap your head around,' as you so put it." A welcoming smile washed across his face. "Blaine, I am aware your questions are many. I am also aware of your mother's choice to keep this world a secret. Her decision brings sadness to us all."

"You know my mother?" Blaine interrupted. "Where is she? Have you seen her? Did you take her or do you know who did?"

The man held his hand up to silence Blaine's questions. Though the smile was gone his expression remained gentle. "I knew your mother once, but that was many pathways ago."

"What do you mean 'pathways'? Are you talking about reincarnation?" She questioned, feeling confused.

"No, Blaine," he answered with a small laugh. "In our life's journeys, we are presented with many pathways. Our decisions of which one to take allows us to change and grow. As these choices are made we forge new lives; thus, becoming different people. I knew your mother many pathways ago." As he spoke Blaine studied the man's face. He appeared to be somewhat older than her mom. His eyes were very blue. When he spoke, they danced with joy and at the same time reflected peace.

"So, you knew her when she was a kid?"

He smiled gently. "Yes, I suppose you could put it that way"

"Where is she?" Blaine questioned.

"Unfortunately, that is a question I am unable to answer for you."

"What do you mean you are unable to answer that?" demanded Blaine, angrily.

"I simply mean I do not know her whereabouts. Elian was on his journey here. He was drawn to the dark forest when he detected your crossover to our world."

"Who is Elian? Oh wait, the boy, I assume. Now you tell me?" Blaine snorted sarcastically.

"There are reasons for his secrecy. He experienced many Tellings of your coming but it was unclear which pathway you would choose."

Blaine stood there confused, silently trying to process what she had just been told; Tellings, crossovers, pathways. "What is a Telling?"

The man paused and seemed to contemplate the question, then finally answered, "A vision of sorts."

"Elian had visions of me?"

The man nodded.

"And the term pathway, you used that when speaking of my mother. I'm not sure I am following you here."

The man shifted his gaze to the flowers for a moment, seemingly pondering his reply. A slight smile of amusement crossed his face as he refocused on Blaine. "Life and who we are is like a forest full of pathways and directions. We can choose to remain on the pathway that has been taken by many, or select some pathway few have traveled. They each can take us to a different destination in the forests. Often these pathways all arrive at the same destination, just some being more difficult to travel. Some others may lead us into the darkness of the forest where there may be no pathway out. Every choice we make determines which pathway we travel."

"Okay, so basically you can take the easy road, or you can take the hard road."

"That is an oversimplification. There is so much more, Daughter of Sairah—Blaine. As you grow in knowledge of our world you will begin to understand."

Blaine wrinkled her face and shut her eyes. "So, you knew I was coming?"

"We have been aware of your imminent arrival for years." The man spoke mechanically as he turned toward the door from which the boy, Elian, had exited. "Come now, I will show you where you may wash up and rest. The night is here and you must be exhausted."

Blaine's body seemed suddenly bogged down with crushing exhaustion. It felt as if the weight of the world was upon her. As the man crossed the room and stopped at the exit, Blaine's attention was diverted to the door itself. It was made of red mahogany. An intricate pattern created by wrought iron or steel graced the surface and seemed to attach the door to the door frame. A small ornate rose was at the center. Blaine was puzzled by the fact that there was no doorknob. How had Elian opened the door without a doorknob? She cocked her head to get a better perspective of the conundrum.

Just then Blaine heard the man speak a word too quietly for Blaine to understand. The metal began to quickly contract toward the middle of the door. Blaine watched in amazement as all the metal disappeared into the small rose. Now all that was left was wood and with that the door slowly opened. The problem solved, Blaine spoke, "Who needs doorknobs with doors like that. I guess it would be a real problem if you forgot the password, especially if you were stuck inside." Blaine laughed a nervous giggle.

The man smiled brightly at her, and spoke with cheerfulness in his voice, "You are quite the jester of words, Blaine, Daughter of Sairah." The man walked to the door and motioned Blaine to follow.

She walked through the door and into the hallway beyond, the door shutting silently behind her. The metal vines emerged from the center rose and moved into place, locking the door down tight. The hallway they entered had three doors. All three were closed and locked down with metal puzzles. The hallway was bright as if lit by daylight. Yet, a quick glance at the overhead skylight revealed a dark sky. Blaine could see all the stars watching from above.

"Our lighting is all powered by the energy that our sun and moon release upon us." The man spoke without turning around. He seemed to have read her thoughts. The walls of the hallway were decorated with beautifully woven tapestries. As they walked by Blaine held out her hand to touch one. It shimmered in response to her touch. She quickly pulled her hand back to her side. The man had stopped in front of the last door on the right. "This is where you shall slumber for the night." He softly uttered a word and the door quickly performed its ritual of opening. The man made a gesture inviting her to enter first. Blaine, making eye contact with the man, gave a nod and walked through the door.

The room was large and lavishly decorated. It reminded Blaine of pictures she had seen of European castles—definitely fit for royalty.

"I hope this will meet with your approval."

"Hey, it certainly beats sleeping out in the forest," she retorted with a slight smile.

"Very well, Blaine, Daughter of Sairah. I shall then take my leave for the night. Marrette will be along momentarily with your dinner. She will assist you in settling into your evening's accommodations."

"Wait. You're leaving? The boy, I mean, Elian, said my questions would be answered. I assumed you would be able to do that now. I have been more than patient."

"This I do understand. However, the hour has grown late. The conversation you desire is best had in the light of a new day. Eat, rest, gain your strength. Tomorrow will be upon us soon enough." With that he turned to leave the room.

"Aren't you going to tell me how to open and close the door?" Blaine blurted out loudly.

"Until you understand more about our world it is better you do not wander about alone. There are many things in our world that could inadvertently bring harm to you." He walked to the door and it began its graceful dance locking her inside.

CHAPTER 8

"Awesome, so I'm pretty much a prisoner," she spoke out loud as the last metal vine locked into place. She walked to the far side of the room where a four-poster bed stood. She ran her fingers over one of the ornately carved posts. It was the largest bed she had ever seen; large enough that five people could probably sleep comfortably on it. On either side of the bed were nightstands that displayed the same ornate carving as the bed.

Sitting down on the bench that resided at the foot of the bed, Blaine continued surveying the room. One area had been designed as a sitting room with two overstuffed high-back chairs set in front of an enormous carved stone fireplace. It was so clean Blaine doubted it had ever been used. To the left of the bed, there was a vanity with an attached mirror adorned with the same ornate wood work as the bed and night stands.

On each side of the sitting room there was a closed door. Each had a doorknob, which peaked Blaine's curiosity. She stood and walked toward the first door. She reached out and turned the small, metal, egg-shaped doorknob. Expecting it to be locked, Blaine was pleasantly surprised to find it turned freely. As she pushed the door open, she automatically felt the wall for a light switch. It quickly became apparent that no switch was necessary as the lights graciously came on by themselves. An immaculate bathroom finished in beautiful cream-colored stone stood before her. She exited the room, returning the door to its original resting place.

As Blaine made her way to the second door, she almost tripped over one of the elegant woven area rugs that complemented the sitting room floor. She was pleasantly surprised to find that this door opened as freely as the first door. The room was illuminated as she entered. She was surprised to find an enormous, well-stocked, walk-in closet. There were dresses and blouses of every color. One wall, lined with shelves, housed only shoes; Blaine had never seen so many in one room before. "Clearly a woman's closet." She mumbled to herself.

"This is obviously someone's bedroom—kind a weird," Blaine spoke out loud, again. She wondered who was giving up her room, or rather suite, for her.

A knock on the door broke the silence of the room and startled Blaine. She quickly stepped out of the closet and closed the door behind her. "Come in," she called. She wanted to add, *if you are so privileged as to know the password*, but decided against that. Up to this point, her sarcasm had not been well received.

The door opened and a large wooden cart emerged through the doorway. Behind the cart was a small waifish girl. Her size caused her to struggle as she navigated the cart. "I'm sorry to disturb you, my lady." She spoke as she carefully maneuvered the cart toward the sitting room, stopping briefly to seal the door behind her. The cart rattled as it went over the grouted lines of the elaborate stonework on the floor. Placed carefully on the cart were several silver domes covering a variety of plates. The inviting aroma of food soon filled the air.

Blaine closed her eyes and took a deep breath to get the full effect of the amazing odors. She watched cautiously as the girl pulled the cart in front of one of the overstuffed high-back chairs. While the girl quietly continued her task of setting up the eating area she looked up and noticed Blaine watching her. She gave Blaine a shy smile, nodded, and then continued the duties at hand. "I will leave these covered to keep the warmth longer," she stated matter-of-factly. Then stepping around the chair and facing Blaine she continued. "There are fresh towels prepared for you in the washroom. In the wardrobe, there is an array of clothes that should be to your liking."

"Those are all for me?" Blaine questioned in a shocked tone as she pointed to the closet behind her."

"Aye, my lady," the girl nodded. "My name is Marrette. I will be happy to attend to any of your needs." Blaine thought it strange that as Marrette spoke she did not make eye contact.

"Thank you very much," Blaine graciously replied. Blaine, who was extremely hungry, had to use every bit of her will power to keep from attacking the delicious smelling food like a ravenous mountain lion. Instead, she slowly approached the overstuffed chair and sat down demurely.

"Unless you require my further assistance, my lady, I will take my leave."

Blaine cringed a bit as Marrette referred to her as "my lady." She appeared to be only a few years Blaine's senior. "No, everything is fine. Please don't worry about me." She quickly smiled at her, trying to conceal how uncomfortable the slight girl made her feel.

Marrette approached the door. "If you find you need any assistance, just place your hand on the rose in the center of the door. It will summons me in my quarters."

Blaine nodded as Marrette took her leave. Blaine didn't even bother waiting for the door to be sealed before she lifted the first silver dome that revealed a small roasted game hen. The hen was artfully surrounded by carrots and potatoes. She quickly removed one of the legs and began eating. After removing all the meat from the leg, she lifted another dome from its resting place to discover a platter of fresh fruit and a variety of breads. Carefully stowed on the lower shelf of the cart was a pitcher of water and a goblet, both made of delicate glass. Blaine poured herself some water and continued to inhale the food that had been prepared for her. After she had devoured nearly everything from the cart she carefully returned the domes to their original places, stood up, and then gently pushed the cart away from the chair.

Blaine raised her arms to stretch. As she turned her head to the side she suddenly became aware of an unpleasant odor. "Ugh!" She groaned out loud. "Time to take advantage of that beautiful bathroom."

She made her way to the bathroom, pulling a towel and washcloth from the stack of linens that lay neatly on a shelf. Next to the linens was a complete assortment of toiletries. From these she selected a bottle of shampoo and a small bar of soap. Inspecting the huge bathtub which could easily have accommodated three people comfortably, she opted for the shower and laid her collection of necessities by the enclosure.

She walked over to the door and closed it; locking it from the inside. As she walked toward the shower she noticed a white fluffy bathrobe that was carefully hung on a hook next to the shower.

She quickly finished her shower, dried off, and wrapped herself in the comfortable robe. Blaine picked up her clothes and shuddered at the thought of wearing her extremely dirty garments.

She walked back into the bedroom, hastily folding up her

clothes and placed them on the bench at the foot of the bed. She ran her hands over the cream-colored bedspread that encompassed the huge bed. It was made of the softest material she had ever felt. It seemed to be a cross between silk and cashmere. She then allowed her weary body to flop freely onto the bed.

Lying on her back gave her a perfect view of the large skylight that was centered above where she now rested. She gazed up at the dancing stars. They seemed so vibrant and so very close. In this serene environment Blaine found herself deep in thought. The surreal feelings generated by the events of the last few days made her doubt her own senses. What she knew had only been days seemed like months. As she thought of how much she missed her mother her eyelids began to grow extremely heavy. She could feel herself drifting off. *I should get up and turn out the lights, except there are no light switches*, she thought to herself. She turned her attention to the bronze-colored floor lamp next to the bed that warmly lit that part of the room. *I should check to see if there is a switch on that.* That was the last thought Blaine had as sleep overcame her.

CHAPTER 9

Blaine ran breathless through a dark forest spurred on by a desperate urgency to get somewhere. She was in the forest, which she had traveled through earlier with the boy, Elian. She leaped over fallen trees, avoiding low hanging branches, as if the knowledge of the path was engraved into her soul. The smell of smoke filled her nostrils. Ahead she could see ominous shadows dancing in the light of a hastily built fire. Every muscle in her body tensed as her gaze locked on a figure tied to a stake on the far side of the fire. The figure, bound and gagged, was Elian! Blaine was about to lunge forward to untie him when she suddenly realized that another figure stood by Elian in the shadows. She was instantly overwhelmed by an evil sensation. It was the same dark evil she had felt the day she and Elian crouched in the bushes, hiding from the men on the horses.

From the darkness emerged another shadow; both had their backs to Blaine. One figure was chanting in a low guttural growl. Blaine hesitated just a moment, gathering her wits. She took a deep breath. Leaping toward the figures, Blaine produced a dagger from her waistband. One figure immediately turned towards her. In mid jump Blaine dropped to her knees, landing hard on the forest floor. Shocked, she screamed out, "Mother!" Blaine's cry disturbed a nearby flock of sleeping birds. They rushed from their hiding place and took to the air in surprise. Then to Blaine's horror, Sairah picked up a large sword that lay on the ground next to her. The blade reflected the flames of the smoldering fire. Sairah hesitated briefly then effortlessly plunged the weapon through Elian's heart.

"No!" Blaine shrieked.

She sat straight up in bed drenched in sweat. She frantically looked around trying to gain some sense of where she was. As she caught her breath memories of the last few days flooded her thoughts. A feeling of relief came over her as she realized that even though it all felt so real, it had only been a horrible nightmare.

She lay back down and closed her eyes briefly, hoping that the overwhelming feeling of uncertainty and horror would leave her. She opened her eyes and gazed up at the skylight to view the beautiful violet sky now bright with sunlight. She watched in awe as random white clouds drifted by.

There was a light knock at the door. Blaine sat up and swung her feet over the edge of the bed and stood up. She adjusted the robe she had been wearing when she fell asleep the night before. Trying to calm her voice, she called, "Come in." The door opened and Marrette entered.

"Good morning, my lady. I trust you slept well." Marrette's cheerful chirping morphed into a serious tone accompanied by a slight frown and a wrinkled brow when she looked past Blaine to the bed. "My lady, there was no need for you to make the bed. It would have been done for you," she said as she walked over to the bed and begin straightening the wrinkled bedspread.

A little embarrassed, Blaine mumbled, "I didn't make it. I mean, I would have, had I slept in it."

Puzzled, Marrette looked up from her task and inquired meekly, "Sorry, my lady. Did the bed not suit you?"

"Oh, it's not that. I was just so tired last night I had lain down on top of it to relax a moment. Then the next thing I knew it was morning."

"Oh, very good, my lady," Marrette answered. Relieved she finished straightening the bed then walked back to the door, which she had left open. She reentered the room, pulling a smaller cart than the one from the previous night. She moved the larger cart and replaced it with the new. Quickly shifting back to her cheerful mood, she gleefully announced, "My lady, your breakfast."

Blaine cringed once more in objection to being addressed so formally. "Please call me Blaine," she pleaded. "I am definitely not royalty."

Marrette once again gave a puzzled glance.

"Thank you for bringing my breakfast this morning and dinner last night."

Marrette's puzzled look turned to a look of pure confusion. "You are welcome my ... Blaine. May I ask, were there no clothes suitable to your taste?"

Blaine subconsciously ran her hands down her robe. "I really didn't get a chance to look, and I have to admit it's a little uncomfortable borrowing clothes from a stranger. Perhaps, I could just wash my clothes and put them back on."

Marrette's face lit up with a large sincere smile; a small contagious giggle escaped her lips. She might have been a very plain girl, but when she laughed the twinkle in her dark eyes lit up her whole face. "No, no Lady Blaine. You don't understand. These were all brought in for you."

Now Blaine was the one with a puzzled look on her face. "Okay! This is just another brick in the wall of confusion and mystery that seems to surround this place," Blaine said with a heavy sigh.

"I'm sorry. I'm not sure I quite understand. However, Lord Alderon will call on you after breakfast. I am positive he will clear up any confusion that may exist."

"So at what point were you told I'd be here?" Blaine stared at Marrette as she shifted uncomfortably under Blaine's intense stare.

"I am just a hand maiden, my lady. I am not privileged with the intricacies of the Manor." With that being said Marrette turned and guided the large cart from last night out the door.

"I'm sorry," Blaine called after her. "I'm just ... I don't know ... just need some answers."

Marrette stopped in the doorway, turned, and then smiled at Blaine. "Yes, my lady ... Blaine. If you are in need of any assistance from me, place your hand on the rose." With a swift turn, she was gone.

Blaine stared blankly at the sealed door for a moment. There was a hollow feeling in her stomach, but not from hunger. She had not yet been able to calm the uneasy sensation generated by her nightmare. Although Blaine had a history of bad dreams with some turning into full-fledged nightmares, she had never experienced such a lingering feeling of dread.

With a heavy sigh she walked to the closet and opened the door. She stood in the doorway, trying to grasp the concept that this bountiful wardrobe was designated just for her. It confused her that she was riddled with worrisome thoughts instead of being filled with sheer delight to receive such a magnificent gift. *Why is it that I'm so anxious?*

"I suppose I should get dressed," she muttered out loud. She walked into the enormous closet. Dresses, slacks, and blouses were grouped together. Each category was sorted by color. As she ran her hands over the items of clothes she felt a variety of textures, which all seem to be spun from natural materials. She opted for a pale blue cotton peasant shirt and a pair of woven pants that were as close to a pair of jeans as she could find. One wall of the closet was lined with drawers. Blaine curiously opened them to discover they contained accessories, undergarments, and pajamas. "They thought of everything, didn't they?"

She got dressed and exited the closet. The sunlight entering through the skylight above now flooded the room, giving it a warm inviting glow. She closed the closet door behind her. As she crossed the room toward the sitting area, a brilliant light blinded her briefly. Turning in the direction of the flash, she realized the sunlight from the skylight reflected off the mirror that hung over the vanity. She caught a glimpse of her reflection in the mirror. "Yikes!" she blurted out loudly. Her long, thick hair gave new meaning to the expression 'a rat's nest.' "That's what I get for falling asleep with wet hair." She picked up a brush that was eloquently displayed on the vanity. After a torturous few minutes of merciless brushing she managed to produce only a small semblance of style until she noticed a small glass object on the vanity that housed hair ties—perfect for containing her mass of hair. Quickly choosing one that matched her blouse, she gathered her hair into a low ponytail. "Good enough," she murmured and went into the sitting room.

The breakfast tray left for her once again contained several plates covered with silver domes. She lifted the first one, which revealed an assortment of pastries. The second dome concealed a variety of fruits and berries; some she recognized while others were completely foreign to her.

The last dome took her by surprise since it didn't reveal food, but a leather-bound book. On its cover, it bore a raised metal symbol: a triangle with loops at each point. Blaine ran her fingers over the geometric figure, which seemed vaguely familiar to her, although she was unsure where she had seen it before. It reminded her of an odd infinity symbol.

She opened the cover, revealing pages of yellowing parchment paper. The script was hand written in black calligraphy. She read the first paragraph out loud. "As the guardians of many worlds, we hold our beliefs sacred and the balance of life holy. Our world will forevermore remain steadfast and strong. This is the Telling of the journey of the people of Renault."

She carefully turned the page. As she attempted to read the beautiful script on the second page, she realized it was written in a language she did not recognize. Puzzled and slightly annoyed, she plopped into one of the chairs and absentmindedly took a pastry off of the plate, popping it into her mouth. Picking up the book again, she was disappointed to find that as she gently thumbed through it, the remaining pages were also written in the same foreign language.

She closed the book and returned it to its place on the tray. Taking another pastry before leaning back in her chair to contemplate its odd contents, Blaine's attention suddenly got diverted by the skylight casting a rectangular patch of light onto the area rug. Mesmerized by the geometric shape, she allowed the birds' morning praise songs to wash away the unsettling feeling in the pit of her stomach. Unfortunately, the serene setting lasted for but a moment since it was difficult for her to veer away from the menacing dream the night before. Just thinking about it turned her blood cold. She was greatly relieved when a soft knock at the door brought her back from such a dark place.

"Come in," Blaine said turning toward the door. She expected it to be Marrette, but was quickly caught off guard, holding her half-eaten pastry as Alderon walked into the room.

"Lord Alderon," she spoke while bowing her head.

"Oh my," he chuckled. "Please, only Alderon. I must apologize for not properly introducing myself last night. I am relieved to know that Marrette has at least informed you of my name."

Blaine relaxed a bit as his jovial laugh lightened her mood. Even the unsettling feelings she had experienced while remembering the nightmare about her mother seemed to retreat deep into the shadows of her mind. Blaine smiled as she spoke. "Yes, she did mention your name and also that you were the one who arranged for my wardrobe. I want to thank you. It was great to have something clean to change into."

He acknowledged her by nodding. Then noticing the food that remained virtually untouched, Alderon questioned, "Was the breakfast not to your liking, Blaine?"

"Oh, no it was just fine. It's just that I'm not a breakfast kind of person."

"Oh, I see, Very well then. Would you care to join me for a walk in the garden? As soon as you finish, of course."

Blaine followed his gaze and was a bit embarrassed as she realized she was still clutching her half-eaten pastry. She quickly set it down on the plate and said, "No, I'm finished. I'd love to go for a walk."

"Shall we go about our way then?" He asked as he turned toward the door.

As they exited the room Blaine took the opportunity to ask about the book. "So, I'm curious about the book. I'm assuming you sent it."

"Yes, I did." Alderon answered. When they took a left turn, Blaine paused allowing him to take the lead.

"I'm a bit confused. It was in a different language."

They continued to walk, passing a closed doorway to their right. It wasn't until Alderon turned left into an open doorway that he answered her. "It did appear that way, didn't it?"

Hoping for a better explanation, Blaine added, "I was able to read the first page but not the rest." Blaine followed Alderon through the door to find herself on a very large landing that was open to the floor below. There was a staircase with a beautifully crafted metal and wood banister that curved its way down to the bottom floor.

"Yes, some of our books can be quite crafty. They like to reveal their contents to those who try to read them, but only at the appropriate time."

"Reveal their contents? You mean a book can pick and choose who will read it?"

"Yes, you could put it that way. The books have a protective mechanism that prevents access to information for those not ready to receive it," Alderon answered as he began his descent down the staircase.

Blaine listened attentively while glancing around the elegantly furnished landing. It reminded her of a photo from *Architectural Digest*. Everything was so perfectly placed and well appointed. The white loveseat that set caddy corner to the staircase looked as though it had never been sat on. "Oh, such clever books," she said a bit sarcastically as she too started down the staircase. She looked around trying to absorb as much as she could of the very detailed area into which she was now descending.

She followed Alderon through an archway that led to a short hallway. At the end of the hallway were wooden double doors, which swung open as he approached. Without missing a step, he crossed over the threshold. Blaine followed closely behind him.

They had entered a huge room. Three of the walls were lined with bookshelves reaching two stories high. The fourth wall was adorned with huge French doors that allowed warm sunlight to fill the room.

Blaine spun slowly around looking at all the books that occupied every single shelf of the bookcase.

"Oh, I love those," Blaine blurted out as she pointed to the rolling library ladder.

"Yes, it does provide great assistance, especially when I must retrieve a book from the top shelf," Alderon pleasantly joked.

"Have you read every one of these books?"

"Yes, most of them at least once; some, more than that."

"Wow! Impressive."

Alderon walked over to the French doors and pushed them open. A light fragrant breeze danced about the room. Blaine took a deep breath.

"After you," Alderon motioned towards the open doors, flashing a brilliant smile as he spoke.

Blaine stepped through the door and onto a covered patio area. She could hear birds singing their well-rehearsed songs to the morning sun as they fluttered about the trees and bushes that resided in this paradise.

As Blaine stopped to take in all the beauty, Alderon walked past her and seated himself at a table, which resided in the middle of the stone patio. "Would you care for some tea?" He asked as he poured himself a cup.

"I think I'll pass if you don't mind," Blaine politely answered as she continued to survey the area. "It's beautiful out here." The flower-bordered patio consisted of large square stones designed in a diamond pattern. A six-inch carpet of thick blue-green grass bordered the diamonds.

Blaine walked across the patio and sat in the chair next to Alderon.

"This is my meditation garden."

"I can see why. It's very peaceful here," she answered as she directed her gaze from the alluring flowerbeds to the towering hedge that lay beyond. "These hedges are huge. They must be at least twenty feet tall. I'd hate to have to keep them trimmed."

"They have been here a very long time. This house has been in my family for several generations."

Blaine turned her attention toward Alderon and locked eyes with him. "So, any news about my mother?"

"Alas, we have heard not a word."

"Oh," Blaine replied disappointedly.

Alderon broke eye contact with Blaine and stood up. As he walked to the edge of the patio an awkward silence fell between them. Blaine's attention drifted back to the splendid variety of flowers that now surrounded her. The colors were so vibrant they seemed to radiate their own light source. The array of colors rivaled those contained in the largest box of crayons. Every hue was displayed boldly. Something hovered above the flowers in abundance.

"Are those butterflies or fairies?" She looked at Alderon who still stood at the edge of the patio with his back to her.

Alderon turned and faced her. "Those are butterflies. Fairies are not as common as you have witnessed here in Renault. They only reveal themselves to a selective few."

No sooner had Alderon spoken these words that a small fairy appeared. As the fairy fluttered about Blaine's head and face she was able to view the beautiful creature up close. The fairy stared directly into Blaine's eyes. Bowing her head politely, she then moved closer to Blaine and kissed her on her nose. Surprised by this, Blaine looked up at Alderon. His expression showed surprise as well. The fairy then quickly flew away.

"Absolutely astonishing," said Alderon. "I have never seen a fairy show such admiration for a human before."

Blaine couldn't hide her excitement as she displayed a beaming smile, which seemed to stretch from ear to ear.

Gaining his composure and deciding not to address what he had just witnessed, Alderon turned his attention to the purpose of the morning's walk, "Blaine, I suppose there is really no delicate way to approach a subject that will probably leave you with many more questions than you have now. However, time is a concern and it grows shorter by the day." As he spoke these words the smile faded from Blaine's face and she suddenly felt a knot in the pit of her stomach. Alderon continued, "We are not certain if your mother did in fact cross over into Renault. What we are certain of is that the Dark Legion that is plaguing Renault is aware of your crossover. You have become the main focus of their attention and they will not rest until you are in their possession."

Blaine suddenly felt as if she were going to be sick. She swallowed hard. "Why would they be interested in my crossover? Even more important, why would they want me in their 'possession'?"

"To try and make you understand I must tell you something of the history and legacy of our world. Eons ago Renault was entrusted with the guardianship of the gateways that connect many worlds together. These gateways were used freely by all inhabitants to pass from world to world. The elders of Renault have been responsible for the monitoring of these portals. One of those gateways led to your world. Over the past few decades Renault has been engaged in a great struggle, which has caused extreme upheaval for her people."

"Did I use one of these portals to cross over?" Blaine asked, interrupting Alderon.

"No, my dear. You see, the gateways have been sealed for a very long time, disallowing the once normal crossover."

The response to her question gave rise to more confusion. It was all Blaine could do to remain silent as Alderon continued. "Unfortunately, your world experienced an overwhelming shift in belief systems. As science grew, people abandoned the mystical and magical ways. They could not understand that gifts of faith and belief are not separate from science. The universe encompasses all and if this is not understood and embraced the fear of what we cannot understand becomes its own force, giving way to folklore and fantasy. Science demands proof. Once proof is required faith is lost. That which we fear is labeled as evil. The only way to deal with evil is to destroy it. The Elders were saddened by this shift. The most cherished beliefs of our world were now almost non-existent in your world. We could not allow this fear to spiral as we knew it would. The elders felt as if they had no other choice but to seal the gateway for the safety of Renault and all who called it home." Alderon paused. Walking over to Blaine, he seated himself in the chair next to her.

"So, all the gateways were sealed?" Blaine questioned. "No, not at that time. Only the one leading to earth was sealed. The elders knew that eventually an invasion from your world would be launched to destroy what was viewed as evil. The elders could not risk an invasion. Since the need to conquer and control had grown so rampant on earth they knew it was only a matter of time. Ours was a peaceful land. We had no armies or weapons." Alderon looked in Blaine's direction as if waiting for her next question.

Blaine sat quiet for a moment. There were so many questions going through her head she hardly knew where to begin. "Was that gateway common knowledge for everybody?"

"Here on Renault, yes. On earth only a few knew at first, but as your world's population grew more and more learned of its existence. It was apparent that its location would soon be common knowledge. You must know that the decision to close the gateways did not come easy for the Elders. We had always considered ourselves as watchers and historians for the different worlds. We never intended to interfere."

Alderon directed his gaze to the garden. He closed his eyes and took in a deep breath. "Oh, how I love the fragrant smell of this garden. It is so calming."

Blaine decided to take this opportunity to ask the one obvious question she had been holding back since Alderon first mentioned the sealed gateway. "If the gateway was sealed, how did I crossover?"

Alderon opened his eyes and turned to face Blaine. The sunlight reflected in his crystal blue eyes making them appear almost hypnotic. "Although I am not sure of the details of your crossover I am sure of one thing, your crossover was one of ancient magic." He then looked directly into Blaine's eyes as he continued speaking. "My dear, I must share that it has been an absolute honor to be in your presence." With that, he stood up. Taking two steps forward, he raised his arms over his head and began chanting words Blaine could not understand.

Confused, Blaine looked around the garden trying to find some kind of explanation for his strange behavior. "Alderon?... I don't ... " Her sentence was cut short by a horrible screeching in the distance. The smell of sulfur filled the air and Blaine thought she heard shrieks of terror. Suddenly a rumble shook the ground. Alderon stood unmoved in what appeared to be some sort of trance. To the left of Blaine came a brief, blinding light. She turned toward the light to see Elian walking quickly toward her. "We must go now." His voice expressed urgency, but his eyes were as calm and collected as always.

"What?" Blaine started to question him, but before she could say another word he took her hand. There was another flash of light, a moment of falling uncontrollably, then nothing.

CHAPTER 10

Blaine could feel warmth on her right cheek. She opened her heavy eyes and blinked several times as she tried to adjust to her surroundings. She was lying down. She could see a slated wooden ceiling above her. As she took a deep breath she noticed the aroma of smoke. She turned her head slightly to the right and focused on a fire burning in a small stone fireplace. She detected some movement in the room. Able to see only shadows in the dim light cast by the fire, she uttered softly, "Hello."

"Hello, Daughter of Sairah."

A sigh of relief escaped her as the familiar sound of Elian's voice reached her ears. Her head was beginning to clear, she sat up and demanded, "Elian, what happened?"

"Alderon detected an attack on the elders. He summoned me and we were transported here for your safety."

"Attack?" Blaine asked as she strained to see Elian in the darkness that hid him.

"Yes." As he stood up he softly uttered words Blaine did not recognize, and suddenly a warm glow filled the room chasing away the darkness. Elian walked across the room to a small counter that had a sink in it. He produced a glass from the cabinet and filled it with water. He turned and walked toward her holding out the glass. "Water?"

Blaine frowned, "Yes, please."

"The Sanction is searching for you," Elian continued.

"The Sanction? Is that the dark Legion Alderon started to tell me about before you brought me here?" Taking the water, Blaine swung her legs off the side of the couch and sat up. Her muscles felt sore and achy. She wavered as she tried to stand.

"Your body is adjusting to the zone jump. Drink the water as it will help you recover. To answer your question, yes, it is one in the same that of which Alderon spoke."

"Alderon had not yet explained why this sanction or dark legion is looking for me. He said they want me in their possession. I don't understand what they could possibly want with me. I'm just a normal teenager." She took a drink of water, locking her gaze on Elian as she drank.

A slight smile had formed on his lips. He sat down on the couch next to her and leaned back never losing his focus on Blaine. "Do you truly believe that?"

Blaine cocked her head to the left a bit. "Believe what?"

"Believe that you are just a normal teenager?"

"Well, yes." She paused as she brought to mind the events of the last few days. "I mean, I guess so.... "

Elian's smile widened a bit. "Okay then, you have me totally convinced, so let us continue on that assumption." He laid his head back on the couch and looked at the ceiling.

"Was that a bit of sarcasm I detected in your voice?" Blaine giggled. He didn't respond. "Okay, I have to admit things have been a bit strange. I'm in a world that is shrouded with magic and mystery. No one here has been at all forthcoming with helping me understand what has happened. My questions go unanswered and information has been minimal at best."

"Please understand we had to resort to secrecy for our own safety until we were sure where your interests were vested. It would have been unwise to tell you too much."

"Now that I've passed the test are you finally going to share all your secrets with me?" Blaine retorted sarcastically.

Elian remained silent for a moment as if carefully planning his next words. "As Alderon has stated before, time is growing short and we are hard pressed to remain vigilant. We must do what we can to keep our promise to protect the worlds with which we have sworn allegiance."

Blaine stared down at the glass in her hand. She put it to her lips and swallowed down the remaining water. Elian stood up effortlessly and took the empty glass from her hand. As their fingers touched a bright green aura appeared and then quickly faded. Startled, Blaine drew her knees into her chest. "What was that?" She questioned as she looked up at Elian.

He didn't appear to be surprised at all. "Emulsion," he replied and turned toward the small kitchenette.

"Emulsion? As in chemistry?"

"Yes, but not as on the level you know."

"Okay, explain it to me on your level."

He turned and leaned against the small counter where he had set her glass. "You explain to me what you know of it. Then I will elaborate on your theory."

"Okay. The basic definition is that when two liquids meet and don't mix such as oil and water, you have emulsion. Now you elaborate."

"We believe the true self of every individual surrounds the outer body. This field is known by many names such as energy, auras, and life forces. Emulsion is the meeting of these forces. I like to think of it as the appendages of the soul."

Blaine raised an eyebrow and asked, "So this flash of light happened because our auras touched and didn't mix?"

"No. Actually auras never mix. Some encounters are more explosive then others when brought together." Elian stated matter-of-factly.

"So, is that a sign that we should not be friends?" Blaine teased flashing a smile as she met his gaze.

Elian offered further explanation. "It simply is a mark of two souls on the same pathway—intertwined destinies, as the elders labeled it."

The words "intertwined destinies" echoed in Blaine's ears. Her smile faded from her face. "You didn't seem surprised to see this happen when we touched. This must happen to you a lot."

"No," he replied as he turned and filled her glass with water again. "I never have experienced it before. However, I have always known and felt a connection with you, Daughter of Sairah." He walked toward her and handed her the glass. "Rest now. We must take to travel once again." He turned toward the front door and began opening it.

"Wait," Blaine exclaimed as she jumped up to stop him. The exertion left her lightheaded and weak, but she remained standing. "You can't just tell me you've always known of our connection then walk out! There's so much I don't understand. So many questions, Please, Elian, enough of the secrecy!"

He paused but didn't look at her. "I am aware of your concerns, but for now you must regain your strength before we leave. I promise you all will be answered soon. Please rest now before your body loses consciousness." With that he walked out the door, closing it behind him.

As the door closed a cool wind blew in from the outside. Blaine could smell the cleansing scent of rain. She sat back down on the edge of the couch. The breath of fresh air seemed to clear her mind momentarily. With a deep sigh of frustration Blaine lay back down. She stared blankly at the ceiling; the image of her mother driving the sword through Elian's heart flooded her mind and caused her to shudder. "If it was just a dream, why does it remain so vivid in my mind?" She questioned out loud. A small voice in the back of her mind seemed to answer, "Visions are like that." Then perhaps it was more than a dream, she thought. Trying to lend some logic to the whole subject, she assured herself that her mother would never do a thing like that. She couldn't hurt anyone. These thoughts filled her head as she drifted off to sleep.

When she opened her eyes again she directed her gaze toward the door Elian had exited earlier. Bright sunlight squeezed its way through the cracks, framing the door with a golden brilliance. The inside of the house, however, remained dark. Blaine suddenly realized there were no windows in the room. Sensing Elian was not in the room, she stood up and walked over to the door. Unlike the doors in Alderon's house this one had a doorknob. She pulled the door open. The bright daylight flooded the room, blinding her for a brief moment. Blaine's eyes quickly adjusted and she went outside. She scanned the lush green that dominated the landscape in search of Elian. She took a few steps forward and then turned to face the house she had just occupied. To her surprise there was no evidence of a house. All she saw was the door that led straight into a moss-covered hill. The door was camouflaged by moss and mushrooms. This explained the absence of windows in the house.

Once again, she scanned the area looking for Elian. She spotted him sitting peacefully in a small clearing in the woods. His eyes were closed. *He must be resting or perhaps meditating,* Blaine thought to herself. Blaine walked toward the clearing. As she approached it, she caught a glimpse of the violet colored sky and once again became mesmerized by its beauty. After a brief pause she continued toward Elian. His eyes were now open and he seemed to be studying her. "Sorry to disturb you," she softly addressed him.

"You're not disturbing me."

"Good, because I need to find out about the attack. Is Alderon safe?"

"Unfortunately, I do not know," answered Elian.

Blaine could not help but feel disappointed. She had assumed Elian would have knowledge of the outcome of the attack. Now she had two people to worry about—Alderon and her mother.

Elian's voice interrupted her thoughts. "What was it that held such fascination for you a moment ago?"

"It was the color of the sky. In my world the sky is blue.... Oh, but you probably know that." She muttered a little embarrassed.

"No, I did not have knowledge of your world's sky color. I am not an elder. I know of all the worlds we are trying to protect. However, I do not have access to those books that contain the details of each world."

"Oh," Blaine blurted out in surprise. "I just assumed that you had been to my world before."

"No. Now that the portals are sealed there are very few that have crossed. It requires great magic and if not executed properly it could mean death."

Blaine locked eyes with Elian. "So, you were not the one that brought me here?"

"No."

His answer once again caused a knot to grow in the pit of her stomach. "But I saw you in my world twice right before I was brought here. Are you saying that wasn't you?" She dropped down and sat on one of the mossy patches that covered the forest floor. "Who was it then?"

"I do not have an answer for you, Blaine. Perhaps your mother sent you here."

"Yeah right. With what magic? How would that even be possible? You said it takes a powerful witch to cross over."

"Witch?" He cocked his head slightly as he spoke.

"Yes, people who practice magic. What do you call them here?"

"Everyone in Renault is taught basic magic. Also, they are taught about the universal life force that binds all living things together. However, not everyone is born with magic as were you and your mother."

"Wait! Are you telling me my mother was not just taught basic magic but that she was born with it?" Blaine questioned exasperatedly.

"Yes, Sairah is one of the most powerful spinners to have been born in centuries."

Blaine absentmindedly picked at a mushroom that took root in the moss. She sat silent for a moment. "That's not possible. She never spoke of magic, let alone performed it."

"Your mother is known to have hidden many a secret from even the most powerful tellers and spinners." As Elian spoke his tone shifted from normal to one of distain.

Blaine quickly looked up at him. Defensively, she stood up and exclaimed quite loudly, "You make it sound as if she is an evil person."

Elian sat silently for several minutes keeping his eyes focused on Blaine's demanding gaze. At last he spoke gently and deliberately. "When we are brought into this world we are a blank canvas. We are constantly required to make choices as we navigate our life pathway. With each choice we forge the direction of that pathway. Some of those choices may lead to dark regions of the universe. However, since life is not predetermined by making positive choices we have the ability to redirect ourselves toward the light once more."

Blaine's dream leaped back into her thoughts. She gasped slightly as a dizzying array of pictures flashed before her. It was as if she were watching a slideshow in fast forward. All the images were of her mother performing horrific acts of war against her own—one betrayal after another played out in her head. No matter how she tried to halt the assault of the images, they just kept coming. She lost awareness of her body as she was forced to witness scene after scene of horror with her mother as the star. She watched aghast as her mother silently slipped into a sleeping man's bedroom and slit his throat. "Please, make them stop," she screamed as she reached out to Elian.

Blaine felt Elian gently take her hand as she slowly regained feeling throughout her body. The visions began to dematerialize. She felt Elian embrace her. As he whispered an inaudible phrase a white light encompassed her and the visions stopped. She crumpled into Elian's arms. She suddenly became aware of everything around her as if she were experiencing life for the first time. She felt the cool breeze on her cheek and the earthy smell of moss and mushrooms and the warmth from Elian's body.

She realized she was lying on the ground and Elian was holding her in his arms. Blaine quickly rolled away from him and bounded to her feet. "What the heck was that?" She demanded.

After remaining seated on the forest floor for a few moments Elian slowly rose to his feet. "It was a Telling; an extraordinarily powerful one." Elian seemed drained. His normal olive complexion was now grayish and dull.

Then suddenly to the left of them came a commotion, which broke the serenity of the forest. Soldiers charged the clearing where Blaine and Elian stood. The soldiers grabbed them. Their uniforms were identical to the ones worn by the men Blaine and

Elian had encountered by the river.

"Blindfold and gag the spinner," one soldier shouted. The soldier that stood near Elian quickly complied. "Bind his hands also. We don't want any tricks."

Another soldier grunted as he walked over to Blaine. He put his finger under her chin lifting it slightly. Blaine glared angrily at him. "So much fuss over this?" He said under his breath. "Do you want her bound and gagged as well, sir?"

"No, that will not be necessary at this time," replied a booming voice that came from the forest. A tall, broad shouldered man emerged from the shadows and entered the clearing.

"Sir, I mean no disrespect, however, if she is the threat that Lord Tevis says she is, shouldn't we take precautions with her as well?" replied the soldier that stood in front of Blaine.

The commander glared back at the solider. "If she was the powerful spinner my father said she was, this capture would not have gone without incident."

"Sir, yes Sir" the solider replied while saluting.

Blaine looked over at Elian who now stood gagged and blindfolded with his hands tied behind his back. Both arms were firmly held by soldiers that stood on either side of him. Then from behind Blaine was seized by a soldier also. She struggled, causing him to tighten his grip on her.

Blaine shifted her gaze to the commanding officer who was now staring at her intently. She met his stare with a defiant glare. Blaine immediately recognized the intense green eyes that now seemed to be piercing her very soul. This was the same man who destroyed all the fairies in the flower field. An immense anger began to rise inside of Blaine.

"Yes." The commander uttered. "This is the cause of the disturbance I had been feeling. Lord Tevis will be most pleased. Secure her and take her back to the horses," he barked his command as he turned to re-enter the forest.

"Commander, what about the spinner?"

The commander stopped and looked back over his shoulder, "Kill him!"

"No!" Blaine screamed as she simultaneously broke free from the grip of the soldier. Throwing her hands out in front of her, Blaine was shocked as a blinding white flash shot out from her fingers. The earth cracked with a deafening crash that filled the air. All the soldiers fell to the ground motionless. The trees creaked in distress as the blasts pulsated into the surrounding trees, causing leaves to rain down on the mossy forest floor.

CHAPTER 11

Blaine quickly ran over to Elian who remained standing. She pulled his blindfold off and untied his gag. A blue light surrounded them both and gently levitated them. Then in a flash Blaine and Elian found themselves standing in unfamiliar surroundings.

Blaine glanced around the forest they now occupied. She was extremely disoriented but continued untying Elian's hands. "Thank goodness you were still able to do magic while bound and blindfolded," she whispered while fumbling with the unruly knot.

"I cannot perform magic while bound. I do not possess ancient magic. No spinners do anymore."

"What do you mean ancient magic?" You mean it wasn't you that toppled the soldiers and brought us here—whatever here is?" Blaine exclaimed confused and exasperated.

"No, it was not I. I am not familiar with this forest," Elian stated softly looking around the densely treed forest that now encircled them.

"The trees look like a type of weeping willow," Blaine stated as she walked over to a tree and ran her hand up and down the trunk. "Wow, Renault never ceases to amaze me. This bark feels like velvet, and some of the leaves are so purple while others appear to be fuchsia—amazing!"

"Yes," Elian replied flatly as he looked up. "The canopy they create is so dense you cannot view the sky above."

You're right. There are no breaks in the trees yet the forest is lit. How is that possible?" As she spoke she noted a look of dismay that had now settled across Elian's normally placid face.

"Lavisian Recata," Elian spoke loudly.

"Your magic will not work here, Elian, Son of Righteousness."

Startled, both Elian and Blaine quickly turned toward the direction of the pleasant voice. Blaine scanned the surrounding forest until her eyes locked on to a brilliant silver object moving toward them.

"Show yourself." Elian called out firmly while taking a defensive stance.

"But of course, weary souls. I must assure you my intentions are pure."

"Then why do you conceal yourself in the darkness of the forest?" Elian questioned. For the first time, Blaine detected uncertainty etched in his voice.

"I am not hiding, dear ones. I am just giving you a few moments to re-orientate yourselves from your journey." The silver object gracefully came into view. Blaine gasped in disbelief. Out of the corner of her eye she saw Elian drop to one knee and bow his head in respect.

"Elian, please rise," the magnificent unicorn spoke. "It is I who am honored to be in your presence."

Blaine stared, mesmerized as the majestic creature moved closer to them. Elian slowly rose to his feet, "I am at a loss for thoughts and words," Elian struggled to form the words that came out of his mouth, "I would have never imagined I would be honored to be in such a presence of majesty."

"Elian, perhaps our legend has been overinflated through the absence of the unicorn. We are all creatures of a greater power, just from different realms." Elian nodded uncertainly, still processing the reality that stood before him.

The unicorn turned his attention towards Blaine, "my lady, it is a defining moment for me to be face-to-face with you." His horn emitted a warm blue glow as he spoke to Blaine. "I know your questions are many; however, let me start by introducing myself. I am Kern."

Blaine glanced in Elian's direction, their eyes met briefly. A slight smile occupied Elian's normal stoic expression. Seeing Elian's posture relax brought a wave of relief to Blaine. She returned her gaze back to Kern. "So you are the one who brought us here?" she questioned meekly.

"Yes, it was my doing." Kern gently pawed at the forest floor. It took every bit of will power for Blaine to control the urge to wrap her arms around this beautiful creature that stood in front of her but she stood steadfast and held her composure.

"And the soldiers in the other forest, you were the one who struck them down allowing us to escape?" Blaine inquired.

"Oh my, no, that was all you my dear." Kern responded admittedly as he tossed his head in the air in a playful gesture.

"Me?! That is not possible!" Blaine blurted out loudly.

Kern chuckled lightly, "Oh, but it is, and now that you have returned to Renault your binding spell is beginning to lose its effectiveness over your many gifts, which are slowly surfacing. It will take much focus and dedication for you to be able to truly wield these powers."

Blaine stared blankly at Kern then shifted her stare towards Elian, "Were you aware of 'my gifts'?" She questioned accusingly.

Elian remained silent for a moment before answering cautiously. "I was aware of the possibility of your full potential;

however, as I have indicated before there was no evidence of what pathway you were to be on. The existence of the binding spell, I am without knowledge of. I do know in order to bind such powers, that you have just yet begun to demonstrate, would require the skill of a powerful spinner. So, I can only speculate that your mother is the one who set the binding spell upon you."

Blaine shifted her weight uncomfortably, staring down at the ground, attempting to digest all that was being told to her. "Lady Blaine," Kern spoke soothingly, "a binding spell is often used by spinners in order to hide themselves from other spinners. When magic is used it leaves a brief imprint on the natural surroundings of where the act took place and the type of magic used. It then manipulates the flow of energy that connects every living thing in the universe. This energy flows through everything that was created from the same source. This imprint that is left behind can be seen by other spinners."

"So, my mother knew I was born with magic and she wanted to hide me? Who was she trying to hide me from?"

Elian stood silently watching the interchange between Blaine and Kern.

"I am not privileged with the answer of her knowledge of the scope of your gifts. It may have been a precautionary tactic to keep you safe. There are many factions in this universe that would stop at nothing to control someone with your abilities and use them for the benefit of their cause." Kern stated gently.

"The Dark Legion?"

"Yes. That is the largest threat to us all at this time; however, I do not think your mother had a true grasp on how dangerous they truly are." The unicorn added, "Please let us walk as we converse. There are many who await in joyous anticipation of your arrival." Kern began walking toward a pathway which seemed to have suddenly appeared before them.

Blaine met Elian's eyes as he held out his hand slightly. "After you, Lady Blaine."

Blaine rolled her eyes at him even though his tone showed no sign of sarcasm and followed after Kern.

Kern spoke as he walked. "As you may have guessed from the experiences of the last few days, a terrible evil has crept into the gateway kingdom of Renault. This is personified in an individual fueled by his hunger for power. He gained entrance into Renault under false pretenses and has used the fears of the good people of Renault to dominate."

"How can someone use the fear of good people to turn them evil? It would seem to me that evil would already have had to be there," Blaine questioned as she followed Kern. She was in constant awe of the beauty and harmony displayed in every movement this magnificent creature made.

"Fear is a poison constantly coursing through the under-current of our lives. Truth and faith are the antidote. Fear of the unknown has the strongest hold on the human soul. It can tether the soul causing an individual to choose an unsavory pathway. Faith and truth bring light and that light breaks the tether allowing a positive choice of pathways. Faith and truth require strength, and most often harder choices. Many choose to take the easier path, refusing the antidote. Without the light the poison takes over and the soul becomes lost. Still looking for the easy way, these lost souls are manipulated by others touched by evil. These evil ones achieve their goals of power and domination because they use fear mongering to keep these lost souls from ever finding the light."

An odd feeling overcame Blaine as she listened to Kern's words about fear and lost souls. Somehow, she could not stop thinking about her mother. Suddenly, she could no longer deny the truth she had seen in her "telling." "My mother did horrible things—

things I could not even imagine doing to another living thing!"
Blaine could not stop the tears as she blurted out these words.

Kern stopped. Giving Blaine a sympathetic glance, he spoke
gently. "Yes, my child, she has been led down an extraordinarily
dark and encumbered pathway."

Blaine's breathing became short and labored. She closed her
eyes tightly and prayed she would wake up from this horrible
nightmare. Everything she believed about her mother had to
be a lie—everything! Her body began to shake uncontrollably.
Then she felt Elian place his hand on her shoulder. Instantly, a
calming warmth engulfed her. She opened her eyes and looked
at Kern. "I'm so sorry." She spoke softly while wiping the tears
from her cheeks. Feeling embarrassed, she continued, "Learning
these truths about my mother makes my life with her seem like
such a lie. It is a lot to process."

"There is no need to apologize," Kern responded sincerely as
he continued deeper into the forest. "Your mother had the ability
to send that evil one back to his old world—your world—and end
the darkness which plagued her land. Her faith wavered. The light
was extinguished as she chose the easy, self-serving pathway."

As Kern spoke Blaine's heart grew heavy with sadness for
her mother. "I understand about having doubts, but how could
she ever justify doing such unspeakable evil?"

"Ah, you see that's when the manipulation becomes so easy.
The transition which allowed her to become the cold and hard
person you saw in your telling happened before she left Renault
and over a long period of time. It began with perceiving the
horrible truth about the abandonment by her own parents. The
feelings of emptiness and betrayal created by this act were used
by the evil one, Tevis. She filled this void by mistaking his false
promises and lies for expressions of love that set her onto a very
dark pathway. He needed her to fully mature and develop the

ancient gift with which she was blessed. Once he controlled her loyalty and devotion he had in his possession the abilities of a very powerful dark spinner."

Their journey through the forest continued as Kern spoke. There is no way to describe how Blaine was feeling. She had wanted answers but they were coming at a very high price. As they walked Blaine glanced back at Elian. His silence was confirmation that he already had knowledge of her mother's dark legacy.

Blaine decided she needed some clarification of information in order to process all that was being told to her. When Kern paused she quickly addressed him, "Then Tevis, who is the leader of the Dark Legion, is a being from earth with no magic."

"That is correct. You see, without the aid of magic it would seem he has no power here. His power, however, is in his ability to prey on the weakness of the spinners. He has manipulated them and set them all on paths of darkness. Their perception is that he holds the key to their happiness, and by pledging their loyalties to his evil plan, they will be rewarded beyond their wildest dreams. So, in essence he does possess them and therefore possesses magic. It is quite evident; however, he does not have the key to accomplish his primary goal. Otherwise, the gateways would have been open by now."

Kern had now stopped in the middle of a beautiful meadow. Turning to his guests he continued speaking. "We have arrived. I believe it best we finish our conversation after you to get some rest."

Blaine took a few steps forward and stood next to Kern. Puzzled, she looked around the meadow. "Pardon my ignorance, but it would seem to me an open meadow would not be a safe place for us to take a rest. Shouldn't we seek shelter?" Blaine timidly questioned.

Kern let out a hearty laugh. "I assure you we are perfectly

safe here. I owe you an apology for not explaining when you first arrived here that we are no longer in Renault." Kern took a few steps forward then disappeared.

Wide-eyed and frantic, Blaine turned toward Elian. "What the ...?" She was surprised to see Elian was calm and collected as always.

"I have heard of this place. I always believed it to be legend." Elian's voice sounded almost giddy with excitement. He stepped forward. As he approached the spot where Kern had disappeared he called back over his shoulder, "Come along, Lady Blaine." Blaine caught a brief glance of his smiling face as he, too, vanished.

"Fantastic!" Blaine spoke out loud. "Here we go again."

CHAPTER 12

Throwing her hands up in surrender, Blaine approached the spot where Kern and Elian had disappeared. She stepped forward, bracing herself for some sort of teleportation travel. Surprisingly, her surroundings did not change. She was in the same meadow. She looked back and saw the view behind her was distorted as though she was gazing through a sphere. In front of her stood Kern and Elian.

"It is a protective shield. Only those with a pure heart may pass through it," Kern explained.

Blaine reached out to touch the shield. A low hum was emitted as she made contact with it.

"The forest we came through is Alatis's gateway to Renault and other worlds," Kern offered.

"There is a gateway that is still operable?" questioned Elian.

"The present elders have no knowledge of this gateway, though it was known to elders of long ago."

"So, you have the ability to visit other worlds? Do you not fear that invading forces may come here too?"

"You are speaking of the overwhelming urge that courses

through the very veins of mankind to dominate and conquer. We have witnessed the consequences of the dominant characteristics as civilization after civilization of man has destroyed themselves in the quest for power. Mankind's belief that happiness comes with power has always been very puzzling to us. Because we have no wish to bring this negative trait to this world, very few humans had ever been allowed to pass through this gateway. You and Lady Blaine are the first in a very long time to be allowed to pass," Kern stated with sadness in his tone.

Blaine was confused by this tone of sadness. As she saw it, only good could come from not letting mankind into this serene world. Man would only bring chaos and destruction. Given the choice, who would possibly want her race in their world?

Blaine's attention was then turned to surveying her surroundings. In the distance she could see what seemed to be a city. "Is that where you live?" she asked.

"No, that is the elfin city of Roe. However, that is our present destination. Gathered there are many who excitedly await your arrival."

"So, elves brought us to your world?" Blaine inquired.

"We all brought you here. It was a collective process bringing you to Alatis."

Elian remained silent as they walked through the meadow toward the elfin city. Blaine's thoughts drifted toward her mother again. "Kern?"

The unicorn slowed his steps and turned slightly to look at Blaine. "Yes, My Lady?"

Cringing slightly, Blaine asked, "Do you know where my mother is?" She heard Elian take a deep breath as though preparing for bad news.

"Her exact location is being veiled by her magic. However, we are aware that she crossed over into Renault shortly after you."

"Do you know if she has resumed her alliance with the Sanction?" She quietly asked.

Elian broke his silence. "It is highly unlikely she would be allowed to take refuge with any member of the Sanction. Sairah's abandonment of her position as second in command was the ultimate betrayal punishable by death."

"Oh!" is all Blaine could say. This new information was not expected. Concern for her mother once again flooded her mind causing her to continue the remaining journey to Roe in silence.

As they approached the city the dirt path they were traveling transitioned into a beautiful cobblestone road. They continued on toward the entrance of the city. From a distance it appeared to be walled. It was only as they got closer Blaine realized it was not a traditional wall. Instead, the city was surrounded by the same type of weeping willow trees they had encountered when they first entered this new world. These trees stood so close together, however, that they gave the illusion of one continuous tree that encircled the perimeter of Roe.

The entrance to the city was framed by a black metal archway. As they drew closer Blaine could see letters worked into the ornate arch. She read them out loud, "The High City of Roe." Elian gave her a surprised look, causing her to give him a questioning glance.

However, before Blaine could question his strange reaction Kern interjected, "I am very taken aback that you are able to read elfin."

"I can't," Blaine retorted.

"Well, evidently you can for the wording on the archway is in the ancient elfin language."

"No, it wasn't," defended Blaine. "It was clearly written in English."

"It makes no matter. Let us go now." Kern urged them on.

Upon entering the city, the impression formed from a distance that the city was an array of traditional buildings soon gave way to a strange reality. The dwellings instead were composed mostly of trees and plants.

"Does the entire city consist of this type of structure?" She asked Kern.

"Yes, with the exception of some stonework. The universal relationship the elves have with the plant world is truly remarkable. Their whole existence is in complete harmony with all living things. It is the ultimate coexistence."

"Spectacular!" Elian exclaimed as he looked around in complete amazement. Hills appeared to be multilevel houses. To give support huge tree trunks were ornately mingled with the dwellings. Elian walked over to one of the structures and ran his hand across it. "It's covered with moss!" he stated surprisingly.

Blaine, although fascinated by the beautiful and strange elfin city, experienced great enjoyment in watching Elian. She had grown so accustomed to his stoic nature that she could not help taking delight in his sincere expression of emotion.

Anticipating their curiosity, Kern explained. "Elves are able to communicate with all growing things. They are able to respectfully request plants and trees to grow in a 'specific manner' to form shelter for the elves. In return the elves protect the plants and trees, allowing them to thrive."

"Tell me more about this ability the elves have?" Blaine asked keeping in step with Kern as he continued to walk. Elian lagged behind, completely absorbed by his surroundings.

"All who live here in Alatis dwell in harmony. Most of us use the spoken word to communicate. However, it is the elves that are able to communicate with even the smallest insect by using the energy force that connects all living things."

As they journeyed farther into town Blaine noticed how

quiet and almost deserted it seemed. "Where is everyone?" She whispered softly. "It's kind of eerie here."

"They are all at the Great Hall in the center of town. You have to remember it has been a very long time since man has been here. Curiosity and excitement combined have caused the inhabitants to gather to view man, many for the first time. Their wait will soon come to an end. The Great Hall is just around the next corner."

Elian had rejoined the group and the three continued in silence. They turned the corner and a magnificent structure came into view. Large redwood trees lined each side forming walls. They stood at least three stories high. Lush dark green vines delicately wove their way around the enormous red trunks. The vines continued upward forming a graceful tapestry, which intertwined with the branches of the redwoods.

The massive "tree structure" was nestled up against a soft rolling hill. The murmurs and whispers of those gathered in the Great Hall gently filled the air.

Kern signaled Elian and Blaine to stop. He spoke softly. "The elves' culture is very rich in tradition and ceremony. Please wait here a moment while I announce your arrival."

Blaine watched as Kern entered the hall passing between the two huge flowering willow trees that stood on either side of the entrance. Their long sweeping branches had been carefully tied back creating elegant curtains, which cascaded down each side. A warm light engulfed Kern and he disappeared into the hall.

"See how the vines intertwine up and across all the trees? They create the walls and ceiling," Elian whispered as he stepped closer to Blaine.

"I know. They are so dense light from inside the hall doesn't penetrate them," Blaine said. Then as she turned toward Elian she asked, "Are you scared?"

"No, of course not," answered Elian with a puzzled look on his face. "Does this situation cause you distress?"

Before Blaine could answer Kern reappeared accompanied by a tall slender woman in a flowing blue gown. "Welcome to the High City of Roe." The lady spoke as she delivered an eloquent curtsy.

"Thank you, My Lady. Also thank you for allowing our passage into your magnificent city," Elian answered bowing down on one knee as he made a wide sweeping open-handed gesture.

Blaine quickly followed suit delivering an awkward curtsy as she spoke. "Yes, thank you." Blaine could not help but feel very strange. She had no clue as to protocol in such a situation.

"Let me introduce myself. I am Lyra, Queen of the elves and head of the United Council. It was the Council's unanimous decision to open our gateway for you. Come now and greet the rest of the Council and the many others wishing to meet you." Her voice was lilting. Her words were delivered in an unemotional and guarded manner.

A light breeze rustled the nearby leaves that littered the cobblestone road. It also carried the sweet fragrance of the blossoms that covered the willow trees. Closing her eyes, Blaine took a moment to inhale the intoxicating scent. When she reopened her eyes, she was aware Lyra's gaze was locked on her. Blaine involuntarily felt her own eyes lock on Lyra's intense glare. She felt herself being drawn into the deep violet pools that were Lyra's eyes. The breeze stirred again breaking the spell. Blaine tried to gain her composure as Lyra gracefully swept back a strand of Raven black hair the breeze had caused to dance in front of her eyes. Blaine smiled with no response from Lyra.

Blaine saw Lyra turn and motioned them forward as she said, "Come this way." The party of four led by Lyra entered the Elfin's Great Hall. As the inside of the Great Hall came into view Blaine was able to see row after row of carved stone pews. Every seat was filled. Lyra walked down the center aisle toward the front of the hall where a stage was located. All eyes were on Blaine and Elian. As they continued down the aisle they could hear quiet murmurs and gasps of amazement coming from the seated congregation.

The look of amazement of those seated seemed to pale compared to Blaine's overwhelming sense of astonishment as she passed row after row of what, up until that moment, she regarded as mythical beings. She met admiring gazes with the likes of griffins, elves, fauns, and at the back and sides of the Great Hall were lined with centaurs.

Slowing her pace, Blaine looked ahead to observe how the cobblestone aisle managed to seamlessly intersect the carved steps leading to the stage where Lyra now stood. Kern had turned to the right at the foot of the stairs and joined a small group of creatures gathered there. Blaine and Elian stopped at the foot of the stairs not sure how to proceed. Their question was answered as Lyra motioned to them to join her on the stage. They ascended the stairs and took their place next to the Queen.

"My fellow Atlatisians, I wish to thank you for coming here to welcome our honored guests. It has been all too long since mankind has walked among us. That changes today." Lyra's voice filled the hall. Then indicating the group Kern had joined at the right of the stage, she continued. "The United Council has brought them here to help defeat the Sanction that grows stronger with each passing day and poses a threat to all." A round of applause filled the Great Hall. Lyra held up her hand and all fell silent again. "This is Elian, Son of Righteousness, and this is the prophesied daughter, Lady Blaine, The Bringer of Light." Applause once again filled the hall. Lyra held her hand up to once more silence the crowd.

Before Lyra could speak again a voice from the back of the hall shouted, "How could you have compromised our very existence by allowing the bloodline of man to step into our world?"

All heads turned in the direction of the voice. Lyra searched the back of the hall to see who had so blatantly broken protocol. "Come forward!" She demanded.

A short stocky figure emerged from the shadows. Stepping into the aisle, he took a few steps toward the front of the hall, and then stopped. In the light that was being emitted from the globes at the end of each pew the figure came into view. His russet beard was long and matted. A tattered hat was pulled over his eyes casting a shadow upon his face as he spoke. "You are allowing an evil to threaten the harmony, which is the very heart of this land."

It took Queen Lyra only a moment to recognize the figure who had taken such liberties. Speaking with impatience in her voice, she addressed the figure. "Rumpkin, you have made us all very aware of your concerns with our decision to allow man into our realm. As I have stated before, your fears are archaic and your beliefs are tainted with hatred for a whole race that is being unfairly judged for the actions of a few."

This response prompted an outburst. The dwarf stamped his foot as he stammered angrily, "Ha! Judgment of a few? You most of all should support this so-called judgment. How can you ignore the spilling of your own blood line?"

An elf in the front row leaped from his seat and confronted Rumpkin. "That is quite enough. How dare you reference a matter that brings such deep personal pain? We have tolerated your outlandish conspiracy theories and prejudices. You and your people are privileged to have so graciously been allowed sanctuary in our land. We, however, will not stand for your disrespect to our Queen."

Unaffected by these words, Rumpkin continued his rant. "So, we hear from the mighty Armel. You claim this to be a peaceful land as you train your army of elves for battle, all the while denying any threat. You can't tell me revenge for your sister's death has never crossed your mind. Now you and your own mother have welcomed the very same bloodline of man into our land. Worse yet you have endangered all of us. You know the evil intent and power of the man that stole your sister's life. Even now he searches frantically for the two that you and the Council have brought here."

Blaine and Elian stood and watched as two other elves joined Armel. They lifted the small dwarf by his arms and carried him toward the exit of the Great Hall. This did not discourage him from continuing his protest. "Tevis will find a way here and he will destroy us all. You will rue the day you allowed these two into our lands, Queen Lyra." His voice became inaudible as he was expelled from the Hall.

Lyra turned to Blaine and Elian. "My sincerest apologies to you both. Rumpkin is a very misguided soul who harbors archaic beliefs taught to him from his world of Orr." Not sure how to respond to all they had witnessed, Blaine and Elian smiled politely and nodded. Lyra faced the audience again. Many of the members were talking loudly amongst themselves. Others stood in silence with looks of disbelief on their faces.

The Queen held up her hand and motioned for silence. The crowd was instantly quieted. "I do not feel the need to defend the Council's decision to bring our honored guests here. To ease any fear, I will offer that the barrier, which has protected our land for eons, be not compromised. Moving on, we must not dwell on past events. Instead we must always keep love in our hearts. This love brings the gift of forgiveness. Rumpkin has not learned this. His fear and anger are all consuming. Do not let him influence you."

Lyra paused to clear her mind. "I had hoped to offer a proper welcome to our guests, but this interruption has dampened the event. So, I will only say we are honored to have Blaine and Elian in our presence. Please make every effort to make them feel at home during their stay in Alatis. I bid you a good day. Please go about your daily rituals. Thank you."

Lyra turned to address Blaine and Elian. "Rumpkin is a relic from another world. After his world was all but destroyed we gave sanctuary to him and the remainder of his clan. He holds humans responsible for the destruction of his world. However, truth be told, the inhabitants of Oritz are as much to blame as the humans."

As Lyra spoke Blaine thought she detected uncertainty reflected deep within the Queen's eyes. Before Blaine could give more thought to this impression, an elfin soldier approached Lyra and spoke softly to her. When they had finished their conversation, Lyra turned to Blaine and Elian, "You must excuse me. Something has occurred that needs my attention. I do apologize, for I had intended to show you about our city and help you get settled. I am sure Kern is up for the task."

"Get settled?" Elian questioned. "We were not aware we were to stay."

Calmly addressing Elian, she stated, "At this time, it is not safe for either of you to return to Renault. We are monitoring the situation. Lord Tevis is outraged that his general let you evade capture. His anger is now being taken out on all of Renault. The atmosphere is very tumultuous and dangerous."

"I do understand the ramifications of our escape. However, I have trained my whole life for these events. In actuality I am part of the catalyst that set these actions in motion." Elian responded passionately.

"Elian, I have watched you for years. Your gifts combined with your extreme dedication and training have made you the warrior and spinner that stands before me today. Unfortunately, your very strengths have made you an extreme threat to Tevis. He will use all his power to destroy you. We must keep you safe until we formulate our defense against his evil."

Blaine watched as an expression of disappointment washed across Elian's face. Blaine was struck by Lyra's use of the word warrior. Certainly, in all their time together Elian's action were nothing less than heroic. The word warrior indicated formal training. Renault had no army to speak of, so who would have trained him? Blaine sighed to herself. Just as she thought, she was not surprised that another mysterious facet to Elian was added to the mix.

Lyra placed her hand on Elian's shoulder. "Soon enough." She turned and nodded to Blaine. "I will join you again tomorrow," she said as she left with a soldier.

"Lady Blaine and Sir Elian, if you would please join me," Kern politely called to them. Responding to his request, they left the stage and joined Kern at the bottom of the stairs. He stood with a centaur, a griffin, and a faun. Blaine was very familiar with all these mystical characters from her hours of reading fantasy stories and folklore. "The United Council represents the tribes, clans, and races that inhabit Alatis," Kern explained as he prepared to make introductions.

"With the exception of the dwarfs," the griffin chimed in. "They are a bristly combative clan," he added, slightly ruffling his feathers.

"Always arguing just for the sake of arguing, there is no reasoning with them, especially Rumpkin. Please do not think we share his views on mankind," the faun interjected as he stepped forward playfully. He bowed deeply. "I am Venistious, but call me Veni. My name is an old family tradition--too long and too formal. I much prefer Veni. It fits me so much more appropriately." He hopped slightly from hoof to hoof in a childlike manner as he spoke.

"Enough now, Veni! They don't need to hear your complete family history." The griffin admonished.

"Maorga is right. I am sure with the events that have already taken place, our honored guests are feeling a bit overwhelmed. Your trivial banter will not help matters, dear friend," said Kern kindly.

A flash of color arose in Veni's cheeks. "I am terribly sorry. I have a tendency to babble on when I am nervous or excited. I have always done it ever since I was a wee one. I don't know why I do it; I just do. I'm very aware that I do it but I just can't seem to stop myself."

"Uh umm," Maorga interjected. Veni responded with a nervous giggle.

Blaine shifted her gaze to the centaur that stood a step or two behind the others. He had his arms folded across his chest. His long, black, flowing tail swished slightly from side to side. His expression was stoic. Blaine made eye contact with him but quickly looked away. His immense stature was quite intimidating.

Maorga noticed Blaine looking at the centaur. "Do not mind Savar. He is one of few words. His silence takes some getting used to. However, it evens itself out when Veni is here." They all chuckled lightly with the exception of Savar. He cracked a small pretense of a smile. "Very well.then, let me take them to their guest quarters. My friends, I will meet up with you at a later time," Kern directed to the other members of the Council.

"Again, welcome to Alatis," Maorga said bowing slightly.

Blaine answered politely, "Thank you."

CHAPTER 13

Kern carefully navigated the narrow center aisle of the Great Hall as he led the group to the exit. His hoofs echoed throughout the now empty hall as they made contact with the cobblestone path.

"How long do you think our stay here will be?" Elian asked.

"That is a question we cannot answer at this time. Our priority right now is in locating Sairah. We believe that she is now powerful enough to weaken the magic that protects the gateways. If she has once again formed alliance with Tevis it would mean his armies could have access to all the worlds."

"Yes, that would be a disastrous situation," Elian added. Blaine detected impatience in his tone.

They exited the Great Hall, passing by several groups of elves still lingering about. Blaine made eye contact with several of them exchanging polite smiles. They followed a small path that veered to the right, leading them just outside of the city's center. They stopped in front of a stone house.

"This is where you will be staying," Kern offered.

Elian thoroughly examined the structure before entering through the artfully crafted arched door. Blaine remained outside with Kern and took a seat on an ornately carved wooden bench that set underneath a paned glass window. She could smell the earthy aroma of the moss that gracefully covered the steep roof of the cottage. "So Tevis killed Lyra's daughter?" Blaine asked timidly.

"Yes. He has the blackest of souls. All light was extinguished long ago. It would seem redemption will never be an option for him."

"How did it happen? Perhaps in battle?"

"Oh no, much worse. Daria, Lyra's daughter, had a great fascination with the human race. She was able to see the goodness in their souls. She felt she could be a beacon of light in their dark world; helping them to choose positive pathways. Lyra allowed Daria to cross over to earth. Living among mankind, she brought light to many lost souls. Then her path crossed with Tevis. Even though very young, Tevis had already lost his way. His ambition and tremendous lust for power had set him on a dark pathway. Daria was determined to connect with the spark of light she saw still existed in his soul. Daria was convinced she could direct him to a new path that would offer him a life of light and love."

"And he killed her for that?" Blaine asked staring at Kern wide-eyed.

"Oh no, not for that. I truly believe at one time, Tevis was very fond of Daria. She was incredibly beautiful and quite engaging. A simple smile from her would lighten even the darkest mood."

"So, he fell in love with her?" questioned Elian who had joined Blaine on the bench.

"I am not sure Tevis knows the meaning of the word love. We do know that Daria fell in love with Tevis. This did not make Lyra happy. When it was time for Daria to return to Alatis, Lyra refused her daughter's request to allow Tevis to join her. Daria felt she had no choice but to remain on earth with the man she loved."

"Yikes!" Blaine exclaimed as she shifted in her seat. "That must have made Lyra very mad!"

"Elves do not show emotion as humans do. They are very poised and calm even in the most trying situations that pertain to everyday life. However, I am told that when Lyra discovered that Daria had revealed her true heritage to Tevis and had broken confidences by teaching him practices of the elfin way, it was a breaking point for Lyra. Against strong protests from Armel, Daria's younger brother, Lyra broke all communications with her daughter."

"The situation escalated when Lyra learned that Tevis had in his possession a book of dark spells that had existed from the dawn of time. This book was considered so dangerous that in order to make sure it did not fall into evil hands many attempts have been made to destroy it. However, even the most powerful magic had no effect. The book was deemed indestructible. So, it was decided the only way to prevent it from being used was to hide it. It is believed the leaders of the many worlds decided to conceal it on earth. Using strong magic to ensure its hiding place seemed to provide the ultimate protection since the inhabitants of earth did not possess magic."

"Well clearly that was a bad decision," Blaine muttered. "How did Tevis obtain the book if it was so well hidden?"

Kern circled a bit then lowered himself to a green patch of grass that grew in front of the bench where Blaine and Elian sat. "We believe Tevis somehow tricked Daria into summoning the book, an action that ultimately resulted in her death."

"I have heard stories about this book since my childhood. In Renault it is referred to as the Book of Death because according to legend to perform every spell requires the soul of the living and the soul of a spinner," Elian stated flatly.

"Yes, Elian, every realm is aware of the book's existence and it has been given many names. The spell used by Tevis required a potion made with the 'spilling of blood of an elf.' If executed correctly, the spell would result in a life of longevity of the one performing the ritual."

"Oh, my goodness!" Blaine explained leaping to her feet. "He killed her for the lure of a longer life?"

"I am afraid so. Sadly, it would seem his lust for power ultimately outweighed any feelings he had for Daria," Kern answered. "Having gained knowledge of the gateways from Daria he was careful not to reveal his true nature until once again using deceitful methods he persuaded her to allow him to pass over into Renault."

"How was that possible? I thought the gateways were sealed," Blaine queried as she repositioned herself next to Elian.

"You have to remember that Tevis has been alive for a very long time. When he crossed over the gateways were still free for travel for those who had knowledge of them."

"Daria betrayed us all by showing him the gateways," Elian accused.

"Oh, dear one, please don't judge so harshly. You have to remember that one who loves purely never has evil in their intent. However, love can be blind to deceit. I'm sure Daria somehow thought she was doing the best for her cause of bringing light to mankind. Her actions were dictated by the belief that Tevis had responded to her and that there had been an alliance formed."

"Did Tevis pass over into any other worlds?" Blaine asked.

"No, fortunately for all the other worlds but unfortunately for Renault, since the gateways were sealed shortly after Tevis's arrival in Renault. The elders' decision to close the gateways denied him any other crossovers and confined him to Renault."

"What happened to the Book of Death? Is it still in Tevis's possession?" Elian asked.

"It is assumed so, Elian," Kern answered.

"If this book contains so many powerful spells why hasn't Tevis used them to gain ultimate control and to break the seals on the gateways?" Blaine questioned.

Elian responded quickly, "Tevis's rise to power was based on deceit. The gateways were closed by the elders for the protection of the worlds. However, Tevis has convinced the populace that the elders sealed the gateways to keep control of all who lived in Renault. He claimed he was fighting for their freedom. They truly believe his cause was just and followed him blindly. Tevis is an extremely manipulative man."

"You are quite right, Elian. That is why his ownership of the book is a closely guarded secret. It would be hard for Tevis to justify ownership of such an evil. Knowledge that he owns the Book of Death would expose his true nature. That is something Tevis cannot risk until he has possession of the magic he needs to achieve his goal. Then it will be too late for those who had been so easily duped. It is my belief that no spinner under Tevis's influence has magic strong enough to execute the spells contained in that book. Your mother seemed to possess the most promise. She was still young when she left Renault. She had not yet achieved the full potential of her magic. Now, however, it is more than reasonable to assume she possesses the maturity and skill to execute those spells."

Blaine remained silent for a moment then gazed intently at Kern. "What happened to my mother that allowed Tevis to possess her? I need to know the truth about what was so horrible that it led her down such a dark pathway."

Kern tossed his head slightly, the late afternoon sun reflecting off the strands of his silver mane. "I will do my best to help you understand your mother's descent onto the dark pathway. Renault had remained one of the few civilizations of humans whose inhabitants had not been fully consumed by greed and the lust for power. Tevis, however, being from earth, possessed this dark nature. Once he arrived in Renault he was quick to realize that control of the gateways would be the means by which he could obtain unlimited power. Tevis realized his first step to his rise to power was to dominate Renault. It was not long after his arrival that the elders decided that as guardians it would be in the best interest of all worlds to seal the gateways."

Kern let out a long breath before he continued. "As Elian mentioned, Tevis used this decision to convince the good citizens of Renault that the elders were taking away their freedom. Backed by these misguided souls, Tevis rose to power. Knowing that he needed magic to open the gateways, Tevis set out to obtain the means by which he could put his plan into action. He had to be careful not to reveal his true motives. This plan to possess magic impacted your mother's life immensely because he began by requesting all newborn children of spinners and tellers to be screened for gifts. Most did not protest this testing. However, when he began confiscating those children for 'the good of the Sanction,' it initiated a variety of responses."

Tears began to well up in his eyes. Quickly composing himself, he proceeded. "Some gave their children in good faith believing in Tevis's cause, which was definitely an act of poor judgment. It did not take long for some parents to realize all was not as it seemed and that their children were being used. Realizing this, they started hiding their gifted children. The elders set up safe houses where parents could place their children. These safe houses allowed the children to have a childhood free of the brainwashing taking place with those in Tevis's control. The children were visited by their parents in secret."

"Some parents chose to put binding and protective spells on their infants so they wouldn't be detected." Elian added.

"So why didn't all parents just do that instead of hiding their children?" Blaine asked.

"It wasn't that easy." Elian continued, "Magic has an important role in our culture. The binding spell disallows children to ever practice magic. Some parents felt this was wrong because it denied children their heritage and their elevated social standing. In fact some hold the belief that if you don't have magic you have no social standing. This prejudice is held so strong by some they consider anyone without magic to be an outcast."

Elian dropped his head and closed his eyes as if feeling the pain his people were enduring. "As the Sanction grew in power some people began to realize they had been wrong about Tevis. Even though many no longer believed in his cause, fear of the consequences of not complying resulted in many going against their better judgment and turning their children over just so they could be left in peace. These children were molded to fit Tevis's purpose."

Regaining his composure Elian continued. "It was a difficult decision, but Sairah's parents decided to hide your mother with the elders to be taught the enlightened ways. Her parents visited her in secret."

"In the meantime, Tevis became aware that the special spinner he needed to open the gateways was not among those in his possession. However, he knew there was someone in the realm that did have the power of ancient magic. The spinners in The Legion can detect the mark of ancient magic left on the universal thread that connects all living things. Every time your mother used her gift the mark was detected."

"Tevis had calculated the probability of which families could have produced a child of ancient magic and began watching them in hopes of being led to their hiding places. Knowing this, Sairah's parents had to begin limiting their visits."

"Why didn't the elders just keep my mother from performing

magic? Problem solved!" Blaine blurted out.

"If only it were that easy," Elian chuckled.

Kern interjected, "Blaine, think about the way your magic manifests itself without any conscious thought of using it. Now imagine a child prone to tantrums and emotional outbursts as all children are. One of the key factors in the training of magic is control. It can take years of training to achieve control. Some never accomplish it. Even if told, a child could not refrain from an occasional accidental display of the gift."

"Oh!" Blaine responded quickly. She sat in silence for a moment trying to digest all that was being disclosed to her.

"The fear of detection became more dangerous when Sairah's mom became pregnant with her second child. Even though it had been decided to put a binding spell on the infant at birth the fear of being discovered became more intense. Your grandparents wanted to protect their children at all costs. Visiting Sairah was risking it all." Kern offered.

"They stopped visiting her completely? How awful! My mom must have felt her parents were replacing her with a new baby. No wonder she felt abandoned," Blaine said sympathetically.

"Aw, you are so right," confirmed Kern. "That is exactly the way Sairah saw it. She was only 13 when they last visited her."

"Though the elders were aware the visits had to be limited due to the possibility of discovery, he became concerned when many weeks passed without a visit. They began a discrete inquiry to find news of your grandparents' whereabouts. The elders hid their concern from your mother to protect her from worry. To their horror they discovered your grandparents had been tortured and killed by Tevis while trying to learn Sairah's location."

Blaine turned pale. "Why didn't the elders tell her the truth?" Blaine inquired.

"Unable to cope with the feeling of abandonment she ran

away from Alderon before he could tell her the sad news. Her immaturity did not allow her to understand the self-sacrifice her parents had made in their choice to leave her with Alderon. Her overwhelming anger in the belief that she had been abandoned caused her to leave the protection she had been under for all those years."

"Alderon was the elder that hid my mother? That is why he said he knew her when she was upon another pathway. Wait, Kern, do you know if he is okay?"

"Yes, he is in hiding; but safe. The Sanction's attacks have grown more frequent and more brutal." Kern replied.

Elian's body stiffened. His relaxed facial features shifted to the blank, stoic façade Blaine was familiar with when she first met him. She made eye contact with him, attempting a brief smile to ease his thoughts. However, in the back of her mind she could not help feeling that the attacks were her fault. After all they were searching for her.

Seeking more information, Blaine asked, "How did Tevis find her?"

"We think she was trying to find her way to her parents' house when Tevis's spies discovered her and took her to him. As soon as she left the protective bubble that was Alderon's estate she was easily detected. She was never told about her parents' death. Tevis befriended her. By feeding into her anger and perception of her abandonment, she was directed to the pathway into the darkness." Kern answered.

Anticipating her next question, Elian spoke. "When Alderon and Sairah crossed paths again Alderon tried to tell her the truth. Tevis kept her isolated for years until his lies became her reality. So skilled in the art of deception, Tevis was effectively able to sway Sairah into believing that the truth Alderon relayed to her was just a pack of lies."

Blaine nodded her head as she rose to her feet and walked over to a patch of wildflowers that swayed gently in the light breeze. She reflectively stared at them then turned and faced Kern and Elian. She spoke as she walked toward the cottage that was to be her home for an undetermined period of time, "If you don't mind I'd like to have some time to myself. This day has been quite an emotional roller coaster." Not waiting for any response, she made a beeline for the door, roughly pushed it open, walked briskly through it, and then closed it with a resounding bang.

CHAPTER 14

She stood leaning against the front door with her eyes closed. She could hear Elian and Kern speaking softly to each other outside. She opened her eyes and began to survey the cottage. Directly in front of her was a set of narrow stone stairs that led to the second story. To the right of her was a large picture window. She took a step toward it. Looking out, she could see Elian still seated on the bench. She turned to face the interior of the room to see that there was a large wood framed couch in front of a modest stone fireplace. She walked further into the living room, passed the couch, and ran her fingers across the scarlet silken material that covered it.

Stopping in front of a glass door just to the left of the fireplace, she gazed out the window. She could see there was a thriving vegetable garden at the edge of the yard. Beyond that there was an orchard of fruit trees bordered in part by a small creek that wound its way through the patches of trees and bushes that dominated the landscape. Turning to view the rest of the cozy room, she saw two doors. The first door was under the stairwell and led to a small bathroom. The other opened into a bedroom.

Blaine walked toward the bathroom. Her stomach protested loudly, but food was the furthest thing from her mind. Stepping into the oddly angled bathroom, she noticed just as she was about to close the door that down the hallway there was an archway leading into a kitchen.

Blaine turned the water on in the sink. Noticing a mirror above the sink she tried to ignore her image, but her attempts were in vain. The reflection of the girl looking back at her was barely recognizable. The wide-eyed innocence of youth had faded over the past few days since she had crossed over. She sighed heavily and quietly commented to the stranger in the mirror, "It feels like a lifetime has passed." She paused a moment as if waiting for some kind of retort.

The reflection of the shower looked enticing enough to forgo her original plan of simply washing up. Placing a neatly folded towel on a hook, she undressed, and stepped into the glass-encased structure. She flinched as the unexpectedly cold water washed over her before changing temperature. Welcoming the warm water as if it was a long-lost friend, Blaine closed her eyes and allowed the crystal clear liquid to flow down upon her achy head. She just wanted her mind to go blank. However, her thoughts would not be quieted. Her mind kept twisting and turning the pieces of information and trying to fit them into what felt like a crumbling puzzle that represented her life. So much of what Blaine thought to be true was just a carefully orchestrated deception.

One reoccurring thought puzzled her; Sairah went to great lengths to hide her past in Renault. Perhaps she reevaluated some of her choices. Maybe she wasn't that dark evil spinner everyone assumed she was. Her train of thought was interrupted by the nagging protests of her stomach. She turned the water off and opened the shower door. Steam poured out into the remaining bathroom. Engulfed in a fine mist, Blaine gave a slight shudder.

She didn't anticipate stepping out onto a cold stone floor. Grabbing the towel, she quickly dried herself off. She cringed at the thought of covering her newly cleansed body with dirty clothes. But to her surprise, her garments did not seem to harbor the odor of well-worn clothing.

Feeling somewhat refreshed, Blaine returned to the living area of the house. She was in awe of the orange sky that was the featured dusk show of the adjoining window. Magenta highlights danced as the sun orchestrated a final light display before settling beyond the horizon for the night. An enticing aroma came from the direction of the kitchen. Blaine made her way to the archway to see Elian standing over the stove with his back to her. He spoke without turning around. "I retrieved some vegetables from the garden. I assume that you are drained and hungry as am I."

"You have no idea," Blaine responded enthusiastically. "It smells amazing!" She lifted herself effortlessly and sat on the small counter next to the stove where Elian was busy preparing the meal.

"So many talents," she teased. "First I learn that you are a trained warrior and now I discover you can cook, too! I'm truly impressed. You'll make a fine husband someday, young man," she giggled. He glanced up at her and flashed a shy smile.

While Elian finished showing off his culinary talents Blaine busied herself setting the small round table that was situated under a large picture window at the back of the kitchen. "Is there anything I can help you with?" She questioned.

"No, I am just finishing up." He brought over two large bowls and set them in the middle of the small table.

Blaine was now seated at the table inspecting the contents of each bowl. One contained a variety of vegetables in what appeared to be a type of red sauce. The other contained a fruit salad. "Looks yummy!" she exclaimed as she grabbed the serving spoon and loaded her plate from the contents of the bowls.

"Elves are vegetarians," Elian explained as he began dishing up his meal.

"Oh!" Blaine said as she shoveled the first bite into her mouth. "Oh, my goodness! This is incredible." Blaine gushed trying to keep the food contained within her mouth and speaking at the same time. This made Elian laugh. The two spent the remainder of the meal in silence tending to the task at hand of satisfying their neglected appetites.

When they had both finished Blaine pushed away from the table and began clearing the dishes. Blaine protested when she realized Elian pitched in. "No! No, you made dinner. I got the dishes." Elian responded by repositioning himself in his chair.

"So what were you and Kern talking about after I left?" Blaine asked as she began filling the sink with soapy water.

"Logistics," Elian replied flatly.

"Oh, sounds intriguing," Blaine remarked.

"Not really. He was just informing me that the elves feel they can efficiently and quickly train you to bring about the full potential and control of your talents."

Blaine stopped and faced Elian. "I thought our magic wouldn't work here." Blaine said.

"True, my magic will not work here. However, *your* magic draws on a universal energy. It holds such power it can be used anywhere," answered Elian. "In fact, it is very surprising your mother was able to put a binding spell on you since this type of magic is very tricky to bind."

Elian spoke as he walked over to the sink and began drying the dishes, "May I ask you of your father?"

"You may ask, but I assure you it won't be a long conversation. I was told he was killed in a car accident before I was born." Blaine answered.

"And what of his family?" asked Elian.

"Again, not a long conversation. I don't know anything about his family. Every time I asked my mother she would stonewall me. I just stopped asking. I suppose in the long run it really doesn't matter. Why do you ask?"

Elian hesitated for a moment before he said, "the elves have a different record of your father."

"What does that mean?" Blaine asked as she walked over to the stove and collected the soiled pots and utensils to take. They were next in line to get washed.

"The elves believe that Sairah was pregnant with you when she crossed over. She put a binding spell on you before she left Renault. That being true, your father must have been from Renault. His death due to a car crash could not be possible as Renault has no cars," Elian offered.

"Well, why am I not surprised. It would seem my mother found it impossible to tell me the truth about anything." Blaine continued to speak as she scrubbed a particularly grimy pot. "So, do they believe my father isn't really dead?"

"Kern didn't enlighten me on that detail. It is known that your mother went to a great deal of effort to hide you. The binding spell she used was not only very powerful but also very danger-ous. She took quite a risk using it. Even though the elves knew your mother was pregnant before she left Renault we believe no one in Renault knew she was with child when she disappeared. Anyone knowing of your existence would assume your father was from earth," Elian offered as he dried the last pan.

As Blaine absentmindedly began putting the clean dishes away she added, "I suppose then my father was a spinner also. That's why my gift is so powerful."

"Perhaps," said Elian as he neatly folded the towel and hung it on a hook near the sink.

"You obviously don't support that theory," Blaine observed out loud.

Elian let out a sigh. Just as he was about to give an explanation, there was a hearty knock at the door.

CHAPTER 15

"Hold that thought," Blaine quipped as she left the kitchen to answer the door. Blaine opened the heavy wooden door to see a tall, broad-shouldered elf standing on the lower step of the porch.

"Lady Blaine," he said as he made a wide-gesturing bow causing his long blonde hair to fall gently to the front of his shoulders. When he stood up Blaine recognized him. It was General Armel, the same elf she had seen briefly when they were in the Great Hall.

"Hello," Blaine replied timidly.

"I am very sorry to disturb you, My Lady. However, I did not get a chance to introduce myself to you earlier. I am Armel, son of Queen Lyra and general of the High Elfin Army."

"It is very nice to meet you," Blaine stated clumsily. "Would you like to come in?" she said, turning sideways and gesturing toward the living room. As she did this she saw Elian standing in the archway of the kitchen.

"No, I do not wish to impose upon your evening." His voice was soft and melodious.

Blaine looked up into Armel's deep violet, soulful eyes and offered a small shy smile. "Oh, you're not interrupting anything. We just finished eating."

"I was wondering if perhaps you would like to join me for an evening stroll. The city is particularly beautiful at this time of the evening." Blaine and Armel locked eyes as Blaine let out an involuntary girlish giggle. From behind Blaine heard Elian clear his throat. "Of course, the invitation is for both of you," Armel added as he shifted on the porch step.

"Naturally," Elian replied. Blaine shot him a warning glance. Taking the hint, Elian continued, "But I must graciously decline."

Realizing she had been lax in performing the social grace of introducing Elian, Blaine quickly stated, "Oh, this is Elian."

Armel stepped into the house and approached Elian, "It is an honor to meet you."

"I am also honored, General Armel," Elian stated flatly as he gave a half-hearted bow.

"Perhaps you will join us next time?" Armel spoke politely as he held out his arm to Blaine.

"Perhaps," Elian muttered.

Blaine slid her arm through Armel's. Looking over her shoulder, she called back to Elian, "We won't be too long." Flashing him a quick smile she exited the house and closed the door behind her.

Even though the sun had already set, the sky glowed with a hypnotic pink tint. They turned toward the city. As they walked their path was illuminated by small lights strung throughout the branches of the trees. It reminded her of Christmas lights. The air was sweet and intoxicating.

"I hope your quarters are suitable." Armel stated matter-of-factly as they walked.

"Oh, yes. The house is quite lovely," said Blaine cringing as she heard the words leave her mouth. She didn't know why she was so nervous, but her stomach was full of butterflies. "Please, I would appreciate it if you would just call me Blaine. I'm no lady." *Ugh*, she thought to herself as she tried to explain. "I mean I am a lady; you just don't need to address me that way, General Armel." She placed the palm of her left hand on her forehead and shook her head slightly.

"Very well, Blaine," he said laughing softly. "And please skip the formalities with me as well. Armel is just fine."

"Okay, thank you." They walked in silence for a moment. "Your city is beautiful, and I love that all the buildings are interfaced with nature. It is quite remarkable," Blaine gushed.

"Thank you, it is the elfin way to live with nature in complete harmony. It is one of the reasons our world has survived so long while many others have fallen in ruins."

"Like man in other worlds?" Blaine quietly mused.

"I do not mean in any way to imply that all man's ways are wrong."

"No need to explain," Blaine replied. "I am not blind to the destructive ways of earth."

"Oh, it's not just humans on Earth. It seems to be an innate occurrence in the makeup of humankind." Armel stopped and looked at Blaine.

"Not all humans are blind to the wasteful and destructive nature that accompanies innovation," Blaine said meeting his gaze. While Armel's face remained placid and pleasant his eyes revealed his disdain for the ways of man. "There are rays of hope that shine through the greed and destruction." Armel smiled and began walking again.

Blaine, perceiving Armel's desire not to pursue the present subject, fell silent as they walked further into the city. She began observing the many different styles of housing. Some rested high in trees that moved with the wind. Some were set deep into the rocks. No matter the location, all were gracefully integrated into the surrounding environment. When their conversation resumed it was lighthearted small talk about the houses and the elaborate gardens they passed as they walked.

They came to what Blaine observed to be the city's center. The shops on the main square were lit with strings of lights even though most had closed for the evening. A beautiful fountain stood in the center of the square. Blaine walked up to the edge and gazed at it dreamily. The spray of water that was carried in the breeze felt cool and refreshing. "It's beautiful. The lighting is so magical," Blaine said not looking away from it as Armel joined her at the fountain. She was mesmerized as she watched the water shoot into the air and fall playfully into the awaiting pool below.

"Water is a wondrous gift of life in our culture," Armel responded.

Blaine noticed the ornate plaque set in the wall of the fountain. " 'To the future our eyes remain. The knowledge of the past is our guide to the roads that may lie ahead,' " Blaine read out loud. "I like that!"

"You read high elfin?" Armel questioned, quite puzzled.

"No, why would you ask?" Blaine said turning toward Armel, confused by the second inquiry today regarding her knowledge of the ancient elfin language.

"That plaque is written in high elfin. Evidently our speculation of your abilities has clearly been underestimated," he chuckled to himself.

Blaine wasn't quite sure how to respond so she remained silent. She turned her back to the fountain to look at the surrounding shops. One was a clothing store. She involuntarily screwed up her face as she recalled having to put on her soiled clothes after her shower. She realized too late that Armel had been watching her.

"Is something wrong?" He questioned.

"No, nothing is wrong—just admiring the shops."

"Oh, but your facial expression said otherwise. I was concerned."

This caused Blaine to giggle. The thought that the general of a great army was concerned with a girl's facial expression was very amusing. "No, nothing is really wrong. I was just thinking perhaps I could wash my clothes. I only have what I am wearing and they could really use freshening up. I can figure it out tomorrow."

"Oh, I see," he responded.

"Perhaps we should start back. I don't want Elian to worry, and I am sure you have much more important things to do than babysit me."

"I don't consider this babysitting by any means. However, you are right. We should head back. It is getting late and your day will start early tomorrow."

They turned and started walking back to the guesthouse that Blaine would now call home for an undetermined amount of time.

"So, an early day for me tomorrow, huh?" she asked light-heartedly. "More walks and tours?"

"No, one of our elder elves will be meeting with you to determine the extent of your binding spell. She will also begin your training. It is imperative you learn how to use your incredible gifts," Armel explained.

"Awesome," Blaine retorted sarcastically. "So, tomorrow I become a science project."

"I do not understand that reference," Armel stated. "However, I promise you that it is in your best interest to learn to use the gifts that have been bestowed upon you, Blaine"

Blaine knew what he said was true. Still she could not help feeling like a case study who had lived in a glass room her whole life. "I suppose you are right." A cold gust of wind blew across the meadow they were passing, causing Blaine to shiver.

Armel observing this asked, "Are you chilled?"

"A little bit but I'll be fine. We're not far from the house."

Armel, concerned about her discomfort, removed the cape attached to his uniform and wrapped it around Blaine's shoulder. "This should help. This time of year, the night temperatures can drop quite quickly. A nice fire will take away the chill."

They walked the rest of the way in silence. The events of the day began wearing heavily on Blaine and sleep sounded like an amazing luxury right now.

As the guesthouse came into view Blaine could see warm light shining from within and smoke spiraling from the chimney. The comforting aroma of burning wood filled the air. Elian was sitting on the bench by the front door, completely absorbed in the book he was reading. When Blaine and Armel arrived at the house Elian glanced up and then continued reading.

Blaine turned to Armel. "Thank you. It was a lovely walk." She then lifted his cape off of her shoulders and handed it to him.

"It was my pleasure," he said smiling down at her. "I hope you enjoy the rest of the evening. I will check in with you tomorrow."

"You don't have to worry about fulfilling any social obligations. I understand that Queen Lyra wants us to feel welcome but I know how busy you must be. I would completely understand if you are not able to keep checking in on us," Blaine said as she shifted nervously while tugging subconsciously at her shirt.

"Oh, it is no social obligation that I fulfill. It is by choice that I wish to spend time with you."

"Thank you," Blaine replied lowering her head. She could feel the color in her cheeks rise.

"General Armel," Elian spoke firmly as he approached unexpectedly from behind. The sound of his voice startled Blaine causing her to jump. "Thank you for the things you sent over. The messenger said it was at your request that they be delivered."

"Yes, and I am pleased that they are to your liking. The hour grows late so I will bid you both a good night. He gave Blaine a quick brilliant smile and nodded at Elian. Then turning, he began his journey back to the city center.

Blaine stood and watched him walk away. She glanced at Elian. He rolled his eyes then returned to the front bench and resumed his reading. Blaine took that as a hint he wanted to be alone. She, however, could not resist the temptation to defy him. She started toward the door then stopped in front of Elian. "What cha reading?" She playfully asked.

"A book that Armel sent over," he replied without looking up at her.

"Oh, is that all he sent over?"

"No, he sent over fresh garments as well. He also sent you a book of basic magic."

"Hmm, sounds intriguing," she commented as she lightly kicked his outstretched foot. There was no response.

"Are you upset with me?" She asked as she sat down next to him.

"No. Why would I have reason to be?" he said continuing to study his book.

"Well, I don't know: maybe because I went with General Armel? You seem, I don't know, short with me."

"Short? As in my height?" Elian asked, looking at Blaine with a puzzled expression on his face.

Blaine giggled. "No, you know—aggravated. It's just that before we came here your feelings and emotions were so unreadable. But ever since we arrived here you seem to have let down your guard. Now I detect that you are upset with me."

"Here I am able to let my guard down. I have no need to worry about being discovered by Tevis's spinners. Unchecked emotions can cause one to lose control of their magic," Elian responded.

"Okay, that accounts for the change in you. Now why the silent brooding bit?"

Elian sat there for a moment and took a deep breath before explaining, "After the last few days of my constant vigil over you, you going off with a complete stranger caused me pause."

"You left me with Alderon. He was a complete stranger," retorted Blaine.

"Unlike Armel, Alderon was not a stranger to me. Besides, even though I was not with you physically I did remain vigilant in my protection of you during our time in Renault."

"Armel is the general of the Elfin Army. I was in very capable hands," Blaine offered.

"And not to mention very attractive," Elian mumbled under his breath.

"Ah ha!" Blaine exclaimed as she jumped to her feet. "You're jealous!"

"No." Elian softly stated, closing his book as he stood up and met Blaine's accusing, but playful stare.

As they stood there in silence just staring into each other's eyes, a wave of warmth overcame Blaine. Elian cracked a small smile as he told her, "I need to attend to the fire. There is going to be quite a chill in the air tonight." He then turned and went into the house leaving Blaine a bit perplexed about what had just occurred.

Blaine remained outside for a few moments then went into the house. There was a blazing fire in the fireplace. The flames crackled and popped as Elian added more wood.

"I put the things General Armel sent over for you in the upstairs bedroom. I thought you would be more comfortable there," Elian said.

"Thank you. If you don't mind, I think I'll turn in for the evening. Armel said that it will be an early morning tomorrow. I guess they are sending someone over to work with me and my magic."

"Yes, that is what I understood from my conversation with Kern also." Elian took a seat on the couch. "I will be going to bed as well. I am to meet with Queen Lyra and General Armel tomorrow."

"Oh? About what?" Blaine questioned.

"To be perfectly honest, I am not sure. They just said they had things to discuss," Elian answered.

"Good night, then. I don't suppose there is an alarm clock in my room?" She playfully added laughing as she made her way up the stairs. Hearing Elian respond with laughter made her smile.

The stairs lead directly to a large room. A warm glow from a small fire burning in the corner fireplace filled the room. To the right there was a stained-glass window. A four-poster bed stood against the far wall. Neatly placed on the bed were several packages wrapped in brown-woven cloth. Blaine walked over to the bed and began inspecting them. Blaine was more than pleased to discover they contained clothing and shoes. Setting aside a night gown, she draped the remaining garments over an arm chair that sat in front of the fireplace. She picked up the books that had been stacked under the packages and set them on the chair as well. It only took her a few seconds to remove her soiled clothing and change into the soft clean night gown. "Much better," she spoke out loud.

She picked up one of the leather-bound books and walked over to the bed. Pulling the covers back, she climbed in. She fluffed the pillows against the headboard, allowing her to sit comfortably. And adjusting the lamp that rested on the small nightstand she began reading *The Principles of Magic*. "Great, a textbook," she mumbled under her breath as she read the first page.

Blaine, uninspired by the book, turned her attention to the fireplace. She loved the sound of the dry wood popping loudly from the heat of the flames. She stared hypnotically at the red-hot embers. Laying the book down, she reached over and turned off the light. Sliding down further into the bed, she readjusted the soft down pillow. She stared up at the pitched-wood beamed ceiling. The last thing she remembered before sleep overtook her was watching the shadows dance in the glow of the fire.

CHAPTER 16

Blaine awoke with a jolt, causing her to sit straight up in bed. She sat for a moment trying to get her bearings. The glow of early morning light filled the window, welcoming her to a new day. She could hear the birds singing their homage to the light. She wondered what had awakened her so suddenly.

Swinging her legs off the bed, she stepped down onto the cool wooden floor. She walked over to the pile of clothing. Sorting through it, she found a loose-fitting tunic and pants. She quickly changed. Slipping on her shoes, she quietly made her way down the stairs. The house was still cloaked in shadows as she walked into the kitchen and fumbled in search of a light switch with no luck. Then she noticed a warm glow slowly lighting the globe that hung from the ceiling. Blaine looked up and smiled; *motion sensors*, she thought. She walked over to the counter where a bowl filled with fresh fruit sat. She removed a plate from that cupboard and selected several pieces of fruit for her breakfast.

After having sat down in the dimly lit kitchen for just enough time to eat the fruit, she crept silently into the living room. The door to the downstairs bedroom was closed. Not wanting to wake Elian, she slipped quietly out the front door intending to watch the sunrise. As she closed the door behind her, a voice startled her, "Good morning," Elian called in greeting.

"Oh, my goodness, you just about gave me a heart attack," she blurted out as she turned in the direction of his voice. Elian was standing near an old tree to the left of the house. Blaine noticed that the sun had made its full appearance above the horizon, painting the sky in magnificent fashion. Elian was smiling widely at her. His dark hair, which was not pulled back into its ponytail, fell softly below his shoulders.

"I apologize. I didn't mean to cause you distress. I was hoping you would rest a while longer."

"No, it's okay. I just thought you were still asleep," answered Blaine.

"I slept a bit, but my thoughts are much too consumed with the state of Renault to allow me to rest much."

Blaine walked over to the tree where Elian stood. "I understand. My sleep was rather restless as well. I was quite preoccupied, trying to process all the information I received yesterday. I can barely comprehend how my mother so easily allowed Tevis to manipulate her to choose her devastatingly dark pathway. I guess her age played a big part in it. Her fear allowed her to jump to conclusions, which gave Tevis the tools to win her over. What I do not understand is how mature, good people would allow themselves to be swayed by Tevis's lies. It seems as if it was all too easy for him to convince the general populace that by joining him they are fighting for a just cause. The truth is that they aren't."

Elian thought a moment then responded. "Perhaps the elders did not present their reasons for closing the gateways to Renault in the proper manner. Ignorance breeds fear and that kind of mindset is easily manipulated by darkness."

"I sort of understand that. I just don't get how they don't see right through his game and turn against him. Then there would be no problem."

Expecting Elian to expand on her last words, she was surprised as he took her hands into his. Blaine didn't pull away. Instead she gazed up at him. The early morning light reflected brightly in his dark soulful eyes. The touch of their hands emitted a green light that grew until it completely surrounded them.

Elian spoke softly, "Fear holds no power on your soul, Blaine, Daughter of Sairah. You are truly all that the prophecies have foretold. The love in your heart conquers all. That is why you don't understand how fear could manipulate those souls who do not let the light of pure love in. You know no other way. This is why you are such a threat to all that is dark and evil. Your light is so strong it will spread from world to world, unfaltering."

Blaine stood silently, gazing into Elian's eyes. She had never felt such complete contentment. The green light danced and swirled as it continued to surround them. Elian slowly dropped his hands to his sides, breaking eye contact. As he did, the light changed from green to blue then back to green again.

"We're not touching any longer. Why is the light still here?" Blaine whispered.

"This I am not sure. I have never witnessed anything quite like this," Elian answered.

They stood there a moment longer watching as the light began to slowly fade. There was a brief blue flash, and then it was gone. Blaine, feeling confused by what had just occurred, tried to bring some normalcy to the situation. Turning toward Elian, she asked, "Did you eat? There's some fruit in the kitchen. If that is not enough, I can go pick some more for you."

Elian laughed softly, "No, I am perfectly fine. Thank you, though."

"Okay, I'm going to go in and get ready for my lesson. I'm not sure what time my teacher will be here." Blaine made quotation marks in the air while saying lesson. She took a few steps toward the house when she noticed a figure coming up the pathway.

"Good morning," the figure called.

"Good morning," Blaine and Elian called out in unison. Blaine looked over her shoulder at Elian and gave him a shy smile.

As the figure came closer Blaine could see it was a female. She came up the path and stopped at the front walk leading to the house. "Blaine, Elian, I am glad to see you are already awake this morning. I am Fayendra, the Elder Magus." Her frame was small in comparison to the other elves Blaine had seen. Her white hair was streaked with silver. It had been casually pulled back into a loose bun. She approached Blaine. Taking Blaine's hand, she said, "Come, come, let me look at you, child." Looking her up and down, she motioned for Blaine to spin in a circle in front of her. Blaine shot a wide-eyed glance in Elian's direction, and then complied. "Yes, yes. I can work with this but we have a lot of work to do," she mumbled to herself as she scurried quickly up the path and into the house. Leaving the front door open behind her, she called to Blaine. "Come along, child. There is much work to be done and the day already has a head start on us."

Blaine looked at Elian again. He shrugged his shoulders, giving her an unsure smile.

"Blaine!" Fayendra gave out an impatient call. Blaine entered the house. Peering around the empty living room she noticed that the back door to the garden was open. Assuming Fayendra had gone outside, Blaine stepped through the open door to the patio. Blaine spotted her standing in the vegetable garden. Pointing to a small group of chairs on the patio, she motioned for Blaine to be seated. Taking a seat on one of the chairs, Blaine watched as Fayendra went from the vegetable garden to the herb garden then to the fruit trees. Blaine observed that she spoke quietly to herself the whole time she'd been collecting various fruits, vegetables, and herbs. Returning to the patio, she stood in front of Blaine. Taking a red berry and raising it over her head, Fayendra spoke an inaudible word while smashing the berry across Blaine's forehead. Blaine stood up and backed away in surprise. Wagging her finger at her in disapproval, Fayendra indicated Blaine should return to her chair and sit down.

Fayendra then began chanting words that Blaine did not recognize. Blaine sat motionless until the chanting stopped. Stepping back, Fayendra then stared intently at Blaine. Looking her up and down, she slowly circled the chair in which Blaine was seated. Not sure what she was supposed to do, Blaine remained in her seat and began looking around nervously. She caught a glimpse of Elian standing in the back doorway, observing what was taking place. A shadow fell across Elian's face so she was unable to make out his expression.

"No, no, no. This will not do!" Fayendra had stopped chanting and was now waving her arms quite erratically.

"What won't do?" Blaine asked annoyed.

Turning toward Elian and pointing, she demanded, "You must leave! I underestimated your magic, young one."

Elian said nothing but Blaine quickly asked, "What? Why can't he stay?"

"His protective bond with you is too strong. It is interfering with my ability to free you from your binding spell," Fayendra answered.

Blaine turned to Elian and gave him a slight nod to confirm that it was okay for him to leave.

Fayendra then called to Elian, "She is in good hands. No harm will come to her. General Armel had requested you to join him later this morning to test your abilities on the battlefield. Perhaps you should meet him at the Royal House and begin early." She made a gesture in the air waving him off. Not waiting for his response, she began chanting again. Blaine watched Elian turn and go back into the house closing the door behind him.

Fayendra continued chanting and dancing about Blaine. Her expression was soft but determined. Her round face grew rosy with all the activity. After several minutes of intense chanting Blaine felt a small gust of wind blow across her face, stirring the loose leaves that were on the patio. The gust became stronger, picking up the leaves and causing them to encircle the chair where Blaine sat. Then as suddenly as it came the wind stopped. The leaves dropped forming a wreath around Blaine's feet. Fayendra stepped back to admire her work. "It is done," she whispered. Pulling up a chair in front of Blaine, she took Blaine's hand in hers. "Now the real work begins. Do you see that pumpkin on the far side of the garden?"

Blaine looked about then spotted the pumpkin. "Yes."

"Bring it here," Fayendra demanded flatly as she leaned back in her chair.

"Okay," Blaine said as she stood up and took a step toward the pumpkin.

"No, no, no! Not that way," Fayendra exclaimed shifting in her seat. Seeing the puzzled look on Blaine's face, she giggled, "With your thoughts!"

Blaine stood there staring at Fayendra a moment in disbelief. "Oh, I can't do that." Blaine replied.

Fayendra was now picking at her fingernails, not even looking at Blaine. "Yes, you can," she stated matter-of-factly.

"No disrespect to you but, no I can't."

Fayendra stood up and went over to a patch of flowers that grew in a pot close by. "Have you ever tried?" She questioned as she bent down and smelled a flower.

"Well, no. But I'm sure I can't," Blaine replied.

"So, try!" Fayendra demanded.

Blaine turned toward the pumpkin again. "Okay—whatever," she mumbled under her breath. "Pumpkin, move over here!" She spoke determinedly.

"Not with your words," Fayendra directed. "Do it with your thoughts."

Feeling slightly aggravated, Blaine said, "Okay." Then she thought to herself, *pumpkin, move here.* Nothing.

"Keep trying," Fayendra sang out.

Blaine pressed her lips together and shot Fayendra an annoying glare. After a few minutes of trying with no success Blaine looked at Fayendra. "I know nothing of magic. I was never taught on earth. They don't believe in magic."

"Again! Try again!" Fayendra responded without even giving Blaine a look.

Blaine's aggravation slowly turned to anger. *This is supposed to be my teacher of magic and she's not teaching me anything,* Blaine thought. "I'm sorry I can't. I don't know how to do this," She pleaded with Fayendra.

"Again, now!" Fayendra demanded. Her tone was harsh and unsupportive. Her face contorted angrily as she stomped her foot on the patio.

"Ugh!" Blaine shouted in anger as she turned toward the pumpkin. Suddenly, the pumpkin lifted off the ground and flew across the garden, passing Blaine and just missing Fayendra as she ducked out of the way. It smashed against the wall of the house with such force that the window shook and the birds that rested on the roof flew away with a start.

Blaine stood there with her mouth wide open and stared in disbelief at the shattered pulp that had once been a pumpkin.

Fayendra seemed unfazed by it all. "See, you can do it," she said as she took her seat once again.

"I am so sorry," Blaine said as she turned toward Fayendra, embarrassed by what had just happened.

"Sorry for what, dear?" Fayendra responded sweetly, taking Blaine's hand and patting it softly.

"I almost hit you with that pumpkin, and look at the huge mess I have made on the patio!" Blaine replied.

Fayendra let out a melodious laugh. "You see, young one, magic isn't learned! It's just there. For you it is more readily available than for most. You are twice blessed; once with the elfin way and twice by ancient magic. This makes it imperative that we work on melding these gifts that have been locked up for too long. After all, you don't want to hurt yourself or someone else," she giggled as she gestured toward the remains of the once robust pumpkin.

Blaine laughed nervously still a bit embarrassed by the whole situation. "Yes, I suppose—wait ... What do you mean blessed by the elfin way? You mean because I'm being taught your way of magic?"

"Oh, dear me ... I just assumed you were aware of your lineage. I suppose I should have discussed this more with Queen Lyra."

"How could it be possible that I'm elfin? I'm sure my mother never visited here. Did someone from here go to Renault and that's where they met my mother?"

"Oh, I am not entirely sure of the details. I sometimes get wrapped up in other aspects of a situation and don't fully pay attention. However, I definitely see the elfin line in your aura, dear."

Blaine was taken aback with this new information. However, as she thought about it, the reality set in that she didn't even know the first thing about her father. So, she supposed anything was possible.

Fayendra studied Blaine. "Dear child, I can imagine all this is causing a tremendous stress on your emotional well-being. However, our time together is so important we must try and stay focused on the task at hand."

Blaine nodded in complete understanding of the importance of what must be learned. The pumpkin was a very strong reminder of that.

"Excellent! I am pleased you are able to push past your own emotional discord and understand the bigger picture. This concept can take a young soul months, if not years, to understand. We are off to a very good start." Fayendra smiled warmly as she spoke. The look she gave Blaine reminded her of her own grandmother—or the one she loved as her own. Blaine's heart ached briefly, knowing she would possibly never see her again.

"The most important thing you must remember is that we are all connected to everything around us—the animals, the plants, the trees, and even the rocks. We are all created out of the same energy. That energy must remain in balance. If there is a strong shift of balance, it results in a lesser body, which loses its energy to the stronger of the two bodies. White magic draws on all energy and combines to create. Black magic destroys the balance by draining the energy from one entity at a time until it creates the chaos it intends. Do you understand that concept?"

Blaine shook her head in complete understanding.

"It is apparent that you draw on your human emotion and the ancient magic. This can have a very strong energy charge—hence the smashed pumpkin."

"That's a bad thing, right?" Blaine mumbled once again, embarrassed.

"No, not bad, just more difficult to wield. Ancient magic is very fickle. That is why you are born to it. It actually picks and chooses who it finds worthy to bless. Ancient magic works in harmony with nature. Human magic is an entirely different concept."

Fayendra stopped abruptly and fumbled with the neckline of her emerald green tunic. She finally retrieved a leather necklace from its hiding place. At the end of the necklace dangled a pale green crystal that sparkled brilliantly in the sunlight "Crystals amplify strength for the use of the elfin magic."

"It's beautiful," Blaine whispered as she attempted to touch the crystal.

Fayendra abruptly removed the crystal from Blaine's reach. Blaine drew her hand back as if she had been burned. "No, no my dear, you must not ever touch a Magi's personal crystal!"

"I'm so sorry," Blaine blurted out.

Fayendra quickly returned the crystal to its refuge inside her garments. "It's all right. There is much to learn. You will make mistakes, but learning from them is the important thing."

Fayendra spent the remainder of the morning explaining the differences between elfin magic, ancient magic, and human magic. By midday, Blaine's head was swimming and she was finding it difficult to concentrate. The more she learned of the elfin ways, the more she found her thoughts wandering to her possible elfin lineage. Perhaps knowledge of that lineage would explain why she always felt more at ease surrounded by nature than surrounded by the modern comforts of man.

Fayendra perceived Blaine's distraction, and trying to direct Blaine's thoughts to the information that was being discussed soon became an impossible task. "Perhaps this would be a good time to cease ... instructions. You need time to yourself to fully absorb all that has been presented to you." Not waiting for a response from Blaine, Fayendra stretched as she rose to her feet. "I will be back tomorrow at the same time."

"Okay," Blaine mumbled as she stood up. Her legs felt a bit unresponsive from sitting so long. "If you prefer we can start a little later tomorrow. I would hate for you to be inconvenienced by having to come here so early," Blaine politely suggested.

"Oh, it's not an inconvenience. I am always up before the sun. It is the best time for learning because the air is less charged from nature's activities that time of the day."

Blaine nodded in compliance but felt disappointed in the answer. Bed time would come early this evening she was sure. "Thank you, Fayendra."

"Yes, yes, but of course." She called over her shoulder as she shuffled down the path and disappeared through the garden gate.

CHAPTER 17

Blaine remained standing in the garden for a moment looking up at a large oak tree that majestically protected the back side of the garden. She watched several birds playfully fluttering from branch to branch singing to all who would listen. Her thoughts drifted to Elian. Wondering where he was, she reflected on the odd yet somehow wonderful exchange they had had this morning.

She drew a deep breath and closed her eyes. Letting out her breath she became very aware of the extreme hunger she felt. Taking her cues from her overly pushy appetite, she walked into the house. As she entered the kitchen she noticed a loaf of bread and several jars of preserves and cheese that had been carefully placed on the counter. She hadn't remembered seeing these things there this morning. *Perhaps they were sent over by Armel last night*, she mused. She took a large bowl from the cupboard and walked out to the garden where she picked a head of lettuce, some tomatoes, and cucumbers. Returning to the kitchen she prepared a large salad. She sliced several pieces of bread in expectation that Elian would return soon. Blaine searched the cabinets and found a jar containing balsamic vinegar. As she turned to finish preparing the meal she was surprised to see Elian standing in the doorway of the kitchen. "Oh, goodness," she exclaimed with a jump. "You startled me. You hungry?" Blaine asked pointing to the bowl on the opposite counter that contained the salad.

"Yes, thank you." Elian answered smiling broadly.

"Could you please get some plates and forks?" Blaine asked as she drizzled the salad with balsamic vinegar.

Blaine set the plate of sliced bread, the cheese, and the jars of preserves in the middle of the table. She then filled each plate with a generous serving of salad. They both sat down at the table to partake of their midday meal.

Blaine took a few bites. "Gosh, I'd really love a steak about now," she said in between chewing.

"Aw, I believe you will find yourself out of luck with that. As I mentioned before the elfin diet consists of no meat. However, you have done well with what is at hand. This is an excellent meal," Elian offered.

"Thank you for the compliment. I know the elfin diet is strictly vegetarian but still a steak sounds amazing. I'll have to wander the garden a little more or maybe venture to some of the shops on the square to plan for dinner. Maybe I'll get all gourmet tonight," Blaine teased.

"Oh, that won't be necessary. Dinner is already planned. We are to join Queen Lyra and General Armel at the Royal Residence this evening," Elian informed her.

"That should be interesting. Speaking of the General, how was your morning with him?" Blaine asked.

"Emotional," Elian answered flatly.

"You say that as if it were a bad thing."

"No, by no means do I say this out of disrespect for General Armel, more so in disappointment of my own skill."

"I don't understand, Elian. I had no idea in the first place that you had even ever trained in combat skills, especially since it is my understanding that Renault has no army to speak of other than that in Tevis's control. That being said, I would imagine that today was never meant to make you think less of yourself."

"No, I do not believe that was the intention. And yes, most of my skills have been self-taught. However, it was intimidating to watch the ease with which the general performed various combat skills—all of which were enhanced by the natural physical gift possessed by all elves. I felt awkward and clumsy. I always thought I would be ready to face Tevis and his Legion—both magic and combat-wise." As Elian spoke Blaine saw the look of disappointment and frustration wash across his face.

"I'm sure it wasn't as bad as you think, Elian. Did you hurl a giant pumpkin at his head?"

"No, of course not!" He laughed. "Why would you ask that?"

"Well, I did. Not at General Armel but at Fayendra. I missed her head by only inches!"

Elian began laughing harder. "No, you didn't!" He said in disbelief.

"Yep, I sure did. The evidence is all over the back patio."

Elian quickly stood up and left the kitchen. Blaine heard the back door open. She could hear Elian laughing heartily. The sound brought joy to her heart. This was the first time she had heard him truly laugh. As Elian came back into the kitchen and sat down he was still chuckling.

"Yeah, yeah, yeah!" Blaine retorted sarcastically. "So, you see your day wasn't as bad as you think."

"I have to ask how did these events come about?" Elian inquired.

Blaine reenacted the events of the morning. When she had finished her story, Elian leaned back in his chair. Stretching his arms over his shoulders he admitted, "You win. Perhaps my day wasn't so bad after all."

"Let's hear it," Blaine egged him on. Elian began his narrative describing his meeting with General Armel. He told Blaine that he was tested on combat skills including sword fighting, agility, speed, and hand-to-hand combat. As he spoke a calm sense of well-being filled Blaine's soul. It was the same feeling she remembered having when she would sit at the table with her mother just talking. She smiled to herself; it was the first time since her crossover that thoughts of her mother didn't bring extreme sadness or anger. She actually experienced a sense of forgiveness, and understanding filled her heart. Before she had much time to analyze this new revelation she realized Elian had finished his story.

"It sounds very physically exhausting, if you ask me," Blaine commented.

"It was. It became very apparent to me that being an elf has its advantages when it comes to battlefield accomplishments. Their agility alone exceeds any of that of human lineage," Elian added.

The mention of the elfin lineage reminded Blaine of Fayendra's serious reference to the fact that Blaine had been blessed with an elfin heritage. Hoping Elian may have some knowledge of this, Blaine decided to mention the comments Fayendra made regarding the subject. Trying not to reveal the feeling of urgency she felt to know the truth, she said as casually as she could, "Oh, I forgot to tell you something Fayendra said to me." Pausing a moment to try to underplay her next comment she continued, "Apparently I am part elf."

Elian sat there in silence for a few moments. Then speaking quietly almost to himself, he said "That may explain the odd conversation I had with General Armel right before I returned home."

Waiting for Elian to go into details about this conversation, Blaine was disappointed as he continued to sit in silence ignoring her anxious stare. Blaine finally spoke. "Okay, first of all that wasn't the response I was expecting from you. I assumed that this revelation would have generated a reaction of surprise. Second, you have added more mystery by mentioning your conversation with General Armel and not explaining what was said."

Elian shifted uncomfortably in his seat. "I apologize—I am surprised to learn of the possibility that you are an elf."

"Part elf," Blaine corrected.

"Part elf. Did Fayendra not offer more details?"

"No, it was apparent she thought I knew. She said I had been blessed with the elfin lineage and that it was reflected quite clearly in my aura and energy. She also made it clear that our focus was to be on the lessons. She did suggest Queen Lyra would be the person to speak to for further answers," Blaine responded.

"This is extraordinary news," Elian responded. "One would have to assume this elfin lineage is on your father's lineage since Sairah's bloodline is well recorded. Plus, there is no evidence she had knowledge of any of the elfin magic or ways."

"You already know that I know nothing of my father, so I suppose anything is possible. I mean, just yesterday we were spending time with a unicorn. I am beginning to think there is nothing out of the realm of possibilities these days," Blaine commented as she slumped down in her chair crossing her arms in front of her chest.

Elian pushed his chair back from the table and stood up. "Perhaps you will be able to speak of these things to Queen Lyra this evening. By the way, we are to dress for dinner. I am going to go bathe and rest before we need to depart for the Royal Residence." He turned and headed through the kitchen archway.

Blaine, irritated by this sudden end to their discussion,

sprang to her feet. "Wait a minute. You didn't tell me about your odd conversation with General Armel."

"Oh, it's not all that important," Elian quickly responded without looking back.

Blaine quickly maneuvered herself in front of Elian, blocking his entrance to the bedroom. "It is important. Now spill it!" She demanded.

"No, it really has no relevance to anything of importance." He mumbled as he tried to step around Blaine.

"Huh! Nice try but let's hear it." Blaine poked at his chest playfully as she shifted from side to side in the bedroom doorway.

Elian finally took a defeated step backward. "Fine. He spoke to me about our connection. Then he reassured me that his interest in you wasn't as I had interpreted it." He spoke without making eye contact with Blaine.

Blaine stood silently displaying a small grin. "So, what could you have possibly interpreted his attention to have been?" She mocked easily.

"I assure you I made no assumptions. However, his interest clearly is in the fact that you have elfin in your bloodline and that alone is quite the draw." He smiled shyly at her.

"Yes, of course you would not admit to any assumptions." Giggling to herself, Blaine stepped out of the doorway and made a gesture for him to pass. "So, when you said we needed to dress for dinner you mean I am to actually wear a dress?"

"Yes," Elian called over his shoulder as he went into his room.

"Great! I just love to wear dresses," Blaine murmured under her breath.

She went upstairs and flopped down on the bed. The wooden frame creaked in protest. She looked over at the nightstand where she had placed the book of basic magic the previous night. She rolled over and picked up the top book. Scanning the pages, she began to gain more clarity about what Fayendra had told her during her morning "lesson." The book described in great detail the different types of magic. She was quite amazed that suddenly everything seemed to make sense. It was as if this information was something she had always known inside, but now it was very tangible. She finished scanning the book and excitedly jumped off the bed. She wanted to share this new revelation with Elian. She quickly bounded down the stairs but was disappointed to see the door to Elian's room was closed.

She returned to her room. As she came to the top of the stairs she noticed a package sticking out from underneath the bed. She walked over to it and bent down to pick it up. "Huh, this must have been dropped when Elian brought everything up last night." Blaine unwrapped the brown cloth packaging to reveal a variety of toiletries, including a brush and other essentials. "Well, I suppose I should go shower and get ready," she mumbled to herself. Gathering a few things, she went back down stairs to the bathroom.

After a quick shower Blaine returned to her bedroom. She moved the pile of clothes from the chair to the bed and began sifting through it. She was pleased to discover a beautiful amethyst silk gown delicately adorned with sky blue embroidery among the clothes sent over by Armel. She noticed there was a small mirror above the vanity that sat against the wall. She walked over and stood in front of it, adjusting the gown to try to get a full image.

Satisfied with her selection, she gently set the dress back on the bed. She then relocated the miscellaneous toiletries to the vanity. Sitting down she stared at her reflection in the mirror. In spite of the events of the last week and her lack of restful sleep, she was amazed to find no apparent signs of fatigue. However, as she gazed at her reflection Blaine couldn't help feel as though there was something different about the image gazing back at her. She wasn't entirely sure what had changed, but there was definitely something different there.

She then absentmindedly picked up the brush and began running it through her damp hair. After carefully French braiding it she decided to lay down and see if she could quiet her mind, which seemed to be moving a million miles a minute. Once she laid her head down on the soft down pillow sleep overcame her quickly.

When she awoke it took her a moment to get oriented to her surroundings. She could hear Elian moving about downstairs. After stretching she jumped off the bed and went to the stairs. "Elian?" She called out.

"Yes, Blaine," he called back to her. It sounded as if he were still in the bedroom.

"When do we need to leave?"

"I assume soon. It is late afternoon and that is when our presence is requested. No specific time, however, was mentioned," he called back.

"Alright, I'll be down shortly." Blaine quickly put on the gown she had selected. Sitting down in front of the mirror, she unbraided her hair and ran her brush through it. The braiding had done its job creating soft waves that cascaded down her back. Pulling the sides back loosely she clipped them with a jeweled barrette that had been included in the packages sent over by Armel. She stood up and examined herself in the mirror one final time. The dress fit perfectly as if it had been custom-made for her. The bodice was form fitted. At the hips it gave way to a flowing long skirt. The sleeves were long and bell-shaped. Fussing with them for a moment, Blaine mumbled to herself, "Well, eating ought to be interesting with these." As she shrugged her shoulders and put on a pair of slipper-type shoes, she took one last look in the mirror before proceeding to the stairs.

CHAPTER 18

Blaine carefully navigated the stairs as not to step on her dress. Visions of tripping and falling the rest of the way down kept her focused. She entered the living room expecting to find Elian waiting for her. However, instead she spotted him through the front window. He stood at the gate talking to Kern. She quickly exited the house to join them. They both turned as she approached them.

"Oh, my high heaven!" She heard Elian exclaimed under his breath.

Blaine scowled at him momentarily, "What?" she questioned.

"You look exquisite," Elian answered quietly.

"Whatever," Blaine blurted out sarcastically.

"My lady, I must say the elfin environment suits you quite wonderfully," Kern added. "You look radiant."

Blaine blushed. "Please stop. You're making me more self-conscious than I already am. I am not used to wearing such girly things. I would prefer a pair of jeans and a T-shirt any day. Since I was informed to dress for dinner I decided to opt for a dress as not to offend our hostess." As she spoke she stepped on her dress causing her to stumble. Elian quickly stepped forward to help. "No, I got it—always the klutz," she joked, attempting to change the subject.

"Shall we make our way then?" Kern spoke, tossing his head up and jostling his silver mane.

"Yes," Elian replied. "My lady." He spoke as he held out his arm to Blaine.

Blaine gave him a coy smile. "But of course." Taking his arm, she couldn't help but notice how the sky-blue tunic he wore complemented his olive skin.

As they made their way to the Royal Residence Kern asked, "So how did your first day go?"

Blaine responded first. "Interesting. Do you know Fayendra?"

"I have met with her once or twice. I do not spend much time in Roe. When I am here I am usually in council with Queen Lyra. She is very knowledgeable. A little unusual, but when you have lived as long as she has you're entitled to your eccentricities."

"No, do not get me wrong. She was very nice. I just don't think I was what she expected."

"I'm sure that was not an issue. Knowing what I do of Fayendra, I do not believe she had formed any preconceptions of you. She knows her responsibility is to give you lessons that will bring you along in due time. How about you, Elian? I hear your skills were tested very vigorously."

"Yes, that is very accurate," Elian answered, sounding a bit defeated.

Kern, detecting Elian's lack of enthusiasm, added quickly, "It is my understanding that General Armel was very impressed with what he saw today."

"I am afraid I wouldn't agree with that," Elian offered.

"Really, those were his words. He said for a young man with no formal training in combat you well surpassed his expectations." Kern went on to explain to Elian the physical differences between elf and human. Genetically, elves are just made quicker and stronger. He told Elian that his speed and strength were very impressive considering these differences. Blaine noticed a slight improvement in Elian's mood as Kern continued speaking.

It wasn't long before the Royal Residence came into view. As they approached the amazing structure Blaine was awestruck. The residence itself was forged from limestone and marble. The roofline twisted into a tall tower, which housed an enormous crystal. The warm glow from that crystal surrounded the residence. A beautiful terrace wrapped around the front of the residence. The house rested harmoniously upon the exposed roots of four gigantic trees, which appeared to be redwoods. The two trees supporting the back of the house stood gracefully against a rugged mountain side from which flowed a breathtaking waterfall. The waterfall cascaded down the mountain, creating a stream that flowed under the arched roots of the four trees. From there the stream twisted and turned as it continued its journey into the city and beyond.

They crossed an ornate stone bridge that was gracefully suspended over the stream. Blaine whispered to Elian, "Why didn't you tell me about this place? It's absolutely amazing!"

"I could not find words to do it justice. You needed to see it for yourself." Blaine nodded in complete agreement.

As they climbed the stairs that led to the terrace Blaine could hear the calming sound of the waterfall that was the backdrop for the Royal Residence. When they reached the terrace she looked up at the protective canopy created by the branches of the trees. It was spectacular. "Wow!" Blaine exclaimed as she turned toward the city. "I didn't realize how much we had climbed. What a view! You can see the entire city from here yet the residence is not visible from below. How is that possible?"

"The canopy created by the many trees throughout the city created a natural setting, which was designed to blend the residence with nature," Kern explained. "This elfin gift of creating their world built in complete harmony with nature always astounds me even though I visit here often."

"Good evening to you all." Armel's voice came from behind them.

"General Armel, always an honor." Kern turned slightly bowing his head as he spoke.

"Oh, come now Kern. No need for such formalities," Armel said as he approached them from the large open-arched doorway, which was the entrance to the residence.

"Lady Blaine," Armel addressed her as he took her hand and kissed it causing Blaine to blush. Out of the corner of her eye she saw Elian roll his eyes.

"Sir Elian, good to see you again. Please come in. Queen Lyra is anxious to see you."

They followed Armel into the residence. Armel closed the door behind them. The residence was elaborately decorated in rich shades of blue, green, and purple. Natural light from the numerous windows of the residence flooded the room. A grand staircase curved down from the balcony that overlooked the open two-story entryway. To the left was a closed double door.

Armel approached the closed doors and knocked. The door opened and Queen Lyra emerged. She smiled warmly. "How wonderful to see you again. I am so pleased you are here tonight," she added graciously. She locked eyes with Blaine, subconsciously causing Blaine to shift uncomfortably under her stare. Lyra then directed her attention to Armel. "Please take our guests to the great room. I will join you shortly. Kern and I have a few things to discuss before he takes his leave."

Blaine quickly turned to Kern. "Are you not joining us for

dinner?" She questioned.

"No, my lady, I will complete my business with the Queen and then I must take my leave. I am needed elsewhere. So, unfortunately, this will be goodbye for now. However, our paths will cross again soon."

Uncertain, Blaine asked," May I give you a hug?"

"Of course, my child," Kern replied.

Blaine wrapped her arms around Kern's neck and buried her face in his soft mane. Stepping back, she told him, "Thank you for everything."

"No, thank *you*." He gently nuzzled at her arm. Kern then turned toward Elian. "It has been a great honor to meet you, Sir Elian."

Elian bowed his head. "No, the honor is all mine." he humbly replied.

"General Armel," Kern said, nodding in his direction. He then followed Queen Lyra through the open double door, which closed silently behind them.

"Come, let us proceed to the great room," Armel invited.

They followed Armel to a large archway that was opposite the front door. The hallway gave way to a huge room. The far wall of the room housed a floor-to-ceiling picture window that allowed a spectacular view of the waterfall as it cascaded down the rocky, moss-covered mountainside. The wall on the left of side of the room was lined with large windows. Each window provided a frame for the beautiful view of nature outside. In the middle of the room sat a wooden table that could easily sit twelve people. It was lavishly set for four. A majestic hand-forged iron candelabra hung over the center of the table.

"Please come in and be seated. Queen Lyra will join us shortly," Armel spoke as he directed Blaine and Elian toward a large sitting area containing several sofas and chairs all artfully arranged around a large stone fireplace. Blaine's attention was captured by a beautifully framed picture that hung over the mantel. It was a painting of the Royal Residence with the waterfall as the main focus. Noticing Blaine's interest in the picture, Armel told her, "My sister painted that."

"It's beautiful!" Blaine remarked as Armel walked up behind her.

"Yes, she was extremely talented. She could always see light even when most saw darkness and despair. It shows in her artwork."

As they stood there quietly admiring the peaceful work of art an awkward silence fell between them. Blaine wondered if Armel knew that she was aware of his sister's history and how Tevis had taken her life.

Thankfully, Armel broke the silence. "Oh, I am terribly sorry. Let me ring for refreshments. I know the walk here is somewhat strenuous. He stepped away from Blaine and reached for a small bell that rested on one of the end tables. Blaine turned and met eyes with Elian who had seated himself on one of the luxurious sofas. He gave her an awkward smile as to acknowledge that he too was thinking about Armel's sister.

Almost immediately after Armel had rung the bell a very slight built elf arrived carrying a tray on which rested four jeweled, metal goblets. He offered a goblet to each of them. He placed the final goblets by the setting at the head of the table, which was clearly Queen Lyra's. Nodding toward Armel, he took his leave.

Blaine walked over and seated herself on the sofa next to Elian, being careful not to spill the contents of the goblet. Armel took a seat in an armchair opposite the sofa occupied by his guests.

Smiling warmly at Blaine, Armel asked, "How was your first meeting with Elder Fayendra?"

Blaine could feel herself blush as she tried to answer Armel's inquiry. "Well ... " She hesitated, a bit embarrassed. "Why? Did she tell you something?"

"No, actually she is rarely seen in the city. I was just wondering your impression of her." His tone was light as if egging her on.

"I suppose she wasn't exactly what I had expected. Then again, I don't think I was exactly what she expected either."

"I highly doubt that she had any particular expectations about you. She is considered to be somewhat odd. She is a bit of a recluse—living outside of the city and rarely being seen by the residents of Roe." Armel offered.

"Are we discussing the eccentricities of my dear friend Fayendra?" Queen Lyra's voice came from the other side of the room. Elian and Armel quickly rose to their feet. Blaine struggled to stand while juggling her goblet as to prevent dumping her drink down the front of her dress. She proudly rose to her feet not spilling a drop just as Queen Lyra told them to sit. Lyra walked over to the table and retrieved her goblet. After taking a long drink, she sighed deeply then joined the others in the sitting area. Blaine watched as Lyra gracefully and elegantly found her way to one of the large armchairs and took her place in it.

"Fayendra is quite unique, to say the least. However, she is the most skilled and knowledgeable of all the elders," Lyra explained.

"Was she dressed?" Armel asked flashing Blaine a brilliant smile and causing Blaine to blush once again.

"Armel!" Queen Lyra objected.

Armel threw his head back in laughter. "Well, it's true. I have been told she has given many a visitor more than they bargained for by receiving them less than well dressed."

"In explanation of what my son has just said Fayendra truly believes in the ancient elfin ways. Tradition requires many rituals be done in the nude as to not restrict the natural flow of energy.

There have been many times when visitors to her cottage have been greeted with her free ways. However, I am quite sure she arrived fully clothed to work with Blaine." They all turned toward Blaine to confirm this assumption.

"Oh, yes. She did have clothes on," Blaine quickly confirmed.

Queen Lyra then directed her attention toward Elian. "I am very impressed with the abilities both in magic and combat that you displayed on the training field today."

"Thank you, your Majesty. However, I am no match for your warriors," Elian humbly replied.

"I would definitely disagree with that evaluation, but there is much to be admired in modesty."

Elian, feeling a bit uncomfortable with Queen Lyra's compliments, decided to change the subject. "This view is spectacular," he said.

Armel, sensing Elian's discomfort, took up the conversation. "The Royal Residence was one of the first structures built in the city. It still takes my breath away." Armel stood up and walked over to the picture window that showcased the waterfall. "The waterfall is quite mesmerizing," Armel continued. They all sat in silence enjoying the view until Armel once again spoke. "Dinner should be ready. I had better go and check on it."

"Thank you, Armel," Queen Lyra spoke as she gestured for all to stand and take their places at the table. "We are in need of more wine," she informed Armel as he exited the room through one of the arched doorways.

Blaine noticed Queen Lyra appeared much more relaxed and less formal than she was during their first meeting. It seemed that she became more and more relaxed as the evening progressed. Blaine smoothed her dress as she stood to join Queen Lyra and Elian who had already taken their places at the large dinner table. Elian stood up as Blaine approached the table. Pulling the chair out for her he winked at her playfully. Blaine gave a small curtsy in response and sat down.

"Do your accommodations suit you?" Queen Lyra asked.

"Yes, things are quite lovely," Blaine answered politely.

"If you are in need of anything, please let me know and I will arrange to have it sent to you."

"Oh, thank you. However, all of the items sent over by Armel last night have more than satisfied my needs."

"Very good, and you Elian?" Lyra questioned.

"Thank you, your Majesty. I, too, have been well provided for," Elian graciously replied.

"Please, there is no need for such formalities. You may address me as Lyra. Tonight, we rejoice in the gathering of family." She raised her goblet into the air. Blaine and Elian quickly followed suit. "To family," Lyra toasted. Elian and Lyra both put their goblets to their lips and drank. Blaine, however not knowing what to expect, cautiously took a small sip. She was delighted to find the wine as pleasant as the surroundings. As she swallowed the sweet nectar she could not help but wonder about the odd toast and comments about the gathering of family. Before she had time to consider the occurrence Armel joined them at the table and the meal was served.

Plate after plate was presented and placed on the table filling the great room with a splendid aroma of savory goodness. Blaine inhaled deeply. She hadn't realized how hungry she was. "Everything looks fantastic," Elian said as the last example of gourmet talent was placed on the table.

Blaine viewed each dish. They were more like works of art than like food.

"Armel, would you please honor this dinner?" Lyra asked. Armel nodded then spoke several words in elfin. Queen Lyra thanked him and invited Blaine and Elian to serve themselves.

Elian picked up the platter closest to him and after dishing out a portion passed it on to Blaine. Blaine had no idea what any of the platters contained but she had never been a picky eater. She took a small portion of each as they were passed to her. Conversation was sparse as they all indulged in the lavish meal. Blaine ate cautiously trying very hard to recall her best table manners.

After a short while Lyra pushed her chair back slightly from the table. Addressing Elian, she said, "I am very curious as to how the elders of Renault became aware of when and where Blaine was going to cross worlds."

Quickly swallowing a mouthful of food, Elian replied, "They knew well of the prophecies, and many tellers were experiencing visions of someone crossing unassisted. The details were never clear. My visions of Blaine, however, have always been very clear ever since I was a child."

"Were the elders aware of your tellings?" Lyra gently inquired.

"Lord Alderon was. When I began sharing such clear details about Blaine he feared for my safety. It was his choice not to tell the others about her. He, however, kept a detailed account of all my tellings."

"As you know with tellings the outcome can always change if the one in the vision decides to take a different pathway. Yet it was you that first found Blaine. Did you remain with Lord Alderon until Blaine crossed over?" Lyra continued her questioning.

"No, when I felt I was old enough to protect myself I left Lord Alderon's estate and took residence in my home isolated in the forest. Lord Alderon and I kept in contact on a regular basis."

Blaine realized Elian was referring to the house in the hillside where they had been when the soldiers found them. Blaine listened intently, fascinated by the conversation.

Elian continued his account. "Right before Blaine crossed

over I had several occurrences that were unlike any tellings I had ever experienced. It was as if I actually was in her world in real time. It definitely was not of a future event or past event as most tellings are. I also do believe Blaine saw me."

They all focused on Blaine. Swallowing the last bite of food from her plate quickly, she volunteered what knowledge she had about the events leading up to the crossover. "I know the day before I arrived in the forest of Renault I had seen the image of a man. The image was always accompanied by a blinding bright light, so I was unable to make out details. I can't confirm 100% it was you, Elian, but I could say with some certainty it was. Who else could it have been?"

"Fascinating," Queen Lyra commented. "The connection that links you two is more powerful than even I could have imagined." Armel shook his head in agreement.

Blaine sat there for a moment in silence. After processing this new information, she spoke. "I understand a little about the bond that ties Elian and me. However, I have been told many times that no one knew what pathway I was going to be following when I did cross over to Renault. It would seem to me that our connection would have immediately given Elian that knowledge."

Elian spoke first, "Actually, the protection and binding spells that had been placed on you should have blocked all knowledge of you."

"That is what is so amazing," Armel chimed in. "Blaine, you would have had to be the one to allow Elian to see you from Renault. There is just no other way since Elian doesn't poses ancient magic. His abilities are tremendous but not strong enough to break the spells your mother had used to protect you."

Queen Lyra smiled sympathetically at Blaine. "In other words, my dear, the two of you had been searching for each other all your lives and you were both unaware of it."

Blaine nodded as if she understood. She did to a point but there were still so many unanswered questions. "So, it was Elian who brought me to Renault." Blaine said in a half questioning manner.

Queen Lyra sat for a moment contemplating a response. "Was Sairah aware that you saw Elian?"

"Yes, she knew. She was incredibly upset about it." Blaine answered.

"I can only speculate, but I would imagine she planned on taking defensive action by strengthening her protective and binding spells on you. However, subconsciously you knew it was time for your true self to be revealed. Somehow you engaged the assistance of Elian which allowed you to cross over on your own," Queen Lyra explained.

With all that Blaine had learned about magic, she knew it was at its strongest when the user was surrounded by nature. Remembering the morning she had left her house with her mother, Blaine realized Queen Lyra was right. "That explains why the morning after I saw Elian she chose to go into the woods. At the time I thought it strange that we were making our escape on foot through the forest, but she needed that setting to enhance her magic." Blaine looked at Elian who also seemed to be deep in thought. She recognized the "weight of the world" expression creeping across his face. Nudging his shoulder slightly with hers to get his attention, she attempted to lighten his mood, "Ha, I guess you're stuck with me!"

Armel chuckled lightly as he stood up and retrieved the bottle of wine. He refilled all the goblets, except for Blaine's. Her goblet remained virtually untouched.

Queen Lyra stood up as she spoke, "Let us continue our visit in the other room. I believe we will be much more comfortable there."

Making their way into the sitting room Elian and Blaine waited for Queen Lyra to sit before taking their places on one of the couches. Armel went to the stone fireplace and systematically stacked wood into the large opening. Turning to Elian, he flashed a brilliant smile as he asked, "Would you care to do the honors?" Joining Armel in front of the fireplace, he quietly spoke a single word, the stack of wood immediately burst into a fiery ball of warmth.

"See, Mother, just one word—so impressive," Armel boasted as if it were his accomplishment.

As Elian returned to his seat next to Blaine she could see a flicker of pride reflected in his dark eyes. The feat of magic Blaine had just witnessed brought some confusion to her. "When we first arrived in Alatis, Kern told us that Elian's magic wouldn't work here," Blaine said with a questioning tone.

"Yes, Kern's statement was technically correct. Here, however, did not pertain to all of Alatis. You see, to better protect our gateway Kern has placed a barrier against all magic around it. He calls it a dead zone. Once someone is allowed to pass the dead zone, then the use of magic is replenished."

"I was unaware creating dead zones against magic was possible," Elian remarked.

"As far as I know Kern is the only one with this unique ability," Armel responded.

"The legends in Renault all speak of the great magic unicorns possess. It is said to surpass anything we can comprehend. Perhaps the legends are accurate in that aspect," Elian shared.

"I am not sure if that pertains to all unicorns. Kern is the only one I have ever encountered," Queen Lyra added. "He has been an advisor to the Elfin Royalty as long as there has been recorded history—perhaps longer. He freely travels from world to world without use of the gateways."

"Are there no other unicorns?" Blaine questioned.

"I have asked this question of him many times. I am fascinated by his comings and goings. He always seems to arrive here when he is needed most. I, however, am not quite sure how he knows when to come. He just tells me that he is always here in spirit and that his physical appearance occurs according to need," Armel interjected.

"Does he live here in Alatis?" Blaine questioned.

"The answer to that question is also unclear. His response, too, is always very cryptic. He tells me that a soul may have many homes because a home is somewhere you are loved. Over the years, I have just stopped asking questions. Instead, I have taken advantage of his wisdom, knowledge, and invaluable counsel," Armel admitted.

"Armel is quite right. Kern is quite an enigma, but his counsel has been deeply revered over times past. We have all come to the conclusion it is best not to question the details of his comings and goings." Queen Lyra interjected. Then she surprised Blaine by turning to her and saying, "So, Blaine are you ready to ask me the question that has been on your mind since you arrived?"

Trying to find the right words, all Blaine could say was "Well ... I guess."

"It's okay. Just ask!" Queen Lyra gently urged.

Finally, finding the courage to speak she began. "Okay. So, Fayendra mentioned today that I was of elfin lineage and indicated that you were aware of this. I guess I want to know if this is true and how. I mean I have no real clue as to who my father is—so I have to assume any elfin bloodline would be from his side. But then again, my mother has quite the deceptive soul. It's all very confusing." Blaine stopped, embarrassed in the realization that she was rambling uncontrollably.

Queen Lyra smiled gently at Blaine. "Come with me," she said as she stood up and walked toward the entrance. Blaine stood to follow Lyra. Looking back over her shoulder she realized Elian was not getting up. She motioned for him to come. Elian looked at Armel questioningly. Armel nodded his okay and Elian rose to his feet and quickly caught up with Blaine.

They followed Queen Lyra, arriving back at the entry. They walked into a room whose door had been closed when they first arrived at the residence. It took Blaine a minute to adjust to the dimly lit room. The light coming from the skylight in the huge ceiling was faint due to the setting sun. Blaine's attention was turned to Queen Lyra as she heard her softly speak a word while waving her hand gracefully in the air, "Moonairaya". As she did so the four round crystal globes located in each corner of the room began to glow. Their intensity increased until all darkness dissipated from the room.

Standing side-by-side, Elian and Blaine surveyed the room; several maps hung on the wall to the left of them. The wall on the right supported floor-to-ceiling shelves filled with books and documents. The center of the room was furnished with high-back chairs surrounding a huge table. Queen Lyra stood at the far side of the table with her back to Blaine and Elian. She was facing a wall on which a large grouping of pictures hung.

"Please join me," she requested. They obliged.

Blaine studied the pictures that were artfully arranged on the wall. Several small pictures surrounded an ornately framed large picture that hung in the center of the wall. All of them were artists' renderings of families. It only took Blaine a moment to realize they were pictures of the Elfin Monarchy. Her eyes danced from one portrait to the next finally stopping at the large, beautifully framed picture in the center. Blaine let out a loud gasp. She took a step forward in order to examine the portrait more closely. She could hardly believe her eyes. Queen Lyra, the King, and Armel were posed together smiling brightly and there standing next to Armel was Blaine.

"How is this even possible?" Elian asked. Blaine was at a complete loss for words.

"That is my late husband, King Ortho and the beautiful young lady in that picture is my daughter, Daria,"

Blaine stood there dumbfounded for a moment then finally found her voice, "I could be her twin."

"Yes, genetics are amazingly selective. Imagine my surprise when first I met you at the Great Hall."

Blaine thought back to the expression on Queen Lyra's face and how closely she had examined Blaine. "So, am I part of your bloodline?"

"Yes, Blaine, you are my great granddaughter."

Blaine stood there trying to process everything she was seeing and hearing.

"Daria was your grandmother. She bore a son before her light was extinguished. He is your father."

Blaine focused on the painting. She felt as if time had stopped. Her father was half-elf, and Queen Lyra spoke as if he was still alive.

"Kern told us that Daria lost her life by the hands of Tevis, and that she was in love with him. So Tevis is the father of Daria's son, Blaine's father." Elian spoke deliberately as if thinking out loud.

Hearing Elian's soft voice jerked Blaine out of her dazed state. She quickly turned in Queen Lyra's direction awaiting a response.

Lyra stood solemnly quiet for a moment and nodded her head as she spoke. "Yes, all you say is true."

Blaine felt as though all the oxygen had been sucked out of the room. Her head began to swim as she took a step backward trying to distance herself from the truth of her heritage that hung undeniably on the wall before her.

Elian stepped closer to her and placed his hand on the small of her back in an effort to support her.

Queen Lyra's wavering voice broke the awkward silence that had filled the room as she continued to confirm Elian's statement. "Yes, Tevis is your grandfather. Your father is his son, General Mitchell."

"The General that confronted us at the clearing by your house is my father?" Blaine asked already knowing the answer before the words left her mouth.

"Yes," Elian answered solemnly. "That was General Mitchell."

"So, my mother is a habitual liar, my father is a cold-hearted murdering militant, and my great grandfather is a power-hungry, serial-killing psychopath. What a fantastic family tree I have," Blaine sighed heavily.

"Do not judge your father too harshly, child. He knows no other way. Kern believes there is light in his heart. His love for your mother remained against the wishes of Tevis. That took much strength," Queen Lyra spoke gently to Blaine.

Elian, concerned for Blaine, escorted her to the table in the middle of the room. Pulling out a chair, he gently guided her into the seat.

At some point Armel had entered the room and now stood at the far end of the table. "We know all of this is almost impossible to comprehend. We really understand a portion of what you are feeling. It took a great deal of understanding from us to finally accept this information when Kern disclosed it to us. Please take heart as we did in knowing that Daria was a great light. Her presence filled the universe with great joy and incomparable goodness. Her blood flows through you as well. As for your mother, her decision to sacrifice all and take you worlds away to protect you speaks well of her love for you. We believe she felt justified lying to you in order to protect you from her previous path of darkness. Her love for you changed her heart causing her to change her pathway. She made a difficult and positive decision as she consciously turned away from her dark ways."

Blaine looked up at Armel. His words brought her some degree of comfort.

"Kern assures us that Tevis and General Mitchell have no knowledge that Sairah had a daughter."

Feeling completely overwhelmed by the implications of the knowledge revealed to her during the last few minutes, Blaine was thankful for the opportunity to direct the conversation to a different topic. "How is it Kern knows so much?" Blaine asked.

"Aw, I have often asked that same question," Armel responded.

Seating herself next to Blaine, Queen Lyra joined the conversation. "His knowledge and magic seem to be infinite. Fayendra once told me that Kern is more than he seems, and that his presence here precedes time itself. When I asked her to elaborate she only laughed and told me 'to trust is to believe and to believe is to trust,' so I stopped asking. She tends to always respond to questions by reciting a riddle."

"Yes," Blaine responded. "He is a mystery." Yet somehow the very mention of his name brought comfort to her. Fayendra was right; Kern was so much more than a magical unicorn. This was simply the form he took when it suited his purpose. Deep in her soul Blaine knew Kern somehow fit into the puzzle that had become her life.

As Blaine thought about the truth of her bloodline her emotions escalated. She finally had the answers to so many of her questions. Yet, this knowledge did not bring the peace she sought. Suddenly, just as the ramifications of this knowledge threatened to completely overwhelm her, she felt Elian's protective energy engulf her. He now stood behind her. The sound of his voice soothed Blaine's emotionally-overridden soul as he addressed Queen Lyra, "So you allowed us to pass through the portal into Alatis because Blaine is your great granddaughter."

"No," Queen Lyra answered without hesitation. "I was aware of the prophecy about the Bringer of Light. However, as with all prophecies, specifics are not revealed. It was not until I had seen Blaine that the thought even occurred to me that she would be of elfin bloodline let alone mine."

"Were you not upset that Kern chose to keep such secrets from you?" Elian inquired.

"I must admit I was a bit distraught that I was not aware of the close connection the Bringer of Light would have to me. However, when Kern explained to me that he needed my judgment to allow you to enter Alatis to be one of the mind and not the heart, I understood why he did not disclose the information. He did not want the fact that the Bringer of Light had such close ties to me to be a factor in that decision. It is not for me to question the ways of the universe and its divine powers."

Blaine considered for a moment how she would have handled the situation had she not been informed on such a personal matter. She was positive she would not have displayed the decorum and grace Queen Lyra had. Blaine met Queen Lyra's loving gaze and smiled warmly at her.

"We both understand that your pathway is not an easy one. I can only hope that what we teach you in the little time we have together will ease some of your burden." Gently taking Blaine's hand in hers, she turned to Elian and spoke. "Elian, the bond that exists between you and Blaine is extraordinary. I speak for many when I tell you we are all eternally grateful for the sacrifices you have made throughout your entire life. There are few souls that are blessed with the realization of their destiny so early in the journey. From the beginning you have chosen the pathway, which will bring about the fulfillment of this destiny."

Armel turned and addressed Elian, "If you are willing, we are prepared to help you perfect your combat skills. These must be at their maximum level for I hear the pathway ahead will be even more challenging."

Elian nodded in agreement then humbly responded with a simple, "Thank you."

Queen Lyra looked up at the skylight as she rose to her feet. "The first stars are shining brightly. Fayendra will be at your cottage as the sun breaks the horizon. The events of the evening has been emotionally draining yet rewarding. You both will need your rest. Armel can escort you back to your cottage."

Also rising to her feet Blaine spoke confirming Lyra's assessment of the evening by saying, "Yes, I am feeling very drained and overwhelmed. I must add, however, since I crossed over I am no stranger to these emotions." Blaine smiled wearily at Lyra as she spoke, "I have also learned a good night's sleep does wonders for renewing one's soul. It is not necessary for Armel to walk us back. We can find the way."

"Yes, your hospitality has been much appreciated. The dinner was spectacular, but there is no need to impose on you any longer," Elian added warmly.

Armel and Queen Lyra accompanied Blaine and Elian to the front door. "Elian, tomorrow morning then?" Armel asked.

"Yes sir, thank you."

Armel turned to Blaine and smiled warmly. Giving her a hug he added, "Dear Blaine, I will see you soon." Blaine could not help feel he was expressing his love for his sister as much as for her.

As Armel opened the front door a gust of brisk night air rushed in causing Blaine to shudder. Queen Lyra looked at Elian, nodded, then turned to Blaine. "I will be traveling for the next few days, but I will send for you when I return. I will be eager to hear of your progress." Stepping forward, she gave Blaine an awkward hug then quickly stepped away.

"Thank you," Blaine responded politely feeling somehow uncomfortable.

"Until our next meeting, blessed be the road that runs beneath your feet," Queen Lyra softly added as Blaine and Elian walked out into the darkening evening.

CHAPTER 19

They walked across the balcony to the steps and then down to the bridge in silence. The air was damp from the spray of the waterfall behind them. As they crossed the bridge Elian spoke first, "Are you all right?"

Blaine laughed, causing Elian to scowl at her, "Don't give me that look," Blaine retorted.

"I am confused why the laughter at my question? I don't find humor in it."

"I don't either. It's just such a loaded question." Blaine responded flatly.

"Loaded question?"

"I mean, am I all right? Do you mean am I okay with the fact that a part of my family tree is a page out of America's Most Wanted, or that the other half of that family tree consists of mythical creatures I didn't believe existed—at least, until two days ago? Maybe it's the fact that I was flirting with my great uncle last night, which, by the way, is extremely uncomfortable. Then there's the fact that my life has completely flipped over and it's not done since it seems to be getting weirder and weirder with each passing day. Let's don't forget to mention the prophecy of which I have had no previous knowledge. How is one supposed to deal with the task of saving not just one world but many worlds? If that's what you mean when you ask 'am I all right,' then, yeah, sure."

Blaine had not intended to unload all her emotions on Elian. Looking over at him, she expected to see a wounded expression on his face caused by her rant. Instead he stood there smiling sheepishly at her. "Good, as long as you are all right," he playfully teased.

"Stop! This is serious!" She sputtered between giggles.

"Is it really?" He answered joining in the laughter.

"Yes, really it is!" She pleaded.

Elian stopped laughing and took her hand. "Blaine, it makes no difference who your family is or what they have done. That is not what defines you. The manner in which you have acted and reacted to the choices of your life's pathway plus the love light in your heart is what really truly defines you."

"Thank you," she responded sincerely.

Elian looked a little confused as he asked, "Why do you thank me?"

Smiling warmly, Blaine replied, "You remind me of the big picture which has stopped me from slipping into drama-queen mode."

They continued the journey home, choosing to walk through the town center instead of around the outskirts of the city. The fountain was beautifully lit. There was much more activity in the square than when Blaine had visited it the day before. They received the curious stares and double takes of many, making Blaine feel very self-conscious. However, it didn't seem to faze Elian at all. He stopped and admired the fountain as if he were a tourist on a sightseeing tour.

"Perhaps we should return back to the cottage," Blaine whispered quietly.

"Why?" Elian questioned.

"Because I think we are making the elves nervous being here unescorted."

Elian glanced around then shrugged his shoulders. "They are just curious. You have to remember most have never seen a human before."

"I get that but ... " Blaine's voice trailed off as a little elfin girl approach them carrying a small blue flower. She stopped by Elian and stared up at him.

"Hello," Elian addressed her politely.

The little girl didn't respond. She stood next to Elian nervously twisting the flower she was holding.

"How are you?" Elian attempted again.

Smiling slightly, she then held out the flower to Elian. "This is for you," she said shyly.

Elian took the flower and bowed graciously. "Thank you, my lady." The little girl giggled then ran off disappearing through the doorway of one of the shops.

"Awe, how sweet!" Blaine gushed.

Elian smiled and took Blaine's hand. "Come let's get back to the cottage. Tomorrow morning will come all too soon."

Blaine loved the serene feeling that came over her when Elian took her hand. Deep in thought, they walked in silence the remainder of the way back to the cottage. Blaine's burdened thoughts were interrupted as she glanced at Elian. Studying his expression, she knew he was struggling with the fact that he was safe in Alatis while others were suffering and dying in Renault. As they approached the cottage, Blaine squeezed Elian's hand. "It's going to be all right."

Elian responded with a weary smile. He held the door open

for Blaine then followed her into the cottage.

"I'm going to turn in for the night. I'm beat!" Blaine said to Elian as he closed the door behind him.

"I am as well," Elian responded. They stood there for a moment awkwardly staring at each other.

"Okay then, good night," Blaine blurted out after giving Elian a quick hug and a kiss on the cheek. She then bolted up the stairs.

Well, that was awkward, Blaine thought to herself. She walked over to her bed and sat down. Pulling off her shoes, she laid across the bed. She could hear Elian making a fire downstairs. She looked at the darkened fireplace in her room. *I should get up and start a fire, too,* she thought. It was the last thought she had before falling asleep.

CHAPTER 20

Blaine woke up surprised to see the warm glow of embers in the fireplace. She sat up causing the blanket, which had covered her, to slide off the bed. She smiled to herself realizing Elian had come up and started the fire and had covered her with the blanket. Looking toward the window, she could see the sky had started to lighten.

Stretching for a moment before getting out of bed, Blaine got ready for the day by changing into a fresh outfit. She went downstairs anxious to see Elian, but was disappointed to discover he was not there. She opened the front door and found the porch empty. She went to the kitchen and prepared a light breakfast. There was a light knock at the front door just as she was finishing her meal. Shoving the last bit of hot bread into her mouth, she hurried to open the door only to find on the other side a smiling Fayendra.

"Good, good, you're up and ready." Glancing over Blaine's shoulder, she added, "Even better—no distractions today."

"Distractions?" Blaine asked puzzled. "You mean Elian?"

"Yes, yes the boy—the boy you have a soul connection to.

I need you to focus your thoughts on what we are going to accomplish today and not on what he is doing or thinking." With that Fayendra walked past Blaine into the living room. She then exited through the door that led to the back garden.

"Okay, I guess we're getting started," Blaine mumbled to herself as she closed the front door and headed for the garden. She heard Fayendra chanting loudly as she walked onto the patio. Blaine stood and watched the comedic scene before her: Fayendra dancing meticulously to and fro while waving her arms this way and that; her long loose-hanging dress magnified her stout stature. Fayendra continued her ritual for several minutes before finally stopping and facing Blaine. Looking quite pleased with herself she proclaimed, "Now we may begin."

"Okay," Blaine stated hesitantly.

"We must always protect the area where a beginner is attempting magic. There are lots of harmful entities in this universe just awaiting an opportunity to manipulate a novice user, especially one of your likes. Such great power! Sit down, sit down! We will talk now, work after." Fayendra pointed to the chairs that they had occupied the day before. Blaine sat down followed by Fayendra.

Fayendra took Blaine's hand as she said, "Yes, yes so strong. So much potential. Your pathway is not an easy one, but I tell you nothing not already known. You must now take control of the ancient magic that you possess. Our time together is short so I don't find it necessary to teach you human magic. I don't want you to use it as a crutch. You must learn to embrace the gift of ancient magic that was bestowed upon you. It is part of our universe. It is everywhere and in every living thing but few are able to wield it. To use such a power without full understanding is a very dangerous thing." Fayendra stopped and looked at Blaine with probing eyes and asked, "Do you grasp this concept?"

"Yes, I think so," Blaine answered back using a tone of uncertainty.

"Good, now explain what you know." Fayendra demanded flatly.

"Huh?" Blaine hesitated, "Okay, so elfin magic isn't really magic at all. It is the manipulation of energy that all living things possess. This energy works harmoniously with nature by communicating with all other living things that draw energy in or give it off."

"Yes, yes, very good—go on," Fayendra encouraged.

"Human magic draws on the same energy but that energy is cued by words. These words allow the energy of living things to be borrowed. However, misuse or abuse of human magic can steal and drain life force energy to the point of extinction. I am still having trouble completely understanding when it comes to that point. Doesn't ancient magic use the energy of others also?" Blaine asked.

"Hmm," Fayendra said as she pondered the question. She then smiled widely as she told Blaine, "You see child, we are all connected—everyone throughout the universe. Energy moves freely and constantly from one entity to another. Throughout the day and night this energy continually courses through you and then moves on. The universal words used in human magic allows the user to manipulate and stop the flow as it actually extracts energy from the objects around it. Then when the spell is done the energy flow goes back to its course as it tries to stabilize the void created by the manipulation. However, one who wields ancient magic doesn't draw on energy fields of those around them. They amplify energy already there and use it that way. Does that clear things up?"

"So ancient magic uses the existing energy by just amplifying it not by draining living things of their energy?" Blaine responded.

"Yes, yes," Fayendra said clapping her hands in delight. "That is why you must always be in control of your emotions. Emotions can involuntarily amplify and manipulate universal energy. You must learn to control your emotions to prevent the chaos that could result were you to lash out emotionally. This will be difficult for your human side because humans are ruled by emotions. That is the weakness that allows them to be so easily manipulated by the dark side. This is also why some with ancient magic have chosen to only use human magic. Ancient magic can be fickle and difficult to wield, so they choose to use human magic as a crutch."

"So, shouldn't I learn to use human magic as well? If ancient magic is so unreliable, it would seem logical to have a backup of sorts?" Blaine said.

Fayendra began to snicker loudly as if Blaine's reasoning was ludicrous. "No, no, no!" She exclaimed. Kern and I have discussed this and we both believe you are the one to fully wield ancient magic. You are the Bringer of Light and with that comes the knowledge that this magic you possess is to be used with discretion.

"So, am I not to use magic on a regular basis?"

"Discretion, my dear, discretion. Power doesn't come from using magic, it comes from the light within. Dark forces use magic to obtain power. They have no restraint—none!"

Fayendra stood up abruptly. "Stand, my dear." Blaine complied. "Now close your eyes and clear all questions from your head. Take a deep breath."

Once again Blaine did as she was asked. As she took in deep breaths she could feel an energy growing deep within her soul. Her hearing became more acute. She was able to discern the sound of the birds as they jumped from branch to branch above her. A breeze gently blew across her face causing the hair on her body to stand up.

"Ahh, yes." Fayendra continued, speaking softly. "I can tell you can feel your connection with the energy of the universe. Now use it to create harmony with all you feel around you."

Blaine stood and listened a moment longer. She heard a baby bird venturing out of the safety of its nest. Blaine opened her eyes and scanned the trees until she spotted a nest. She saw a baby bird hopping as it made its way to the end of one of the branches. Just then a gust of wind caused the branch to move. The small bird lost its footing and began to fall. Blaine gasped. Then using the universal energy to surround the bird she lifted it gently and placed it back in its nest.

Fayendra looked at Blaine and said, "You just used your emotions to wield your gift."

Blaine tilted her head at Fayendra, "What do you mean?"

"Simply this—you acted in fear. You were afraid the bird would get hurt and that emotion caused you to use your gift to react. Fear is the strongest destructive emotion of all."

Blaine thought about this for a moment. "Of course, there was an underlying element of fear. It is a strong motivator. I protect something because I am afraid it will get hurt. If I keep someone warm by creating a fire it is because I want to protect them from the cold. I could give many other examples but surely you understand my line of thinking? How can that be wrong?"

A grin crossed Fayendra's face as she explained, "Your emotion of fear dominated your decision. Do you not see the conflict created when you overthink a situation and complicate it with emotion? You protect because it is the right thing to do not because you fear the consequences of not protecting. When that happens, then your act becomes selfless."

"But that is what I did just now. I protected the baby bird because I could."

"Did you? Were you being selfless?" Fayendra questioned.

Blaine scowled at her teacher not understanding the question. "I saved the bird from being injured or possibly dying," Blaine said defiantly.

"That is an emotional response. How do you know it would not have spread its wings and flown? Perhaps its mother had passed to the other side and this bird now had to face the possibility of starving to death. If that was the case, you extended its pain."

"I still don't understand. I hate to see a defenseless animal in distress. So, I will help if I can. How is that being emotional?"

Fayendra laughed, "You just stated it yourself. YOU hate to see any animal in pain. Your decision to act was about you and how it would make you feel if the bird had gotten hurt or died. The difference is in why you did what you did, not in the act itself. You must learn to act simply because you can."

Blaine's cheeks got red with embarrassment as she came to understand what Fayendra was saying. "I never thought of things in that way before. I see the difference now. I am so sorry."

"No—no sorry and no mistakes, just learning. To walk our pathway with the understanding that there are some things that must be experienced for learning is imperative. As you make decisions you are given the chance to learn as consequences always follow decisions. If you feel your decision resulted in a negative consequence you have two choices. You can learn from it and move on, or you can view it as a failure. Dwelling on failure is reacting with emotion and is the beginning of the slippery path into darkness. Self-pity is also a consequence of dwelling on failure. If these emotions are in place as you use the forces of the universe, you will act without regard of consequences to others. Thinking only of yourself is the purest form of darkness. Souls of darkness do exist and they are constantly working to win over other souls of power to the dark ways. They exploit the self-serving soul by pushing its emotional side and hoping it will act without regard for others. You must not react."

Blaine sat back down. She leaned back in her chair feeling completely overwhelmed. She understood what Fayendra was saying and felt completely unqualified to meet the challenge of selflessness Fayendra had just described. If she could not conceive accomplishing this, how could she possibly fulfill the prophecy. Blaine looked into Fayendra's eyes as she spoke. "I'm not sure I can live up to the prophecy."

Fayendra closed her eyes and tilted her head to the morning sky. She stood silently for a moment. "There is no time for self-doubt, Blaine—no time!" She spoke firmly as she opened her eyes.

Fayendra took Blaine's hand as she seated herself. She then reached down and pulled her crystal from its hiding place beneath her dress. Holding it firmly in the palm of her hand, she whispered a word that Blaine did not understand. An electric shock radiated from Fayendra's hand to Blaine's. It continued up her arm and through her whole body. Blaine resisted the urge to pull away. She closed her eyes as her body went numb to all sensation. When she opened her eyes, she was no longer in the garden of the guesthouse. Instead, she stood alone in a clearing in a dark forest. The air hung heavy with the stench of death. She gagged slightly as she struggled to adjust to the overwhelming pungent smell.

Scanning the area, she looked up. A dense smoke filled the purple sky. "I'm back in Renault," She said out loud.

She then heard a familiar voice behind her. "The gateway!!" Protect it at all costs!" It was Elian's voice. She turned and started running in the direction of the voice while calling Elian's name. As she ran branches rushed by her slapping her in the face. She felt their impact but was numb to the pain. She could feel the ground shake as she drew closer to Elian's voice. He finally came into view. He stood in front of a small group of soldiers with his sword drawn. His face was pale and distorted with anger and determination. Several others stood with him. Looking behind the group, Blaine could see a large militia drawing closer.

Blaine called out to Elian but he didn't respond. She drew closer trying not to be seen. As the approaching Army drew closer several others joined Elian. He turned to the cloaked figure next to him as he asked, "Is this all that remains?"

The figure next to him pulled back his cloak to check his weapon and Blaine recognized him. It was Armel. "Yes, unfortunately it is. Their spinners were too powerful for the rest."

Elian briefly lowered his head in sorrow then placed his hand on Armel's shoulder. "It has been an honor fighting by your side, brother."

Armel spoke as he placed his hand on Elian, "Until we meet again by the Great Father's Gate, my brother!"

The approaching Army bore down on the area like ants flooding into a picnic. Tevis's spinners led the charge. Blasts of blue rays rained down on Elian and the small band of soldiers that gallantly stood before the unspeakable army that flooded the forest.

Attempting to rush toward Elian and his followers, Blaine discovered she was frozen in place. She was unable to help the courageous group.

Elian continued to lead the counter attack against the approaching army while trying to maintain a protective field around the small group. His efforts were futile. He was unable to sustain the level of energy it took to defend his position. As the last spinner in Elian's group succumbed to the power of the attacking troops Tevis's men, with weapons drawn, surged forward engulfing the small group of resisters. Arrows bombarded the area striking soldiers from both fighting forces.

Blaine continued to watch in horror as one by one each of

Elian's armed men fell to the ground until all that remained was Armel and Elian. They swung their swords effortlessly. Each carefully executed stroke of their swords brought down several soldiers at a time. It soon became apparent, however, that the opposing force had endless manpower. Elian, realizing his situation, lowered his sword and stretched his arms out in front of him. Gathering all his remaining strength, he spoke loudly, "Atilimus." A circular blast pulsed from him and shot through the forest. The soldiers closest to Elian dropped in their tracks as death overtook them. Those further back were stunned, unable to move. The forest rang silent with the exception of the moans coming from the stunned and injured soldiers that littered the battlefield.

Suddenly a loud clapping came from the right of where Elian and Armel stood bloodied and defeated. Elian was on his knees obviously drained of all energy. Blaine knew immediately that the tremendous blast she had just witnessed had drawn him to the edge of death. They both turned in the direction of the clapping.

"Impressive, very impressive indeed," a sarcastic voice called out. Three figures appeared from the shadows of the forest. Blaine immediately recognized General Mitchell, her father. The man standing next to him was slight in build, almost mousy compared to the stature of General Mitchell. His dark hair was streaked with gray.

"Tevis!" Armel shouted. "I was hoping to come face to face with you."

"It's over Armel!" General Mitchell responded as he walked toward the defeated pair. "We won!"

"Not yet!" Armel shouted as he raced toward Mitchell with sword drawn. Suddenly Armel became frozen in his tracks as an unseen force effortlessly yanked his sword from his hand. Taking advantage of the situation, Mitchell leaped forward plunging his sword through Armel's heart and twisting his blade as he pulled it out.

"No!" Elian and Blaine cried in unison. Tears flowed down Blaine's cheeks as she watched Armel's lifeless body fall to the ground.

Elian shouted as he slowly rose to his feet. His voice was weak and shaky, "You will answer for the crimes you have committed against the universe." Elian seemed to gather strength as he spoke.

"To whom shall I answer? You?" Tevis laughed as he spoke.

Blaine turned her attention back to Tevis and General Mitchell, who once again stood at Tevis's side. The third figure remained concealed by the shadows of the forest.

"I've had enough of this entertainment. Finish it!" Tevis spoke as he motioned to the mysterious figure behind him.

Blaine felt her heart drop as Sairah stepped next to Tevis. His smile made Blaine sick to her stomach. Sairah looked tired and old. Dark circles framed her once beautiful blue eyes. Blaine thought she detected a trace of defiance radiating softly from within her mother.

"Our bargain did not include the taking of his life! It was only to open the gateways and that was all, Tevis!" Sairah hissed.

Tevis threw his head back in laughter, "You were always so gullible. Now motherhood has made you soft." Tevis mocked. "If you don't want your beloved daughter harmed, you will continue to do as I say."

"I could extinguish your life where you stand!" Sairah replied her eyes blazing with hate.

"Oh, my child, do you think I am unaware of that? I know, unlike your daughter whose hesitation to kill me was her undoing, you would do it in a heartbeat. I am no fool. I have taken all the precautions to ensure my safety. If I don't contact the arch spinner before a designated time, she has been told to execute Blaine. There is no way you could retrieve her in time. The fact of the matter is even as we speak her time grows very short. The longer you keep talking the shorter her time grows. So, if you wish to ever see your daughter again you will do what I tell you! Kill him!"

"Sairah," Elian spoke calmly. "Save Blaine, please."

Blaine continued to watch through blinding tears as Sairah raised her hand. A tear rolled down her cheek as she told Elian, "I'm sorry." Then suddenly a blast pulsed from Sairah's hand striking Elian. All the breath was sucked from Blaine's lungs as she helplessly watched Elian fall to the ground.

"Enough of the dramatics. Unseal the gateway now!" Tevis demanded.

"You'll have to wait, father. Her energy levels have been drained. Opening the gateway could kill her," Mitchell said as he kneeled next to Sairah.

"So be it then. If she dies; she dies. She will have served her purpose. The greater good must be served. Always remember that, Mitchell!" Tevis callously spouted.

Suddenly colors blurred and rushed before Blaine's eyes. She became dizzy and disoriented. When things came back into focus she found herself standing on a hill. The sun was just breaking the horizon. As the early morning rays illuminated the lush countryside, Blaine saw several large stones in a cluster. "Stonehenge! I'm back on earth!" She said out loud as she fell to her knees feeling weak and confused about what she had just witnessed.

All at once the ground beneath her began to rumble. A blinding blast came from within the stone monument. It pulsed through the countryside leveling all in its path. Blaine jumped to her feet. A strange wind whipped around her. She turned her attention to the structure of stone that had once stood before her. All that remained now was a large rectangular shaped portal. Blaine watched in horror as Tevis led his army of spinners through the opening.

In that moment Blaine felt the sensation of moving through time and space. She became aware of screams of pain and terror. Next thing she knew she was seated next to Fayendra in the garden once again. She became aware that she still held Fayendra's hand in hers. Instinctively yanking her hand from Fayendra's, Blaine felt as though she had just run a marathon. She was shaky and unbelievably fatigued. She looked at Fayendra wide-eyed and terrified.

"What the hell was that?" She demanded.

"Hell is the right word, my dear. The coming of it," Fayendra answered calmly as she returned the crystal to the safety of its hiding place beneath her dress.

"Fayendra, I have to know if this was just a telling. I mean, just like my other tellings, it's not set in stone. Please tell me it doesn't have to be this way?" Blaine stumbled for words as her soul searched for affirmation that what she had just seen could be changed.

"You are right; there is not just one possible pathway."

"Okay, then," Blaine quietly mumbled to herself as she replayed in her head every detail of her telling. The words that echoed again and again in her mind were "unlike your daughter's hesitation to kill me." "So, on this pathway I am captured," Blaine said out loud.

"Yes, so it would seem," Fayendra replied while intensely studying Blaine's face.

"How?"

"That is not shown to us. As you know tellings are usually revealed in fragments. It is not within our power to choose what is shown."

"Tevis told my mother that I hesitated to kill him. That choice led to those consequences. If I were not to hesitate, another pathway could open, right?" Blaine questioned.

Fayendra nodded. "That would be a likely assumption."

"Tevis used me to force my mother to kill Elian and open the gateways." It turned Blaine's stomach to speak these words.

"Yes, your mother's decisions were motivated by emotion. Tevis used her fear of losing you to manipulate her. He has the blackest of souls. What little light was there—that glimmer Daria saw and was hoping to use to save him—was extinguished long ago. In absence of light there is only darkness and he is the definition of pure evil. He must be stopped at all costs," Fayendra scolded. "He is obsessed with the desire for power. Only absolute domination over the universe and all those who dwell within can satisfy his thirst. It is all that matters to him. Never forget this."

Blaine sat silently trying to calculate the challenge Fayendra had just so passionately presented. *Talk about the weight of the universe!* Blaine shuttered as she considered that.

"Child, I do realize that there is much that has been settled upon you in the last few days. Processing all seems a daunting task—I know. So, I will give you the rest of the day to absorb all we have discussed. I just need you to remember that hesitation and self-doubt can lead to a very slippery path."

Blaine nodded mechanically as Fayendra stood; straightened her dress, and then turned to leave. "Tomorrow morning, I will be here!"

Blaine sat motionless as Fayendra made her departure. Her mind was a dizzying cornucopia of confusion. All Fayendra had said was true. She knew she would have to face Tevis and find the strength to defeat him. She tried to analyze exactly what she was feeling. She was aware of a haunting feeling. She knew it was not fear of confronting Tevis and his spinners. Perhaps it was simply fear of the unknown—but no, that wasn't it either. Whatever it was it was stranger than that and it was something that had always been there, buried deep in her soul. Somehow, she realized it involved a deep anger toward her mother. Whatever it was it had caused an emptiness she could not explain; and it had been with her all her life.

CHAPTER 21

She stood up and walked toward the back of the garden. Opening up the gate, she absentmindedly went through it and headed toward the happily bubbling stream that passed by the back of the cottage. She approached a cluster of rocks and sat down.

The sun surrounded her in a warm blanket of acceptance. A light breeze played with her dark hair as if trying to reassure her that all was going to be okay. Yet the emptiness seemed to grow. It felt as if it were consuming her. Blaine surrendered to the feeling allowing its darkness to overcome her.

She longed to return to the life she had before. She wished she had never heard of Renault. She wanted to once again feel the love and security like when her grandmother embraced her. She wanted to forget forever what her mother really was and the evil of which she was truly capable. She felt the urge to run. Yes, to run far, far away—away from everything and everyone—from Tevis, Fayendra, Alatis, Renault, and Elian.

Elian! The mere thought of him brought all her thoughts to an abrupt end. Chaos seemed to cease as a warm light began to fight the overwhelming darkness that had previously filled her soul. Suddenly she knew the source of the dark emptiness. It had nothing to do with the events of the last days. It was not caused even from the burden she felt by learning she was the fulfillment of the prophecy about the Bringer of Light. The emptiness, this darkness, had lived inside her for as long as she could remember.

Blaine took a deep breath as she tried to analyze a lifetime of feelings, like she never belonged. *It all makes sense now*, she muttered to herself. Growing up she never felt that she fit in. Deep down she knew she was destined for something more; something greater! The emptiness came from not having the knowledge of her destiny. Without the knowledge of her true purpose her soul felt empty. She had allowed that emptiness to turn to fear.

Suddenly Blaine felt more alive than she had ever felt. It was a time of rebirth. As she took in her next breath it was as if it were her first. A sense of serenity filled her soul. Then an image suddenly filled her mind. She closed her eyes and allowed it to wash over her.

She stood in a small apartment. Blaine recognized it from pictures she had seen of herself as a toddler. Sairah set on an old sofa. Next to her was a young Blaine chattering away about Alatis and the prophecy of the Bringer of Light.

Blaine watched in amazement as she listened to her younger self explain to her mom that the universe needed her to save it from the bad man. Tears were rolling down Sairah's cheeks.

"Why are you sad mommy?" the younger Blaine questioned innocently. "There is nothing to be sad about. It is a good thing."

Sairah attempted a smile as she lovingly hugged the young Blaine. "I love you so much, my Angel. You are truly my soul saver."

Then the vision became a blur of colors that flashed before Blaine's eyes. When images came back into focus Blaine was viewing the same living room. Now, however, the lighting was down. Sairah was sitting on the couch nodding as she held the phone to her ear. Her knees were pulled up to her chest. "I don't know why," she was saying in a defensive manner. "I just feel it's safer for her to be bound again to prevent her from having any more thoughts about saving the universe." Sairah held the phone in her right hand while she subconsciously bit the nails on her left hand. She appeared to be disturbed by what the person on the other end of the phone with saying.

"No, it didn't seem as if she had experienced a vision. I just need to keep her safe. I'll do whatever I can to keep her from harm's way!" Sairah continued. "I could never forgive myself if she fell into Tevis's hands. Over my dead, cold body he will have to step before I allow that!" Blaine could see such hate in Sairah's eyes. As she spoke these words it caused a cold chill to run down Blaine's spine.

"I know. I know. She deserves the stability but staying in one place very long increases our chances of being discovered. I don't know if Tevis has loyalists on this side and if they can even communicate with him, and I'm not about to take that chance. She deserves to live a normal happy life. All I want is for her to know how much she is loved!"

Once again colors blurred. As the vision ended Sairah's voice drifted away. Blaine could hear her mother's laughter and the childish squeals of delight from an exuberant, happy child. Then Blaine heard her mother say, "I love you always, Blaine." This was the last thing Blaine heard as she opened her eyes to find herself once again by the stream behind the cottage in Alatis. A sense of serenity washed over her. The emptiness that had engulfed her was now gone. She felt a renewed sense of confidence. The realization that this pathway was her destiny brought her a new understanding that touched the very depths of her soul.

Her thoughts turned to her mother and the telling of the past she had just experienced. Blaine now believed all Sairah's decisions—right or wrong—were made out of the love she had for her daughter. Though they were clouded by fear, love was the chief motivating force, nonetheless. Blaine felt the burning anger she had had for her mother dissipated.

She remained seated taking in the warm afternoon sun and listening to the beautiful sounds of the birds as they sang in the trees above her. She delighted in the light breeze that rustled the green iridescent leaves of the trees. Everything Fayendra had said seemed to fall into place. She stood feeling lighthearted for the first time that she could remember and began walking up the creek. She strolled along the banks of the creek following its every twist and turn. She came to a point where the denseness of the trees made passage impossible. The creek had now turned into a fast-moving stream.

Blaine glanced around not sure of how far she had traveled. Across the stream the trees had thinned and she could see an open field that was randomly spotted with stone walls. On the edge of the field were what appeared to be targets. A small group of elves gathered near a cluster of structures.

Blaine stood and watched as the elves paired off and began hand-to-hand combat. She marveled at how effortlessly they were able to leap over the walls as they each endeavored to gain the advantage over their opponent.

Her focus was drawn to one pair in particular. They seemed to be equally matched in strength as they jousted. They moved with such grace and agility as they continued their exercise. Blaine felt as if she was watching a well-orchestrated ballet. Just as it seemed one was gaining the advantage the other would maneuver and rebound thwarting the efforts of his opponent. As they continued their combat, one by one, the other elves ceased their practice and also became transfixed by what was occurring on the training field.

As she watched Blaine wondered if this was the same training area where Elian was taking his training. She strained to see if she could spot him, but she was too far away to identify any of the figures.

She glanced up stream to see if there was a bridge she could use to cross the swiftly moving water. No luck. She then mentally analyzed the distance to the opposite bank. "I could jump that," she said to herself confidently.

Backing up, Blaine closed her eyes and took a deep breath. Then opening her eyes, she ran forward as fast as she could. With each stride Blaine imagined herself clearing the stream and landing triumphantly on the opposite bank. When she came to the edge of the bank she pushed off with all her might bounding into the air. She landed successfully on the other side of the stream. Though her landing was a bit clumsy Blaine could not help being pleased as she noted she had cleared the stream with a good four-foot margin. She smiled to herself as she rested against a tree at the edge of the field, basking in the light of her impressive feat.

She then turned her focus back to the training field. She was close enough now to see the battle gear worn by the group in the field; it was formfitting and appeared to be made of a flexible, metallic material. The original small group seemed to have grown. They were all watching the two nimble figures who were now sparring with swords drawn. Blaine searched for Elian among the growing armor-clad group of elves who were observing the extraordinary display of swordsmanship being executed in front of them. She was disappointed to discover he was not there.

Just then the two soldiers who were sparring moved closer to her as one agilely maneuvered himself over to a large trench. She continued watching the two dance about the field. One turned to face her. Blaine took a deep breath as she realized it was Armel. The other must be his opponent. She studied the opponent's movements. Even though she could not see his face she began to suspect that it was Elian.

Blaine watched, mesmerized as Armel's opponent appeared to be gaining the advantage until he was foiled by an exposed tree root. He stumbled slightly. Though he recovered quickly it gave Armel the opportunity to use a swift leg swing to knock his opponent's feet out from under him, ending the contest.

The gathered soldiers all clapped and cheered as Armel helped up his fallen opponent. Armel was smiling widely as they both removed their protective armor from their heads. Blaine's suspicions were confirmed as she heard the other soldier let out a joyous laugh.

"Elian," Blaine called out enthusiastically waving her hand in the air. Elian and Armel turned in her direction. Elian's face lit up as he made eye contact with Blaine.

Jogging effortlessly over to Blaine he greeted her warmly, "Good morning."

Blaine gave him an awkward hug. She was smiling widely as she said, "Impressive sparring."

"Thank you," Elian replied humbly. "I would have taken the match if not for my lack of awareness of the uneven ground," he mumbled, a bit embarrassed.

"You're too hard on yourself. Armel's an elf. Genetically speaking, he should have completely dominated, but you gave him a tremendous run for his money. It was a great feat that you seem to be missing, silly."

Elian smiled. "Perhaps. However, I have my suspicions that Armel may have been holding back."

"I seriously doubt that. Armel does not strike me as someone who would purposely allow anyone to beat him, especially not in front of the soldiers he commands."

Armel now joined Elian and Blaine. "Good morning, my lady," he said bowing slightly.

"Good morning to you, General," Blaine replied.

"Did you come to join us for battle training today?" Armel questioned, smiling playfully at her.

Not waiting for Blaine to respond, Elian questioned, "Are you finished with Fayendra already?"

"Yes. Our time was brief this morning. I had a few things I needed to work out first." Seeing the puzzled look on Elian's face she added, "We'll talk later. I don't want to interrupt your training."

"Oh, you are not interrupting." Armel answered. Then he asked again, "Would you care to join in?

"No, no," Elian answered for Blaine.

"Hey!" Blaine exclaimed interrupting Elian. "Are you insinuating that I am not capable of training in a combat setting?"

Elian's discomfort at her question was apparent as he stumbled over his words to try to rectify the situation. "No, no, of course not. I just, well, figured you would be tired from your morning session with Fayendra, and it's not as if there's extra armor ... "

"Yeah, I get it," Blaine teased. "You think of me as a delicate flower that needs protecting."

"Well, I wouldn't go so far as the delicate flower part," Elian mumbled under his breath.

This made Armel laugh out loud.

"So, what is your point?" Perhaps you are afraid I'll show you up in front of the elfin Army."

Elian shook his head laughing. "Oh my, Blaine, always the combative one."

"Come," Armel said as he motioned for them to follow him. "We were just going to finish up with some archery and agility training." Armel turned and walked toward the other side of the field to join the group of soldiers there.

As Elian began to follow Armel, he turned and looked over his shoulder. "You coming?" He asked as he held out his hand behind his back.

Blaine quickly caught up with him. Holding hands, they walked over to join the others at the agility course. Blaine watched as the first set of elves maneuvered effortlessly: first across a line of tree trunks that were partly submerged in a swampy pond, then over a very tall stone wall. Try as she could, Blaine was unable to see what lay beyond the wall.

Then it was Blaine's and Elian's turn. They stood side by side. Elian turned toward her and winked just as the elf starting the race yelled, "Go!" Elian took a quick lead. Leaping from stump to stump it almost appeared as if his feet never touched the surface of the wooden platforms. Though Blaine's speed was not as fast as Elian's she maneuvered confidently across the pond. Elian had already climbed the stone wall by the time she arrived at its base. She took a running leap and to her surprise she scaled the wall quite easily. Jumping to the ground on the other side, she scanned the next obstacle. In front of her was a large thicket of bushes. She could see Elian sliding along on his belly trying to avoid the sharp thorns that grew on the bushes as he continued his attempt to complete the course.

Blaine dropped to her stomach and began the journey. She could feel her hair being pulled as it became entangled in thorns as she tried to twist and turn her way through the thicket. Pulling herself out at the end of the obstacle she could see Elian about 300 yards in front of her. He stood at the bank of a large pond that was surrounded by trees. He was using a bow and seemed to be aiming an arrow at a vine that tethered a rope to a tree.

Blaine arrived at the pond and noticed another bow and

arrow leaning against one of the trees. "Are we supposed to shoot that vine to free the rope?" questioned Blaine.

"Yes!" Elian answered as he released his second arrow missing the vine once again. "Your target is over there," he said pointing to a second rope and vine. "Once the rope is free, use it to swing across the pond," Elian spoke as he loaded another arrow.

"Okay!" Blaine picked up the bow. "I've never used a bow before," she said as she cautiously loaded the arrow.

Elian let out a growl of frustration as his arrow missed again.

Blaine pulled back the bow string, aimed, and fired. The arrow flew swiftly to the target, freeing the rope.

"Wow, I did it," Blaine squealed with delight.

"Huh ... beginners luck!" Elian grumbled as he let his fourth arrow fly, only to once again miss its target.

Blaine shot him a dirty look. "Beginners luck, is it?" She picked up another arrow, aimed, and released it into the air. She then threw down the bow just as her arrow effortlessly hit its target releasing Elian's rope. Blaine took her rope and running to give herself more lift she propelled herself across the pond. Releasing the rope just at the right moment, she landed at the edge of the pond causing her feet to get slightly wet. She didn't bother looking back. She began running as fast as she could, leaping over the small hedges that grew randomly on the remainder of the course. She could see the soldiers who had already completed the course ahead of her waiting at the finish line. As she pushed herself to go faster she glanced to her side and saw Elian was gaining on her. He overtook her only inches from the finish line.

Armel was laughing and cheering as they both crossed the line. "Well done, well done!" He said as he joined them.

Elian was smiling smugly at Blaine. "Don't give me that look!" Blaine teased. "I would have won had I not shot your vine for you."

Elian began laughing. "Yes, I know. I love how you tried to lull me into a false sense of security by saying that you had never shot a bow and arrow before. Tricky, very tricky."

"That was no trick; that really was my first time," she flatly informed him.

"Must be those elfin genes," Armel added gleefully.

Blaine and Elian remained until the rest of the soldiers finished the obstacle course before they parted ways with Armel and the training group.

Elian and Blaine walked in silence as they made their way back to the cottage. Both were preoccupied with their own thoughts. Elian finally broke the silence. "So, may I inquire as to why your time with Fayendra was so limited today?"

Hesitating, Blaine struggled to find the words to explain the events of the morning. "I had a lot of self-doubt and hesitation about my ability to live up to the prophecy of the Bringer of Light."

"That is understandable, Blaine, but it is most important that you believe in yourself." Elian encouraged.

"Yes, I know." She paused trying to decide if she should reveal to him the telling she and Fayendra had shared. Finally, she said, "Fayendra and I shared a telling."

"Oh?"

"Yes, a very disturbing one."

Elian didn't respond.

"Don't you want to know what it was?" Blaine questioned.

"I already know," he stated without emotion.

She stopped and stared at him. He took a few more steps then looked over his shoulder at her. "Are you not coming?" The expression on his face and his monotone was the same as it had been on the day they met—flat and matter-of-fact.

"No!" Blaine responded defiantly.

"No, you're not coming?" Elian questioned.

"No! You are going to tell me how you knew about this and then failed to mention it to me!" She scolded. "So, you have known about this telling and didn't tell me?"

"Yes," Elian answered as he began walking again.

"Yes. That's it?" Blaine's tone was irritated and hostile. "Stop walking and talk to me!"

Elian stopped but didn't turn around. Blaine caught up with him. Facing him she demanded, "You knew but chose not to tell me?"

"What would you have had me say? Telling you would have only fed into your self-doubt. You are forgetting a telling is just that—a telling. None of them are set in stone. Every choice we make has the ability to change the future."

Blaine was quiet for a moment as she considered his answer. "You are right. I'm sorry."

"It is fine," he said as he began walking again.

"Are you mad at me?" Blaine asked as she followed him.

"No, why would I be?" He snapped back.

"Okay, if that's your answer, we'll go with it," Blaine replied in an effort to lighten the mood.

This time Elian stopped and faced Blaine as he spoke. "I'm sorry, too. It's just that I have spent my whole life preparing and training for the instrumental part I am to play in helping the Bringer of Light fulfill the prophecy. I, however, never imagined the bond I would feel with you. Being here with you in this safe environment has given me a glimpse of life without my mission dominating every thought and action. For the first time the burden of the future has been lessened." Elian paused searching for the words to further describe his feelings.

Blaine took this opportunity to ask, "So is it such a bad thing to take a break from the burden fate has thrust upon you?"

"No, not at all and that's just it." Elian turned and began walking again.

Blaine was now walking by his side. "What's just it? That you are enjoying this short intermission from the weight you have carried all these years. Do you really think it is not okay to enjoy a few minutes of joy and laughter?" Elian glanced at her briefly then quickly looked away. "I get it," Blaine continued. "I get your feeling guilty because you don't want this to end. I get that it would be so much easier if all these responsibilities we have ahead of us would just go away. Only today I was wishing I could run—run far, far away from it all. It was in that mindset I was given the realization that ignorance is not bliss! I know your knowledge of your destiny has been a burden, but imagine going through life not knowing you have a purpose. My whole life I've been protected. I had been made blind to my true destiny. I've lived my whole life in darkness. I felt I never fit in and there was such a feeling of emptiness as if something so important was missing. Now, even though knowledge of this destiny is overwhelming and daunting all the previous emptiness and longings are gone. For the first time my pathway is so clear to me. For the first time I truly feel alive."

Elian slowed his pace and gazed at Blaine. "You make me feel alive!"

Blaine didn't know how to respond to this declaration so they continued their walk along the creek in silence. As the cottage came into view Elian ended the silence. "We should probably cross here. The water appears to be quite shallow and we can use the exposed rocks to cross. Blaine nodded. Elian led the way. "Careful, the rocks are quite slippery," he called back.

"Okay," Blaine replied, happy the uncomfortable awkwardness between them had come to an end. She started across the creek smiling to herself as she watched Elian gracefully navigating the creek by stepping from rock to rock. As Elian was about to reach the opposite bank Blaine splashed water in his direction. She had meant only to sprinkle him, but instead Elian's back got drenched. "Oops," Blaine murmured.

"Really?" Elian replied. Blaine couldn't discern whether his tone reflected anger or just surprise. Regretting her decision to "sprinkle" Elian with water, Blaine stood motionless holding her breath. She then playfully and innocently asked, "Not the right time?"

Elian's reply came too quickly for Blaine to avoid the consequence of her decision. He bent down and with both hands began splashing water at her. Blaine tried to retreat to the safety of the far bank but before she had even taken one step Elian was beside her. He lifted her effortlessly and threw her over his shoulder. Blaine tried to struggle but her laughter thwarted her efforts. "So that's how you want it!" Elian joked. "I should just throw you in the creek," he told her as he walked upstream to deeper water.

"No, no. I'm sorry. I didn't mean to get you so wet. I was just trying to get you to smile," Blaine pleaded. She was already beginning to shiver from that icy water and did not wish to suffer the discomfort of a full dunking.

Elian stopped and loosened his grip on Blaine's waist allowing her to slide down off his shoulder. Her feet touched down softly on the stream bed. She took a small step back from Elian who still held loosely on to her waist. He looked deep into her eyes as he whispered, "You always make me smile." He then leaned down to kiss her. As their lips touched Blaine stepped closer to Elian. However, as she did so she lost her footing. She fell into the water taking Elian with her. They both broke into laughter as Elian clumsily helped Blaine to her feet. "See what I mean?

You *always* making me smile," he joked.

Trying to keep from shivering, Blaine muttered, "Yeah, always the clown. Leave it to me to spoil a beautiful romantic moment."

"That's why I have fallen in love with you because with you, nothing is boring. Now let's get to the cottage. Your whole body is shaking from the cold." Elian took her hand and led her to the other side of the creek.

It took Blaine a minute to realize what she had just heard. *Did he just say he was in love with me?* She giggled to herself as they walked back to the cottage. She was walking on air.

CHAPTER 22

Blaine went into the cottage and retrieved some towels from the bathroom. Returning outside, she found Elian had seated himself and was taking advantage of the warmth of the afternoon. Blaine could not help but notice that the reflection of the bright sun off his wet skin made him look as though he was covered in diamonds. She tossed him a towel. After wrapping another one of the towels around her she told him, "I'm going inside to change. Clearly, I got the worst of that fall." Elian responded with laughter.

Blaine went to her room and changed. She walked back downstairs and into the kitchen as she used a towel to dry her wet hair. She looked out the window at Elian who was now reclined in the chair with his eyes closed. He looked happy and peaceful. Her heart skipped a beat as she thought about his "sort of" kiss. He had really said he loved her. Her elation was, however, short lived as she realized how this complicated things so much. She shook off the reality. "Just one day to enjoy this," she said out loud.

Blaine prepared a small tray of snacks. Returning outside she set the tray on a small table and seated herself in the chair next to

Elian. They spent the remainder of the day enjoying each other's company. They talked about the obstacle course, the weather, and the different flowers that magnificently adorned the garden. They both did everything in their power to avoid conversation regarding the truth of the circumstances that had brought them to this point. Blaine was fine with this. Surely, they had earned one afternoon of "normalcy."

Late in the afternoon Elian excused himself to go shower. Blaine took this opportunity to gather tomatoes and eggplant from the garden. She cut some fresh herbs and headed to the kitchen to start dinner. Preparing the tomatoes with the fresh herbs, she decided that while the sauce cooked down she would also clean up. She went upstairs and retrieved a fresh set of clothing. Elian just finished his shower when she returned downstairs, allowing her access to the bathroom.

Once she returned to the kitchen, she noticed Elian standing over the stove stirring the sauce. "Smells great," he commented.

"Let's hope it tastes okay," she giggled as she walked to the counter to finish preparing the eggplant. Everything should be ready in about twenty minutes," she said as she slid past Elian and placed the eggplant in the oven.

"Anything I can do to help?" Elian asked.

"Nope. Well, I'll take that back. I guess if you want to slice some bread, that would help. I think I saw another loaf in the cupboard," Blaine answered as she placed a small basket on the counter next to him for the slices.

"I thought it would be nice to eat in the garden tonight," Elian suggested casually.

"Oh, that would be great. We'll have to move the table from the far side of the house. I'll go wipe it down," Blaine responded as she picked up a dampened cloth." Could you please stir the sauce for me?"

"Yes ma'am," Elian said as he playfully saluted her.

"Yeah, yeah—everyone's a comedian." Blaine stepped out onto the patio. The sun was low in the sky. Shadows filled the area except for the streaks of a few rays of sun that had managed to avoid the canopy of trees above. They cast brilliant spotlights of sun throughout the garden. She took a couple of steps then stopped in amazement of what she saw. "How beautiful!" She spoke out loud. Elian had already moved the table to the garden. He had set it with silverware and in the center of the table he had placed a beautiful bouquet of flowers surrounded by small candles in glass containers. Several metal candelabras surrounded the table.

Elian came up behind Blaine. "Hope this is to your liking," he said smiling smugly.

"Oh, it's okay," Blaine joked. "You sit. I'll go finish making dinner."

Blaine walked back to the cottage. Looking back over her shoulder she saw Elian take a seat at the table. She thought to herself how perfect this was. When the eggplant had finished cooking she carefully arranged the meal on dinner plates and returned to the patio to join Elian. "Bon appétit," Blaine said as she set the plates on the table. Noticing the puzzled look on Elian's face, she added, "Oh, it's French—another language spoken on earth."

Elian nodded.

Blaine waited for Elian to take the first bite. "Well?" she asked in anticipation. "What do you think?"

"It's fantastic. Clearly ... you could have ... been a ... great chef," Elian complimented between bites.

"Oh yeah, right! I wouldn't go that far. However, I do enjoy cooking even though it is weird not having meat."

"I agree. So, is there anything you can't do?" Elian asked.

"What do you mean?" Blaine questioned in return.

"You are dead-on with a bow and arrow, the first time you even pick one up; you keep up with me on the obstacle course; you cook; you are intelligent and witty; you can perform great feats of magic; and then there's the fact that you are devastatingly beautiful."

This made Blaine blush. "Thank you, Elian, but I'm just trying to make it through dinner without knocking the table over or catching myself on fire," she stated nervously as she pointed to all the candles.

Elian tossed his head back as he chuckled. "I must admit that thought did occur to me while I was lighting the candles, but I decided I was more than willing to risk my life to have dinner with you."

Blaine giggled quietly. "Well, I suppose it is apparent from our time together that grace is not my strong suit."

"Ah, but that's why being with you is such an adventure," Elian said warmly.

The sun had set by now. The flames from the candles caused shadows to dance across the patio as an occasional light breeze softly kissed the flames, making them flicker in near synchronicity to the stars above. Elian leaned back in his chair and gazed up into the sky. "It's strange to see different stars and constellations in the sky."

"Yes, but it's still beautiful," Blaine added.

"I do not disagree. I have always loved the stars. I knew the stars in Renault like the back of my hand. Now being here has been a reminder of how large the universe truly is."

Blaine's gaze moved from the sky to Elian. She set her elbow on the table and rested her chin in the palm of her hand. She studied Elian as he spoke. After a few moments Elian dropped his gaze and locked eyes with Blaine. "What?" He smiled as he spoke. "Am I boring you?"

"Thank you!"

"For what?"

"For today! For tonight. For all this." Blaine motioned to the dinner table and candles.

"You're welcome," he replied softly. They sat silently for a moment gazing at each other. Then Elian whispered, "And of course I am also thankful that we got through it without catching anything on fire."

Blaine burst out laughing. "Hard to believe but true, so true." Just then a breeze made its way through the canopy of trees above jostling free several blossoms from the wisteria that surrounded the patio. The blossoms fluttered to the ground like a light winter's snow. Blaine held out her hand. "Oh look, it's raining flowers."

"Magnificent!"

As the blossoms began falling into the candles Elian stood up. "Perhaps we should not tempt fate. We should go in or we may still see a fire before the evening's end."

"Yes, that is probably an excellent idea." Blaine agreed.

Blaine cleared the dishes from the table while Elian extinguished all the candles. They went inside and after washing the dishes from the evening meal they retired into the living room. Blaine took a seat on the couch and watched as Elian started a fire in the fireplace to ward off the evening chill. Seating himself next to Blaine, Elian put his arm around her. Blaine laid her head on his shoulder. They sat in silence as they watched the fire—both enjoying the tranquility of the moment.

Blaine broke the silence. "I wish this night would never end." Elian responded by pulling her closer to him. Then as their eyes met he leaned down and softly kissed her lips.

Just then their peaceful interlude was interrupted by a loud banging on the front door. "You've got to be kidding me," Blaine muttered under her breath.

Elian rose and walked to the front door followed closely by
Blaine. Opening the door, they were both surprised to see Savar,
the centaur, standing on the front porch. Addressing Elian, he
said, "I am very sorry to disturb you and Lady Blaine this late in
the evening, but Fayendra has sent me with an urgent message
for Lady Blaine." Reaching into a leather satchel that hung across
his body, he retrieved a parchment envelope and handed it to
Elian. Elian turned to Blaine and placed the envelope in her hand.

Blaine carefully broke the red wax seal and opened the envelope. She removed the note from inside.

Blaine—

> It is of the utmost importance that
> you continue your training of the use
> of ancient magic at my house.
> You must submerge yourself in the use
> of your gift day and night until it's full
> potential has been achieved.

Fayendra

Blaine read the short note several times before looking up
at Elian. "I am to go to Fayendra's house. She is insisting I stay
there to complete my training." Speaking these words made
Blaine feel ill. She could not bear the thought of leaving Elian.

"Are you to leave tonight?" Elian questioned.

Savar answered for Blaine. "I am to escort Lady Blaine to
Fayendra's house this evening."

"Very well then," Elian responded, his disappointment clearly
reflected in his tone. Looking at Blaine he instructed, "You will
need to pack for your stay."

Blaine nodded numbly and went upstairs to perform the
task. Entering her room, Blaine searched for something to use to
pack a few necessities for her stay at Fayendra's. She discovered
a backpack in the closet and hastily filled it with clean clothes

and a variety of toiletries. Once again, she was overcome by the sadness of leaving Elian even though she knew full well that time was running out and that she needed to learn a lifetime of magic in a minuscule time frame of only a few days.

Returning downstairs, Blaine found the front door had been closed. Elian was leaning against the back of the sofa staring into space. When he saw Blaine, he straightened up and walked to the door. Blaine took a deep breath, "I'll only be gone for a few days. I'm sure." She sat her bag next to her.

Elian smiled warmly and took her hands. "Until we are in each other's presence again, daughter of Sairah, Bringer of Light, Blaine, my love." He bent down and gave her a kiss on the forehead. Blaine wrapped her arms tightly around him. She could feel tears welling up in her eyes. "I love you," Elian whispered.

Blaine remained silent in an attempt to choke back her tears. She reluctantly broke away from Elian's embrace. Bending down she picked up her backpack. Elian opened the door for her and she stepped out into the night.

"Are you ready then, My Lady?" Savar asked humbly. Blaine nodded in response. "Fayendra would have you at her cottage as quickly as possible," Savar said as he lowered his body to the ground. "To accomplish this, it will be necessary for you to ride upon my back for the journey there."

"Okay," Blaine replied nervously as she glanced over her shoulder at Elian who now stood at the front door. She secured the backpack and then walked over to Savar. She stood there a moment intimidated by the task at hand. She had ridden horses when she was younger but this was certainly not the same. Savar perceived her discomfort and offered his hand. Taking his hand, Blaine was able to support herself as she threw her legs over his wide back. Of course, there was no saddle or reins. Unsure where to put her hand, she decided to rest them between her straddled legs. As her hand made contact with his fur she was surprised to discover how soft it was. Once again Savar became aware of Blaine's apprehension. Turning, he looked over his shoulder at her as he instructed, "You are going to need to slide up and hold on to my torso or you could take a terrible tumble as we travel."

Blaine slid up and wrapped her arms around his torso—*somewhat like riding double on a horse,* she thought.

Savar shuffled his hoofs and Blaine looked at Elian one last time. He forced a smile as he held up his hand and said, "Godspeed!"

Savar turned and nodded at Elian, "My Lord."

Blaine lifted her hand from Savar and waved at Elian as they began their journey to Fayendra's.

CHAPTER 23

Starting at a slow walk, Savar quickly transitioned into a full gallop. Blaine tightened her grip. As they rode, his long black hair was occasionally caught in the mounting wind, which hit Blaine in the face.

They rode out of the gates of Roe and into the night. The air had begun to take on a harsh chill. Blaine drew her body closer to Savar. Turning her face to the side, she rested her cheek on his bareback trying to stay warm.

Savar didn't speak as they traveled, which was fine with Blaine. They soon came to the open meadow where she and Elian had arrived in Roe. Riding across the meadow, they entered an area dotted with trees, but as they traveled the trees became a dense forest. Savar slowed his pace to a cantor, which was great for Blaine since she was now able to sit up and loosen her hold on Savar. The only problem that she had was that visibility was difficult as the darkness seemed to grow denser with every step. Occasionally an opening in the canopy of trees above would allow the light of the moon to penetrate. Savar seemed unaffected by the darkness as he maneuvered with precision around the forest trees, continuing at a steady pace. Blaine noticed the forest was beginning to thin. The light of the moon was now allowing her to view their surroundings better.

The night was alive with the serenades of insects and other night creatures. She could hear the babble of a distant creek. The smell of burning wood came lightly on the cool night air. She could also hear the sound of music somewhere in the distance. It sounded like someone was playing a flute. Peering around Savar's broad back, she could see they were approaching a large clearing in the midst of the forest. A small structure occupied the center of the clearing. Dim light flickered softly from the windows of the dwelling. As they entered the clearing the music grew louder. The light from the windows grew brighter causing the moss-covered cottage to appear as if it were surrounded by a halo.

Savar stopped in front of the cottage and helped Blaine slide off his back and down to the forest floor. Blaine stood next to him for a moment. She placed her hand on his back for support as she tried to gain her equilibrium. She then looked up at Savar. "So, this is where Fayendra lives."

He looked down at her and nodded. "I will bid you good evening, Lady Blaine." Savar bowed gracefully, and before Blaine could respond or ask any other questions he turned and trotted back into the forest. She watched him disappear into the darkness of the night then turned back to the cottage. She approached the door cautiously and knocked. The music she had heard before continued to fill the night air. She stood on the front porch waiting for a response to her knock, but none came. She decided to walk around to the side of the house. Peering into a window, she was able to see the living room. It was illuminated by candles located throughout the area. Blaine then followed the path that led to the back of the cottage. Rounding the corner, she discovered a patio that gave way to a large garden. The whole area was lighted by what seemed to be hundreds of candles.

Veni the faun sat on a large stump that had been crafted into a chair. He tapped his foot lightly as he played his flute.

Fayendra appeared from the shadows chanting as she danced around the candles that encircled the stone patio. It only took a moment for Blaine to realize that Fayendra wore no clothing. Feeling uneasy with what she had just viewed, she quickly stepped back around the corner of the house—out of sight. She hoped that when the ritual was completed Fayendra would cover up and she could greet her teacher with some degree of comfort.

She leaned against the house and closed her eyes. The enticing melodies of the flute seem to wash away the anxiety she had felt at having to leave Elian and the protection of his love.

"There you are, young one!"

The sound of Fayendra's voice caused Blaine to jump and let out a small scream. She opened her eyes to see Fayendra standing in front of her. The hope of a comfortable meeting quickly dissipated as Blaine realized Fayendra was still completely naked. "I'm sorry. I didn't want to interrupt anything," Blaine mumbled trying desperately not to look beyond Fayendra's eyes.

"You are certainly not interrupting. I was just giving thanks for the blessings that have been bestowed upon me today when I felt your presence," Fayendra said as she disappeared back around the corner motioning Blaine to follow. She complied keeping her gaze down toward her feet.

"Good evening, Lady Blaine!" Veni said excitedly as he jumped up from his stump. Setting his flute down, he continued, "I am so happy to see you. I was wondering if I would get the opportunity to speak with you again. I don't go to Roe often. I much prefer the comfort of the woods. The elves have so many traditions I find it quite intimidating trying to understand all of them. Rather than taking a chance of offending anyone with my ignorance, I find it much better staying close to home."

Blaine smiled and nodded politely at Veni.

"Would you like some wine?" he asked as he held up a bottle and offered her a goblet. "It is elderberry and it's quite satisfactory, if I do say so myself. A dear friend of mine made it. I don't drink it often—just on special occasions, and ... well, also when I'm playing music for Fayendra, which I do quite often, so I guess I drink wine more than I really thought. Now that I truly think about it, I probably drink too much. Perhaps I should think about cutting ... "

"Now, now, Veni. Don't overwhelm the girl," Fayendra chimed in.

"Oh, I'm sorry. There I go again," Veni said apologetically as he set the bottle down and took a long drink from his goblet.

"Please sit," Fayendra offered as she motioned to a wood bench that rested against the back of her cottage. "How was your journey here?"

"It was unexpected, but good," Blaine replied as she continued looking down to avoid the sight of Fayendra's nudity.

"Yes, I do apologize for the sudden change of plans. However, after giving much thought to the task at hand I have decided my home offers the best environment for your continued instruction. Here we are far away from that distraction of the modern elfin lifestyle. The isolation will allow you to advance at a faster rate. I do fear our time is shorter than we had first anticipated."

"How so?" Blaine asked shifting uncomfortably as Fayendra moved forward and stood in front of her.

Fayendra, perceiving Blaine's discomfort, let out a light chuckle. "I always forget how uncomfortable the natural body can make some souls. Fabric can disrupt the flow of universal energy. I avoid this disruption by not wearing clothing. If you'll excuse me ... " She took a few steps. Opening the back door to the cottage, she disappeared inside. A minute later she reappeared wearing a white wraparound robe.

Blaine was grateful that Fayendra was now covered. The relief, however, was mixed with a feeling of guilt that the "natural body" made her so uncomfortable. "I didn't mean to disrupt your ritual. It just took me by surprise. I'll be fine—really."

"There was no disruption," Fayendra said as she seated herself next to Blaine and gave her a reassuring pat on the knee. "Now, to answer your question, we have learned Tevis is allowing his most advanced spinners to use 'The Book.' We fear that perhaps we have underestimated the power of those spinners."

"But I thought only those who have ancient magic can execute the spells in that book."

"It would seem we are learning that Dark Magic has a whole different set of rules. If the soul is dark enough it may be able to tap into an undercurrent that will allow it to perform those difficult spells and, rest assured, Tevis would not let anyone touch that book that was not completely corrupted by evil."

"So, it is possible he has spinners strong enough to open the gateways."

"No!" Fayendra exclaimed causing Blaine to look at her in confusion. "The spells in that book aren't that kind of magic."

Blaine processed Fayendra's words slowly before continuing. "I guess I misunderstood. I was under the impression that Tevis has not revealed to his followers that he is in possession of the book because doing so would expose his true colors. I thought in order to have the deep devotion of his followers, he needs to continue to lie to them. Knowledge that he has such an instrument of darkness would expose his deceit."

"You are right. The majority of his followers truly believe Tevis is fighting for their freedom. He has convinced them that the elders are the ones abusing their power. They don't know that the elders are fighting against the havoc that would exist if Tevis was to ever gain free access to the other peaceful, unsuspecting worlds. However, his top advisers, who are also spinners, have been given knowledge of the Book of Death. They share Tevis's lust for power and have traded their last bit of morality for the promise of personal gain they think will be theirs if they follow him. They are pure evil and have combined their abilities in an effort to execute the dark spells. Fortunately, they have been unable to achieve their goals. This is, in part, due to the lack of many of the items that are needed to complete these horrific potions and spells. To compensate they are experimenting with substitutes. This, however, in itself, is so very dangerous. They don't comprehend the extent of the power this pure evil possesses."

"So, Tevis is desperate," Blaine commented.

"Oh, Tevis has been desperate for years. His failure to capture you has pushed him beyond the point of any rational thought—not that there was much of that to begin with."

Blaine nodded. She glanced at Veni who now sat in silence listening to Fayendra. She could see the fear in his eyes. "So, if he can't use anything in the book to break the spell on the gateway, what is in the book that could help him?" Blaine asked.

"He wants magic. He hates having to rely on his spinners for his source of power. When your mother was his ally he used her to control all the spinners. They knew her power and feared it. His ability to manipulate her made him feel secure. She was his closest advisor. The betrayal of her disappearance was something he never saw coming. It rocked him to the core," Fayendra explained.

"Is that even possible? It was my understanding that you had to be born with magic." Blaine responded.

Fayendra nodded grimly. "There are writings that claim it is possible. First it would take the most powerful spinners to successfully achieve the spell. However, the consequence of achievement is far too severe, as it would mean the loss of their lives. Their very souls would be consumed by the spell and transferred to the recipient robbing them of their very existence. Their own blind desire for power would be their downfall. They would not realize what was happening until it was too late. It gets worse because it is not just a one-time proposition. In order to maintain the magic, Tevis would continually have to drain others."

"Like a vampire," Blaine spoke quietly.

"Yes, but enough talk for tonight," Fayendra stated as she waved her hand. She then mumbled a word and the majority of the candles on the patio were extinguished with the exception of a few, which lighted the way to the back door.

Veni yawned loudly. "I will bid you farewell, ladies."

"Thank you for your company, dear friend," Fayendra said as she executed a grand bow. "Sleep well."

"Good to see you again, Veni," Blaine said standing and bidding him a farewell wave.

"Yes, I was so pleased to have seen you again as well," Veni replied as he returned Blaine's wave and quickly trotted off into the woods.

Blaine turned to Fayendra, "Does he live far from here?"

"No, just on the other side of the creek," answered Fayendra. "Come inside now and I will prepare a place for you to sleep." As they entered the house the few remaining candles on the patio extinguished themselves. Fayendra closed the door behind them.

Blaine surveyed the small, one-room cottage. It was furnished sparsely with little decor. A small kitchen was nestled in one corner and there was a loft that overlooked a small sitting area which housed a fireplace. A ladder allowed access to the loft. Walking over to a small cupboard, Fayendra retrieved a pillow and a quilt. Handing them to Blaine she motioned to the loft. "You should be perfectly comfortable in the loft."

"I don't want to take your sleeping space," Blaine replied as she took the bedding from Fayendra.

Fayendra let out a dry cough. "Oh my, young one, I haven't slept up there for years. These old bones would protest to the task of climbing that ladder night after night."

Blaine stood for a moment as Fayendra walked over to the fireplace. Leaning over she stirred a black pot that was suspended over a small fire. Blaine hesitated, then walked over to the ladder and cautiously began to climb while balancing the bedding in one hand. The ladder creaked in objection with each rung Blaine climbed.

Looking over her shoulder at Blaine, Fayendra advised, "We will begin at first light. Sleep well."

"Okay," Blaine responded. Tossing the pillow and quilt up into the loft, she then pulled herself on to the platform." Good night," Blaine called down to Fayendra.

Blaine discovered her new sleeping area was extremely small. A thin mattress covered the entire surface of the loft. Maneuvering herself and her bedding into the center of the mattress, she removed her shoes and backpack, adjusted the quilt over her, and placed the pillow at the top of the mattress. She was grateful for the small round loft window, which allowed moonlight to fill the sleeping area.

She could hear Fayendra moving about in the room below. It was only a short time before all the light from the candles was extinguished leaving just the glow of the fire to light the room. Blaine stared up at the ceiling listening to the occasional popping and cracking of the fire. As she began to drift off to sleep her last thought was of Elian.

CHAPTER 24

Blaine woke up abruptly from a disturbing dream. She was drenched in sweat and her breathing was heavy. She sat up abruptly and hit her head on the low pitch of the roof.

"Ow!" Blaine exclaimed. Trying to gain her bearings, she blinked rapidly in an attempt to adjust to the morning light that flooded through the small window of the loft. Realizing that the day was well underway, she scrambled down the ladder. Fayendra was not in the cottage. Blaine went to the back door and exited into the garden. Fayendra was hunched over a patch of herbs that had been cultivated in a small fenced area. "I'm sorry, Fayendra," Blaine pleaded.

A bit startled Fayendra stood straight up and turned towards Blaine. "For what, dear?"

"For oversleeping. You had wanted to begin at the crack of dawn and it's clearly past that," she said motioning to the morning sun that peaked over the tree line.

"Don't worry. It is fine," Fayendra said waving absently into the air. "Training cannot be maximized when your body is in need of sleep; counterproductive it is." She held out a basket of herbs she had gathered from her garden. "Please take this into the kitchen for me, dear. There are some berries and muffins on the counter. Eat and then join me out here."

Blaine walked across the patio and took the basket from Fayendra. She realized she had descended the loft in such a hurry that she had not put on her shoes. Returning to the cottage, she set the basket down on the kitchen counter. She took some berries. After eating them practically without chewing she selected a muffin and proceeded over to the ladder. Climbing the first few rungs, she reached into the loft and extracted her shoes from their resting place next to the mattress. After descending, she took a seat on the sofa in the sitting room to put on her shoes, finished her muffin, and then headed outside to rejoin Fayendra.

Fayendra was seated on a bench in the shade of a large tree. A scarlet red bird was perched on her shoulder. Fayendra seemed to be having a conversation with the bird. As Blaine approached, the bird diverted its gaze from Fayendra to Blaine. Then the bird chirped quietly into Fayendra's ear "Yes. Yes it is," she heard Fayendra say to the bird. Trying not to startle Fayendra's visitor, Blaine slowed her pace as she approached them. Seeing Blaine, the bird chirped once more then fluttered away.

"Sit. We have much to cover today," Fayendra said cheerfully. Seating herself next to Fayendra Blaine could not help but notice that her teacher seemed much more relaxed and lighthearted in these surroundings.

"So ... yesterday you were very much burdened by self-doubt and lack of confidence. However, I perceive those factors are no longer present. It appears you have found the truth that has been buried in your heart this whole time," Fayendra stated as she stood up to face Blaine.

Blaine nodded.

"Good. We no longer need to dwell on the importance of

this training or the need for you to give all your energy and focus to its success." Fayendra closed her eyes as she spoke. "Now we meditate! Close your eyes and feel the energy of the universe that flows through you." Fayendra remained silent for a moment. Blaine could hear the continuing ballad of the creek in the distance. She focused on the serenity and peace it brought to her.

"Good!" Fayendra stated softly. "Now as energy passes through you, imagine yourself amplifying that energy." Blaine opened one eye and peered at Fayendra. "Imagine how a ray of sunlight passes through a piece of glass. As it emerges on the other side its warmth and light are magnified. That ray of sunshine is now so much more than when it first pierced the glass. Now be that piece of glass."

Blaine closed her eyes again and imagined universal energy as waves of color that flowed from one living entity to another. She imagined the waves of color becoming more brilliant and stronger as they left her body.

Fayendra remained silent for several moments. Then she presented this challenge. "Now, use that energy to manipulate the physical."

Blaine opened her eyes and focused on a pile of small rocks. She then used her mind and methodically stacked them one upon the other creating a small tower.

Fayendra clapped. "Your abilities never cease to amaze me. The way you maintained the energy flow is extraordinary, especially on the first try." Blaine smiled widely at Fayendra.

The rest of the morning consisted of similar exercises, each one challenging Blaine to exert more control and to maintain her energy flow longer than the time before. At times Blaine would lose her control in frustration causing several close calls to Fayendra's physical well-being. Fayendra's response would consist of a giggle as she reminded Blaine to control her unbridled human emotions.

At midday Fayendra allowed a short break during which time Blaine rested and ate lunch. This intermission was, however, short lived as Fayendra surged forward with the training. "Now use your energy to create an aggressive force," Fayendra instructed. "Knock down your stone tower," she said pointing to Blaine's architectural achievement from earlier in the morning.

Blaine turned her focus in the direction of the rocks that gracefully stood in the afternoon sun. She squinted at the rocks trying to direct her energy into a concentrated beam. To her dismay the rock structure barely wavered.

"Use your hand to direct and guide your energy," Fayendra suggested.

Blaine thrust her arm out in front of her. As she pointed to the stack of rocks a pulse of purple light shot from her index finger and raced to the structure. Upon impact the stones were pulverized leaving only a pile of dust to mark the spot where the tower had once stood.

Fayendra was ecstatic. "Wow! That definitely was using your energy as a weapon," she remarked gleefully. Fayendra walked over and stood next to Blaine.

Blaine, however, had a very different reaction to her latest accomplishment. She felt confused and very conflicted. "I'm so sorry," Blaine mumbled. "But this destructive aspect has taken me by surprise and is rather daunting."

Fayendra responded quickly to Blaine's concerns. "Your innate goodness causes you to have concerns, but please never forget you will be battling pure evil. There must be no hesitation—hesitation means death! Now, enough about that, you now need to learn to control this aspect of your gift. You will need to practice that,-but please try not to blow up my house," Fayendra giggled as she walked away. This made Blaine smile and eased her reservations.

Fayendra walked over to a small water pump and began filling several buckets with well water. As Fayendra proceeded to attend to her garden—watering and manicuring the many plants—Blaine spent the remainder of her day attempting to control the force of energy that she had learned to the emit.

Soon shadows grew longer and darker as they faded into eventual night. Fayendra joined Blaine. Having watched her every attempt, she told Blaine as she gently patted her back, "You have done well today."

"Thank you," Blaine replied humbly. In the back of her mind she was thinking how thankful she was that she didn't blow up Fayendra's house.

"Come, now. I prepared dinner." As they walked toward the cottage Blaine became aware of how weary she felt. The thought of food and rest became overwhelming.

Upon entering the cottage, the smell of fresh baked bread filled the air. "I prepared a hot bath for you. Go bathe, and by the time you finish dinner will be ready."

Blaine didn't question the invitation. She headed straight for the bath area, which was divided from the rest of the room by an ornate screen. Undressing quickly, she climbed into the tub. Blaine soaked in the tub until her fingers and toes began to wrinkle. Her thoughts began to drift. She smiled to herself as she recalled the events of her last evening with Elian. Suddenly realizing the bath water had become quite cold, Blaine decided to end her bath.

After dressing Blaine approached the small kitchen. She found Fayendra seated at the table that was nestled in the corner by the back door. She was writing in a journal. In the center of the table was a bowl and a small plate containing several slices of bread. Looking up from her journal Fayendra said, "Sit and eat."

Blaine was once again reminded how hungry she was when she smelled the delightful aroma coming from the bowl of stew that Fayendra placed before her. Fayendra continued to write, looking up occasionally and smiling at Blaine who was enjoying her evening meal.

After finishing her dinner, Blaine realized how tired she truly was. As she headed toward the loft, she turned to Fayendra. "If it is all right with you I think I'll go to bed."

Fayendra paused momentarily from her writing. She gave her full attention to Blaine. "Of course, dear, rest well."

"Thank you and good night." Blaine quickly succumbed to sleep the moment she positioned herself comfortably on the mattress.

The following morning, Blaine awoke feeling rested and ready for a full day. The cottage was dark. The living room, however, was slightly lit by a few remaining embers that glowed in the fireplace. Spotting Fayendra's silhouette on the couch, Blaine walked quietly to the back door and went outside.

The sun, awash with beautiful hues of red and orange, had just begun to peek its head above the horizon. Surrounded by the cool air and morning dew, Blaine let out a shiver.

"Good morning," came Fayendra's voice from the shadows of the trees. Blaine was in awe of Fayendra's swift and silent transition from the couch to the lining of the forest. "Dawn is the best time for picking mushrooms," Fayendra said holding up a small basket. "Today we work on defensive magic. Learning the full potential of this skill will be extremely important as you face Tevis and his army. I'll just put these in the cottage." As Fayendra walked past Blaine into the house, Blaine could smell the earthy aroma of the mushrooms. Fayendra soon rejoined Blaine on the back patio.

"I'm pleased you are up so early," Fayendra chirped. "Come." Fayendra motioned Blaine forward as she entered the clearing where they had trained yesterday.

The area was still shrouded in darkness. Blaine had a difficult time adjusting to the lack of light. She also couldn't discern what Fayendra was whispering. Just when she was about to ask Fayendra to repeat herself, something jolted her, freezing her every movement. She stood there helpless and confused. Unable to speak, she stared wide-eyed into the darkness. She managed to hear Fayendra approach her.

"I caught you with your guard completely down. You were depending on your sense of sight to see into the darkness; you should have detected and drawn from the energy around you as I prepared my attack. Developing this ability will allow you awareness of all of your surroundings and will prevent you from falling prey to your enemies." Fayendra whispered again and Blaine was released from her defenseless state. "Did you feel anything before you were frozen?" Fayendra questioned.

"Yes, a sort of electrical jolt. I assume that was the magic hitting me."

"No. That jolt you felt was actually the unnatural movements of the energy flow. Depending on the spell or the user, the disruption may manifest itself in many ways—a pain in the stomach, a twitch of an eyebrow, the rising of goose bumps can all be signs of the unnatural flow of energy. You must always be in tune with the universe. Not only to detect these unnatural flows, but to assure you are guided down the right pathway," Fayendra scolded.

Blaine shuddered slightly. "How do I constantly stay in tune when life offers so many distractions," she questioned. The sky was now light and the shadows that had obscured Fayendra's face were lifted. Blaine could tell that Fayendra was pondering her question.

"Yes, unfortunately that can create a problem—so many distractions. That is exactly why I have chosen to live outside of the elfin city. Unlike most, however, you are already leaps and bounds ahead. You possess the gift of ancient magic. The universal energy has always been a constant factor in your life. You just need to recognize it then harness it. I have a feeling you already do, but have not yet defined it."

Blaine thought back to instances in her life when she "felt" things before they happened. She always chalked it up as good intuition about people and situations. But now she realized that Fayendra was right: She had always been aware of universal energy. Acknowledging this fact, Blaine subconsciously nodded her head as she made eye contact with Fayendra.

Fayendra continued, "Good! Now that you are a bit more aware of the why and the what, let's practice."

Fayendra murmured another word and instantly, all the hair on Blaine's body stood on end as a violent gust of wind pelted Blaine with dirt and gravel. Blaine winced in objection as she heard Fayendra say over the roar of the wind, "Protect yourself."

Blaine shielded her eyes with her hand as she asked, "How?"

Fayendra stood silent as the wind roared through the trees causing dead twigs and branches to break and come hurling through the air directly toward Blaine. Blaine then heard a loud snap as a particularly large branch broke from the wind's assault. Blaine watched it as if in slow motion as it came relentlessly toward her. Fighting the wind, she raised her hand and screamed, "Enough!!"

The wind stopped abruptly causing the array of debris to fall promptly to the ground. The morning air filled with silence once again. Blaine rubbed her eyes to restore clarity from the assault of dust and dirt Fayendra's spell had brought. She locked eyes with her teacher. Fayendra's expression of shock and confusion concerned Blaine. "Are you okay, Fayendra? Did I do something wrong?"

Fayendra stammered as if trying to find her voice. As she made her way over to a toppled bench she gasped weakly, "I need to sit a moment."

Blaine rushed to her side, trying to detect the presence of injury as she turned the bench to its original resting place. "Are you hurt?"

Fayendra took a deep breath. "No, child. I was overwhelmed by what I just witnessed. I have heard stories of things like this occurring in ancient times, but I never believed the possibility of them really happening let alone being privileged to witness it."

Blaine sat down next to Fayendra. She took Blaine's hand in hers as she stared off into the distance. Blaine struggled to understand the source of Fayendra's amazement. She confessed her confusion. "I'm sorry, Fayendra, I don't quite understand."

Fayendra directed her gaze toward Blaine. Laughing almost to herself, she softly said, "Of course you don't. But where do I even begin to explain? A spell is cast by changing the flow of energy. The manipulation of that energy flow is the responsibility of the person casting the spell. It will continue until that person stops manipulating that energy, or is rendered unable to continue manipulating that energy."

"Yes, I get that," Blaine confirmed.

"What I am trying to tell you," Fayendra continued, "is that you neutralized my spell without incapacitating me. You were able to re-establish the natural flow of energy with one simple command. It was unbelievable!"

Blaine stared blankly at Fayendra trying to process the implications of what she was being told. "So ... what does that mean?" Blaine asked.

"It means all doubt about your being the Bringer of Light has been removed." Straightening her skirt as she stood up, Fayendra surveyed the garden. "Quite a mess I made," she stated gleefully.

Blaine remained seated as Fayendra scurried about in an effort to restore order to the garden. She pondered Fayendra's statement, "All doubt has been removed."

CHAPTER 25

After several moments of straightening the area, Fayendra looked at Blaine who remained seated on the bench. "You seemed troubled? Never a doubt was there about the magic you possess." Fayendra seemed to be reading Blaine's thoughts and most likely she was. "Perhaps you have doubts about you actually being the object of our ancient prophecy. I have to admit the possibility that we may have projected our hopes on you without substantiation was discussed in length among our elders."

Blaine nodded "So you now believe that I am the one of whom the prophecy spoke just because I stopped that spell?"

Fayendra giggled as she walked toward Blaine. "Oh, my dear, you must remember that all things in our universe including magic have rules and boundaries. It doesn't matter if it's elfin, human, or ancient magic. All through history there have been spinners that have processed ancient magic. Your feat today proves, however, that you are the first that IS."

Again, processing more information, Blaine was struck with a new realization about her identity. As a result, her response to Fayendra came out as a mumble. "Wow! That's quite a label to place on a sixteen-year-old."

"Age is irrelevant. You were guided here because deep in the fabric of your being you knew this is where you are needed. You followed your pathway. Now you still have much to learn. I can only teach you that which I know. Very soon you will need to seek the tutelage of others. My task at hand is to teach you how to maximize your ability to protect yourself."

Blaine pushed aside the overwhelming thoughts that began entering her mind. "Okay, where do we start?"

The rest of the day was spent learning protection spells and using energy to create force fields. They worked tirelessly the whole day taking only a brief break at midday for lunch. As the sun sank lower into the horizon Blaine had become frustrated with her lack of progress. After the last failed attempt, Fayendra dismissed Blaine sharply. "We will stop for the night since I feel an immense drain of energy. I need to meditate!"

Defeated, Blaine entered Fayendra's cottage slamming the door behind her. She flopped down on the couch and closed her eyes. She longed to see Elian because she knew his calming ways would ease her troubled mind. Fayendra's relentless warnings of the importance of developing impenetrable walls of protection against the physically harmful spells of other spinners rang in her ears. Blaine was to achieve perfection that allowed her to effortlessly and continuously defend herself against these attacks as well as the attacks on her every thought. It was not going well. She had tried so hard to meet the challenges Fayendra had presented her, but she could not seem to conquer the ability to multitask magic.

Attempting to meditate to clear her mind, Blaine drifted off to sleep instead. She woke with a start to find herself alone in the darkness of the night. Fayendra was nowhere to be seen indoors. Heading outside, Blaine strained her eyes, trying to identify outlines of figures by Fayendra's meditation bench. The night air was cool and moist, which caused Blaine to shiver. She took a seat on one of the patio chairs. The magical Alatisan moon was silver and its light made everything appear as if it had been sprinkled with glitter. Finally locating Fayendra, Blaine looked in the direction of the forest, where a single moon beam had pierced the canopy of trees lighting the area where a conversation was brewing.

Aside from Fayendra, Blaine recognized Maorga, the Griffin, and Kern. Blaine could not help but notice that the light of the moon reflecting off Kern made him appear to be glowing.

Seeing Kern lit a spark deep in Blaine's soul. She wanted to rush forward to hear his words of inspiration that she knew would wash away the feeling of complete defeat she was experiencing. Instead, she hesitated as she observed Fayendra's body language. Fayendra stood motionless, nodding occasionally as she listened to Kern. Kern shot a quick look in Blaine's direction, but then refocused on Fayendra and Maorga.

Suddenly an overwhelming sense of well-being washed over Blaine. It had only been a glance, but in that instance she was given the knowledge that Kern encompassed—far more than any living being could comprehend. Then a voice gently resonated from the depths of Blaine's soul, "I have existed long before time itself." Blaine closed her eyes and focused on the voice. "Dear one, you have learned all you can here. It is time."

Blaine opened her eyes to find the sense of serenity had been but a fleeting moment. She now found herself filled with the all too familiar feeling of uncertainty. As she peered into the darkness in an effort to see Kern she was disappointed as she watched him disappear into the forest.

Seeing Fayendra and Maorga approaching, she asked, "Why did Kern leave? I really needed to talk to him."

Ignoring Blaine's question Fayendra said, "Your time with me has drawn to an end, but you already knew that. Maorga will take you where you are needed now."

"Back to Roe? Back to Elian?" Blaine was almost pleading but deep in her soul she knew that wasn't where she would be going.

"Elian is no longer in Alatis," Maorga stated matter-of-factly.

Hoping she had misunderstood what Maorga had just said Blaine ask, "What do you mean he's not in Roe? Where is he then?"

"Renault," Maorga replied.

Blaine gasped, "Why? Why would he leave without me?" She demanded.

Her demands were met only with silence. Finally, Fayendra spoke, "Before you leave I must give you something."

Blaine stood in disbelief as she watched Fayendra hurry off toward the cottage. Her questions had been completely ignored. She then turned her attention to Maorga who was shifting uneasily from foot to foot. His discomfort was evident as he cocked his head seemingly trying to analyze the current situation but not able to find the words to ease it. Once again Blaine was overcome by the all too familiar feeling of helplessness.

Suddenly her despair and thought of loneliness were interrupted by Kern's gentle voice. "You are never alone. Above all have faith in yourself and the things you hold true in your heart."

The slamming of the cottage door jarred Blaine back from her encounter with Kern. Blaine watched as Fayendra approached her. She was carrying Blaine's backpack and a small wooden box. "This was given to me by an ancient elder from a race that was destroyed by evil. Even though I was very young, I knew it was not to be mine. I put it away and all but forgot about it until last night when it called to me." She handed the dusty, worn box to Blaine.

Blaine ran her fingers over the elaborately carved box now worn with age and decay. The lid resisted her attempts to open it. The rusty hinges creaked as she achieved the task. Peering inside, Blaine discovered the box was lined in white crushed velvet that, despite the obvious age of the box, looked as if it had never been touched. Nestled inside the bed of velvet was a magnificent crystal. Turquoise in color—even in the moonlight—it was the most amazing thing Blaine had ever seen. Its extreme beauty became even more evident as Fayendra waved her hand causing the patio to be lit by the candles that surrounded it.

"It's beautiful. Are you sure you want to give it to me?" Blaine asked.

Fayendra smiled widely. "You are the proper owner. I was just keeping it safe until that day our paths finally crossed. Crystals don't belong to us; we belong to them. Each holds great powers: some protect, some amplify power, some are even needed to balance the soul. Each crystal is unique to the person for whom it was created. That is why it's never wise to let another touch your crystal."

Blaine removed the crystal from its resting place. There was a Phoenix at the top of the crystal. It housed a loop from which a silver chain hung. Blaine slipped the chain over her head. Immediately, the crystal emitted a soft turquoise glow as it touched the skin beneath her shirt. Peering down, she asked Fayendra, "Is this normal?" She then giggled to herself as she realized the word "normal" had no place in her new world.

"Yes. The crystal is acknowledging that it has been joined with the soul for whom it was created. In accepting this crystal, you promise to protect it. It is more precious than most because it is the only one of its kind in existence," Fayendra informed Blaine.

"How will I know what power it possesses and how to use it?" Blaine asked.

Fayendra shook her head. "A crystal will reveal its true self at those times your soul requires its powers."

Blaine nodded in acknowledgment. "Thank you, Fayendra."

"You are most welcome. Now it is time for you to go. Maorga will fly you to the gateway."

"The gateway? Am I returning to Renault as well?"

Having remained silent until now, Maorga answered, "Yes, we must quickly go about our way. Every hour here is a day on Renault. Things have escalated in the time you have been gone. It is feared that Tevis may possess a spinner who can open the gateways. Worse than that, he has grown bolder with the book by openly attempting spells contained in it. That book must be recovered at all costs!"

With that Maorga lowered his body to the ground and Fayendra assisted Blaine as she climbed on to his back. Fayendra handed Blaine her backpack. Not wanting to interfere with Maorga's wings, she adjusted herself accordingly. As Maorga gracefully took flight Blaine waved farewell to Fayendra. She then gripped the feathers around his shoulders and held her legs tightly to his body to maintain balance.

"Equilibrium will best be maintained if you wrap your arms around my neck," Maorga suggested.

Blaine moved forward and did as he indicated. Each thrust of Maorga's wings propelled them higher. The air turned from brisk to bone chilling. In an effort to protect herself from the bitter cold wind, Blaine buried her face in Maorga's soft, warm, feathers. Her body began to shiver in protest of the cold and Blaine found herself praying silently for a quick flight. Time seemed to stand still as they continued their journey into the night. Blaine began to feel lightheaded. "The oxygen is very thin up here." She enunciated every word, hoping that Maorga would be able to hear her against the chilling wind.

Maorga's response was equally as loud. "We will be there shortly. Hold on just a bit longer."

Blaine attempted to nod but her body would not respond. Just when she felt as if she was going to lose consciousness, she felt Maorga began his descent. The air became warmer and Blaine began to regain her equilibrium as her oxygen level stabilized.

"We are here," Maorga announced as he landed in a small clearing near a thick forest.

Blaine sat up. Her legs could feel the strain from having been pressed so tightly against Maorga sides during the flight. This and the cold caused her to stumble after sliding off Maorga's back. She steadied herself against Maorga until she regained mobility. Surveying the area was difficult since the only light available came from the moon that would sporadically pop out between dense cumulus clouds. Totally befuddled, she sought Maorga's advice. "What now?"

"Kern is to meet us here. He will be your escort the rest of the way," Maorga answered as he ruffled his feathers and twitched his lion's tail slightly.

The welcomed answer provided Blaine with a tremendous sense of peace. While awaiting Kern's arrival, an awkward silence developed between Maorga and her. Blaine shifted uncomfortably as she said, "You were saying that Tevis has been attempting spells from the Book of Death? Do you know what kind of spells?"

Maorga shook his head, "No, not really? Unfortunately, there is so little known about the content of this mysterious text. We only know that it is evil—pure evil. No good can come from it being in Tevis's possession. I personally had never believed in the existence of the book. I just thought it was a fairytale created to scare young ones. Why earth was chosen as the hiding place is a mystery to me. It seems an extremely poor choice knowing humans don't have the best track record for resisting temptation."

"Yes. That is a very accurate and sad assessment of human-kind," Kern's voice floated across the night air. Blaine's countenance brightened when she heard his voice. Kern continued, giving a better explanation to the clandestine book than Maorga. "Keep in mind that magic on earth had been nonexistent for a very long time. The idea of the book being discovered accidentally was a circumstance that was not anticipated," Kern explained.

"It was told to me by my great grandfather that anyone attempting to use the book would be driven mad with the lust for power and unnatural knowledge," Maorga added.

"This is the common belief. However, since we don't know exactly what lies between its covers it is hard to say what is true and what is myth. What we do know for sure is that it was hidden away and information about its contents was stricken from recorded history."

Blaine remained silent for a moment then interjected quietly, "So, what you're saying is that it's not just the possibility of Tevis having access to the other worlds, but rather the fact that he is in complete possession of the book and its contents."

"Yes. You see, when he discovered the Book of Death it awakened an undercurrent of negative energy that was felt throughout the universe. We are not sure of the events which led him to possess the book. However, it is believed that Lyra's daughter was an unsuspecting participant to this. We do know at some point she brought Tevis from earth into Renault. It is believed she intended to bring him into Alatis, but the protection spell elves cast long ago against humans passing through the gateway prevented this from occurring," Kern said.

"Hadn't the gateways been sealed before that?" Blaine questioned.

"Time is an oddity," Kern replied. "It is measured differently from world to world. It affects races and species quite differently as well. Humans seem to be the most affected by it. The elders of Renault were in the deciding stages of sealing the gateways when Tevis entered their world. They detected the evil and negative forces that accompanied that event and quickly associated those forces with the book. It was and still is the only entity to cause such a negative vibration. Identifying who was actually in possession of it, however, was a different matter. It may have been veiled by a protection spell. It was decided since the possessor was unknown the least they could do is contain it in Renault with the hope that the means of identifying the owner could be discovered at a later time. The elders contacted me and I assisted in closing the gateways to ensure that the book would remain in Renault to allow elders time to deal with the situation."

"So, sealing the gateways was not due to the fear of an invasion from earth?" Blaine questioned.

Kern was silent for a moment. "The closing of the gateways was initially considered due to the possibility that an invasion may occur. However, the knowledge that the book had entered their world had given them little choice. The invasion of earth was but a possibility. The book, however, was a reality. Therefore, as "keepers of the gates" the choice to seal the gateways could not be avoided. As to what to tell the citizens of Renault, they felt it was in everyone's best interest not to disclose the reality of the book, let alone the fact that it now resided in Renault. They wanted to minimize the fear factor this knowledge could generate."

"It had been our hope that the book would be recovered quickly and once again hidden from harm's way. I believe the Elders of Renault underestimated the resourcefulness of Tevis," Maorga added.

"Perhaps we were all a bit blindsided by the darkness that

runs through and now completely consumes Tevis." Kern's despondent response caused him to drop his head in despair.

"So, it is my destiny to retrieve the book and hide it away?" Blaine questioned.

Neither Kern nor Maorga responded right away. Kern finally broke the silence. "Destiny is a grossly misunderstood concept. All souls have a purpose. This purpose cannot be fulfilled unless the soul abandons all quest for power and worldly ways and starts to understand that the only thing that gives life meaning is to seek the fulfillment of this purpose. Destiny is the grand scheme of creation. Every soul is given gifts, but the decision of how to use these gifts is the choice of each soul—a matter of free will. Destiny will be served to bring about the universal purpose but at the hand of which soul is dependent on choices."

"Everyone keeps talking about the prophecy and claiming I am the Bringer of Light." Blaine said addressing Kern.

"Yes, however, the wondrous thing about prophecies is that they are very unspecific. Let me relay the exact prophecy about the Bringer of Light. An offspring of man—one of many worlds—will grace all with divine intervention and resolve. The ancient ways will course through and bring light to the world extinguishing evil in the wake of this Bringer of Light." Kern paused before going on. "As in most things in life it leaves much to interpretation. Ones pathway is theirs alone to travel. Your choices are of your own making."

"The universe is at a crossroads. In all intelligent life, not just in humans, there has grown a great disconnect from where we've come from. This has allowed evil to flourish and run rampant ... " Maorga stopped overwhelmed by emotion.

"Sometimes even the smallest spark can ignite the miracle needed to bring the light back to hearts darkened by negative forces. This small spark can then spread until the universe can once again bask in the light." Kern graciously finished Maorga's sentiment.

Blaine could not yet grasp all Kern had said, but somewhere in the depths of her soul she knew his words were true. Her choices had led her here. In that moment she knew she was the Bringer of Light; destiny had found its champion. Blaine's thoughts were interrupted as she heard Kern say, "It is time to go."

As Kern nodded in Maorga's direction the majestic Griffin turned to Blaine and said, "Lady Blaine, may your footing remain sure as you travel your pathway. Safe journeys."

"Thank you, Maorga. I hope to see you again soon." Blaine watched as Maorga flew away.

CHAPTER 26

Blaine followed Kern as he turned toward the forest. She shyly asked, "Are you coming with me to Renault?" Even though Blaine already knew the answer, she held on to a ray of hope that Kern would be by her side.

"This path must be journeyed by you and you alone. I will take you as far as the gateway and allow your travel through it." They walked a little further and Kern stopped in front of two fern covered stumps. "We are here," Kern turned to Blaine.

"Really? I was expecting something a bit grander," Blaine responded as she surveyed the area.

"Yes, I suppose one would be expecting more considering all the emphasis that is put on the gateways. However, in reality they are merely links to other worlds. Each world marks the location of their gateways differently. At one point this gate's location was marked in a more obvious way. Having been virtually unused for such a long time, the location has been obscured by the surrounding forest. Now, just a word of warning: once you have crossed be vigilant of your surroundings. Someone will meet you; however, I warn you Renault is not the world you remember."

"Okay, but will I be brought to where Elian is?" Blaine asked.

"That is a question I cannot answer," Kern replied.

His short and vague answer was nothing less than disconcerting. Considering that she couldn't do anything to change the situation, Blaine chose to concentrate on the matters at hand. She geared up for the task that lay before her. "What do I need to do to cross?"

"Just walk between the stumps," Kern answered.

Blaine was hesitant as she began to step forward. Turning to look at Kern, she basked in the soft silver blue light that emanated from Kern's horn, wrapping its warmth around her. Feeling comforted, she nodded her appreciation before continuing forward. As she passed between the two stumps a bright light blinded her briefly. She took one more step and when the light dimmed she turned to look at Kern, but he was nowhere to be found. She now stood alone in the midst of a dark forest.

In her mind she remembered Fayendra's words about being constantly vigilant and aware of her surroundings. Surveying her new surroundings, Blaine quickly guarded her thoughts. She felt warmth against her chest. Through her shirt she could see the blue glow of her crystal. Blaine knew immediately that it was helping to protect her.

The sun was just beginning to break over the horizon and pierce the density of the surrounding forest. The stillness of the morning had a calming effect on Blaine. Her mind wandered to the concept of time, trying in vain to calculate the difference between Renault and Roe. Fortunately, this was short lived since she needed to once again focus on the matters at hand.

Kern had said that someone would be here to meet her, yet the surrounding forest appeared quiet and unoccupied. Suddenly, the hair on Blaine's arm stood on end. She immediately crouched behind some low bushes. A moment later soldiers walking in single file came into view. As she tried to conceal herself better she could feel her heart pounding rapidly. She was extremely relieved when the soldiers passed without incident.

Blaine remained in her hiding spot trying to decide what to do next. "Someone will meet you." She kept replaying Kerns words in her head wondering if she was given the correct information. Aside from the soldiers, there was no one else in sight. Just when she was about to leave the bushes, she saw movement out of the corner of her eye. Scanning the area carefully, she couldn't detect anything out of the ordinary, until she spotted a figure hiding amongst the nearby trees. She very slowly lifted her hand and directed a light wind that effortlessly swayed the surrounding branches that momentarily revealed the figure's identity. Blaine immediately recognized Alderon. She let out a sigh of relief as she stepped out from her own hiding place and quickly made her way to him.

"Blaine!" He said in almost a whisper as he greeted her with a hug. "This area is crawling with foot soldiers. We must be careful."

Blaine nodded her head in response. "Yes, a patrol just passed by. Is Tevis aware that there is a gateway here?"

"We are not sure as to the extent of his knowledge. Things have really escalated in the months since you and Elian departed. Renault has experienced a complete shift in power. Tevis rules this land ruthlessly. He enslaves or kills all that choose to defy him."

Months? Blaine mumbled to herself shaking her head in disbelief. The serene and calm Alderon that Blaine knew now looked haggard and weary. His eyes reflected sadness to the highest degree. Although she did not wish to add to his burden, she desperately needed to be appraised of what had been happening on Renault. "Have you seen Elian since his return?" Blaine asked.

"We had been in contact through messengers. He remains with the elfin soldiers that volunteered to help fight Tevis's tyranny. Their attacks have weakened the hold that Tevis had on the land and have made Tevis even more determined to be in control, no matter how cruel the effort." Alderon took a moment to scan the area, "We must get to a safe place. We can discuss the events of the last few months as soon as we are out of the open."

"Lead the way," Blaine whispered. Following Alderon gave Blaine a chance to observe him. Blaine was surprised that despite his weak appearance, Alderon was very agile. They walked in silence then stopped at the edge of the forest. Blaine gasped as she looked beyond Alderon. They stood on top of a large hill that overlooked much of Renault. It's beautiful purple sky was replaced with a heavy haze that appeared to be made up of black soot and dust. The air smelled of death and destruction. There were patches of scorched earth throughout the area. In the distance she could see the remains of some houses—some still smoldering from attacks. Blaine looked at Alderon in horror. The once beautiful land was now a war zone. She was at a complete loss for words.

Before Blaine had a chance to find her voice a noise came from behind them. They both turned quickly in the direction of the noise, "Freeze! You are in a restricted area!" Blaine immediately realized she had been so distraught at the sight of Renault she had lost awareness of her senses. As a result, she didn't even notice a small armed group of soldiers approaching. Recovering quickly, Blaine sensed a spinner among the group and instantly took defensive action. She sent a bolt of energy into their midst that dropped them—including the spinner—to their knees in pain. She grabbed hold of Alderon's hand, commanding him to take action. "Think of a safe place." Suddenly in a whirl of light, they disappeared from the forest and reappeared inside a dimly lit cavern.

Several figures jumped to attention when Blaine and Alderon

made their sudden appearance. Alderon quickly reassured them. "It's okay. It's me, Alderon, and the woman is a friend." While the figures moved in to get a closer look at them, Alderon whispered to Blaine. "I've never seen anything like that before!"

Still trying to adjust her eyes to the dimly lit surroundings, Blaine responded with a chuckle. "And I've never done anything like that before. As far as I was concerned, it was just a shot in the dark. I'm thankful that it worked." She didn't even want to consider what the outcome would have been if it had not worked.

An older gentleman approached and smiled broadly as he placed his hand on Alderon's shoulder. "I'm glad you have returned safely, brother, and in such a grand manner. Considering your sudden presence, I can only assume your companion is Blaine."

"You are right, and it was only because of her I did return safely," Alderon answered gratefully.

A young figure approached them. "Tell me, how was it possible for you to zone jump through all of the protection spells?" It was more of a demand than a question.

At that moment, Blaine's crystal lit up. She knew that many of the figures in the group that now surrounded her were spinners. She could feel their prying thoughts attempting to push past her protective wall, but to no avail. She answered for Alderon, addressing the spinners calmly but firmly. "You are only going to exhaust yourselves by trying to read my thoughts. I assure you that I am really on your side."

A quiet murmuring arose from the now growing crowd. The younger man stepped closer to Blaine. She knew proximity could allow a stronger connection when it came to reading another's thoughts, "You still did not answer how you were able to zone jump through all the protection spells that are in place." She could tell that the young man's tone had turned hostile as he pushed harder against Blaine's barriers. The crystal around her neck began to glow brighter as the young man locked eyes with hers. She sensed fear, so much fear, not just from him but from everyone in the crowd. Suddenly, Blaine's crystal pulsed, which emitted a strong flash of light that knocked the determined young man back. The cavern grew silent.

In an attempt to defuse the escalating situation, Alderon spoke firmly but reassuringly. "Please, everyone, I tell you the truth. Trust me. Blaine is a friend. There is no need to fear her. She is here to help us put an end to this war with Tevis and his tyranny."

The young man responded again—this time more cautiously, ceasing all attempts to push through Blaine's protective barriers. "Alderon, you have always had the people's respect and trust. So, holding to your word, we will allow her to stay in the safety of our protection; however, she must be aware that we have rules against the unknown magic she is spinning."

"Yes. Yes, of course, Carter." Alderon responded, finally identifying the bold lad.

Blaine heard Carter's words, but they rang empty as the fear of the unknown and distrust that prevailed took on a life of its own. Vibration after vibration hit Blaine, like waves in an ocean. Some were so strong it took all her concentration to prevent them from bringing her to her knees. Nonetheless, she remained steadfast and poised, even though she knew she could overpower them all in the blink of an eye.

Alderon turned to Blaine and motioned her to follow. "Come this way".

Blaine obliged. They walked down a dark tunnel. The air was damp and musty, causing Blaine to shiver. Looking past Alderon she could see that the darkness began to lighten. Soon they came to the mouth of the cave. Blaine felt a sense of relief as they stepped into the morning light. The fresh air lifted her spirits.

Turning to Blaine, Alderon spoke apologetically. "I am so

very sorry for their reaction to our arrival. We have all been through so much. Many loved ones have been taken due to Tevis's treachery and deceit. Suspicion has morphed into an all-consuming fear of anything or anyone unfamiliar."

Blaine contemplated Alderon's apology. She remembered that Kern had said Renaultians were unaware of the book and Tevis's true intentions. She wondered how much Alderon even knew. "I can understand their reaction. I am guessing most are not aware of me or my gifts. Are they at all familiar with ancient magic and its capabilities?"

"They are all aware of the existence of ancient magic; however, as you know human magic is what is taught to all our spinners. At times some display a fleeting moment of the gift of ancient magic, but nothing controllable or sustainable. The existence of one who possesses and is able to control such power is inconceivable by most. However, just the small display of your abilities I have witnessed makes me aware that no other spinner could come close to matching your level of ancient magic. Your mother is the only spinner who was considered to possess some degree of this ability. You have made her magic appear to be parlor games." Alderon smiled nervously at Blaine.

"Do I make you nervous?" Blaine asked with a giggle. "Last time we were together you were the one making me nervous."

Alderon chuckled. "Yes, I suppose that is true. You have changed immensely since our pathways last crossed. You are no longer the insecure teenager, full of unanswered questions. You possess the confidence and poise of royalty. Yet, your eyes reveal the love and kindness of your soul. This is a combination rarely seen. I see no display of desire for personal gain or power."

His words caused Blaine to blush. "Thank you. I don't feel different." Even as she spoke these words she knew they were not entirely true. She still felt clumsy and awkward. Yet deep down she had a tremendous sense of purpose. She knew what needed to be done and she knew she was the one who could accomplish it.

They stood in silence for a moment as Blaine took in her mountainous surroundings. "An extinct volcano?" She questioned Alderon.

"Yes, the area was discovered long ago and as things turned bad it offered the perfect refuge for those opposing Tevis," Alderon answered.

Blaine examined the area. The volcanic walls were steep and very high. "So, the cave is the only way in?"

Yes. Even if one could scale the tremendous mountain, they would have to deal with the sheer drop to the volcano's floor. Those in hiding have created a makeshift village near some underground springs. The spinners take turns guarding the entrance of the cave. Many protection spells have been cast to protect this area," Alderon explained.

"Not much quality of life for those in hiding," Blaine acknowledged. "Are Elian and Armel aware of this location?"

"Of this I am not sure. They have kept their distance for good reason. You have already witnessed the negative reaction your arrival has generated, and you are human. I am not sure what would happen if the good citizens of Renault realized elves had crossed over into their world as well."

Blaine nodded in agreement then added, "They are tracking Tevis to retrieve the book." As she spoke these words she could sense the fear racing through Alderon.

"So, the book is not just a myth?" Alderon inquired timidly.

"No, so I've been told. I wasn't sure of the extent of your knowledge in this matter."

"The ancient elders knew of its existence, but felt safe knowing it had been hidden away. In time it obtained myth status until some suspected it had been discovered and brought into Renault. Spinners felt it, also. No one knew where it was being housed or who had retrieved it, but the change it caused in the vibration of our world was undeniable," Alderon offered.

Blaine walked in silence through the jungle toward the village as she processed Alderon's recounting of the book's history on Renault. She then asked, "How long has Tevis been in Renault. I am having trouble understanding the timeline."

Alderon stopped. "It's uncertain, possibly hundreds of years."

"You mean it has taken him this long to implement his plan to gain power over Renault?" Blaine inquired.

"One of our main duties as elders is tracking history. Tevis was unknown to us for several generations. We suspected he manipulated a spinner to apprentice for him. It was easy for him to manipulate unsuspecting spinners—especially those who considered themselves misfits and those that had been orphaned—to join him. The elders were aware of flare-ups from what we began calling mysterious magic, but we were unable to discover exactly who was initiating them."

"He was using those spinners to attempt spells from the book, wasn't he?" Blaine asked.

"That is our belief. If legends are accurate, those spinners who attempted spells lacked the power to control them. Instead, the spells would drain their life force and cause them to die a horrific death."

"So, at what point did he become a blip on the radar?" Blaine asked intrigued by the history of her grandfather.

"I'm not sure what that means but he began making his presence known several decades ago. He would appear in town and denounce the elders to anyone who would listen. He used the closing of the gates against us claiming everyone should have the right to use the gateways freely. He preached the belief that this was not their decision to make. He claimed it was done to allow the elders to exert power over the population. At first his rabble rousing fell on deaf ears. However, as time went on the seeds of fear grew and took on a life of its own. The fear caused an unreasonable distrust of the elders," Alderon explained.

"Why didn't the elders just put him in jail or step in somehow?" Blaine questioned.

"It has never been our way to control the opinions of our people. We have always trusted their good judgment. We did not realize how fear had destroyed that judgment and allowed Tevis to gain power over people's thoughts until it was too late," Alderon answered.

"But what of the tellers? Were there none who foresaw the consequences of his poisonous ways? Was there no way to keep circumstances from escalating to an all-out war?" Blaine asked passionately.

Alderon paused, taking a few minutes to contemplate his response before he finally spoke. "As you know, tellings are not an exact science. The future is not set in stone. Every decision we make changes our pathway. There were tellings about his rise to power. However, in the tellings his identity was never clear. Tellers were unable to remember what he looked like. It was a very unusual phenomenon and we believe it was possible that he was shadowed by some sort of spell, which was directly related to the book."

Arriving at a small hut Blaine could hear the sounds of the springs bubbling in the distance.

Alderon continued, "It's rather crude but it does protect you from the elements. Even though we knew magic could be used to accomplish that task, the traditional method was chosen instead. Magic has been disallowed here in fear that the mark it leaves on the universe could be detected by Tevis's spinners."

"Makes sense." Then noticing the isolation of her new dwelling, Blaine asked, "Are there no other huts? I was under the impression that there was a village."

"There are several other huts further back. These are used by spinners during their breaks from their watch at the caves. They are still on watch when they are in the village but at a lesser capacity. Considering everyone's reaction to your arrival I thought this isolated hut would be a wise choice," Alderon answered.

As they entered the hut Blaine observed it had a crude stone floor and was furnished sparsely with some makeshift furniture.

Alderon continued, "There is an outhouse about twenty feet behind the hut. The springs are very warm and make an excellent bathing spot. There are several pools allowing for some privacy. I can take you to their location."

Blaine suddenly became aware of how tired she was. The thought of taking even a few more steps was unthinkable. "Thank you, but I really would like to rest for a while if that's okay."

"Of course! I will come by later and bring you some food."

Blaine thanked Alderon again as he made his exit, closing the bamboo door behind him. She walked over to the bed whose appearance reflected its hasty construction; a lumpy, thin pad sat atop the bed. Several neatly folded blankets occupied the foot of it. As Blaine sat down cautiously the bed creaked loudly in protest to the weight. She took one of the blankets and spread it over her as she lay down. Turning on her side, she quickly fell into a hard and dreamless sleep.

CHAPTER 27

She was awakened to the sound of a light knock at the door. "Come in," she muttered as she quickly sat up in bed trying to appear alert.

Alderon stepped through the door carrying a basket. A delightful aroma filled the hut causing Blaine's stomach to growl in anticipation. Alderon set the basket down on the small table in the middle of the room. Blaine stood up and walked over to the table. She sat down on one of the two chairs that accompanied the table. Alderon seated himself opposite her. He began unpacking the basket. He set some bread and a bowl of stew in front of her. "It smells wonderful," Blaine remarked. "Is this meat?"

"Yes. I hope that is okay?" Alderon answered as he motioned for her to eat. "It isn't gourmet but we make do with what we have. Bringing supplies here gets riskier with each passing day."

"Well, it looks gourmet to me. I haven't had any meat since I left Renault. Elves are vegetarians, you know," Blaine commented as she began eating the stew, barely breathing between bites. She stopped suddenly realizing that she was displaying less than poor table manners. She looked up at Alderon and apologized. "I am so sorry. I didn't realize how hungry I was." As she made eye contact with Alderon his blue eyes seemed burdened and sad.

"Is something wrong?" Blaine questioned as she broke off a piece of bread and soaked up some of the stew with it.

Alderon shifted in his chair as he cleared his throat. "I know before you left Renault you were very concerned about your mother."

Blaine stopped eating. "Yes, I was told she was here in Renault, but other than that there has been no information."

Alderon continued, "She has been seen in the company of Tevis's most trusted spinners," Alderon said.

Blaine dropped her gaze from Alderon and stared down at her nearly empty bowl. "Interesting," she murmured. This was definitely not the information she was expecting.

"It may not be as it seems. We have no knowledge of her present relationship with Tevis," Alderon added trying to ease the situation for Blaine.

"For her to be working with Tevis in any capacity is completely unacceptable," Blaine retorted. She paused a moment before adding, "Anyway, it doesn't matter. I have to do what needs to be done and the sooner the better." Blaine knew that time had run out. She must retrieve the book from Tevis and put an end to the fear that had eclipsed Renault, no matter her mother's consequences.

"What are your plans and what can I do to help?" Alderon asked anxiously.

"That is definitely the million-dollar question," Blaine stated, half laughing. "I need to locate the book. Since my mother seems to be back in the good graces of Tevis, perhaps if I locate her I can obtain information about its location."

"I can go with you," Alderon volunteered.

Blaine thought for a moment. As tempted as she was to say

yes, she knew that if she were to succeed in retrieving the book and disarming Tevis, Renault would need Alderon's wisdom and knowledge to unite and lead this fragmented land. "No, Alderon, you are too valuable. Your service lies in a different capacity."

Alderon nodded in disappointment. "I understand. At least let me guide you to where your mother is most likely located."

Realizing Alderon's need to feel as though he were helping the cause, Blaine agreed knowing all the while her intentions were different. "Would it be possible for me to bathe before I depart? I believe a trip to a hot springs would renew me both physically and mentally."

"Yes, of course," Alderon responded almost gleefully. "Actually, that would make the timing perfect. We can leave under the cover of darkness."

Blaine took the last few bites of her dinner. She retrieved a canteen that was in the basket. Slinging it over her shoulder along with her backpack, she followed Alderon out of the hut. "There's a hot spring not too far from here. It's a little closer to the village but very secluded."

"Sounds good to me," Blaine said smiling widely.

They walked along the rugged trail that led to the springs. The closer they got the more difficult the trail became. Blaine assumed that was due to the lack of foot traffic. Alderon pushed past some overgrown bushes that blocked the trail to reveal a small, deep blue pool of water surrounded by lush foliage. Blaine gasped at the beauty of the location. Colorful foliage exploded from every plant and a multitude of delicate flowers filled the air with the sweet scent of honey, "Oh my, it's like a painting. It's so beautiful," Blaine exclaimed.

"Yes, I suppose it is. Sad to say, with the present crisis it is somewhat difficult to appreciate the true beauty that still clings to this land," Alderon mentioned.

Blaine was suddenly overwhelmed by the hopelessness that consumed Alderon's spirit. There was no denying the intense despair he felt for the people that fought gallantly for this land and its freedom from tyranny. She placed her hand on his shoulder, "We can't change events over which we have no control, but we can choose the way we face them. I know with all my heart that you are here to make a difference. Do not allow fear in to your heart. You must stay strong and know that you have been given a gift that needs to be shared and taught. Don't lose sight of this, Alderon, for the moment we lose sight of our true purpose we lose sight of who we are truly meant to be." As the words flowed from her mouth she knew them to be true. However, she was at a loss as to where they came from.

Alderon smiled at Blaine, "Thank you for your kind words. You are truly the Bringer of Light. I will go and gather a few items while you bathe. Then return, allowing us to make way."

"Thank you, Alderon." Blaine watched him disappear through the overgrown path. She knew he was where he needed to be. She also knew that he was aware deep down that when he returned she would be gone. Blaine sat down on a rock that jetted out over the water. She could hear the water as it lapped softly against the edge of the large stone. She looked around thoroughly enjoying the amazing splendor that met her eyes. She wanted to memorize every detail. Taking a deep breath, she tried to refocus on the task that lay before her. She was, however, once again distracted as an insect fluttered past her. It looked like a dragonfly with the wings of a butterfly. The wings were beautifully painted with an array of vibrant colors. She watched as it landed on a nearby bush, opening and closing its wings gracefully, then casually fluttered away.

A wave of serenity washed over her and she smiled to herself. Closing her eyes, she took in one last breath of the intoxicating fragrance that surrounded her, pictured her mother's face in her mind, and disappeared from the rock.

When Blaine opened her eyes again she was seated on the stone floor of a lavishly decorated bedroom. The curtains were hastily drawn over the windows allowing a few rays of sunlight into the otherwise dimly lit room. "It worked!" Blaine said out loud. Suddenly, she heard the opening of a door behind her. She jumped to her feet and took a defensive stance. A figure walked through the door. Startled for a moment to see someone standing in the middle of the room, the figure's face quickly replaced concern with recognition.

CHAPTER 28

"Blaine! Oh, my dear! You're safe. Thank you, God!" She exclaimed as she rushed to Blaine and wrapped her arms around her daughter in a loving embrace. She held Blaine tightly in her arms. Blaine remained silent and unresponsive to Sairah's display of affection, which seemed to go unnoticed by her mother.

"Hello, Mother," Blaine said flatly.

Blaine's lack of response to her mother's emotional greeting caught Sairah by surprise. "What's wrong?"

Blaine stood silent for a moment. It took all her strength to calm the mixture of emotions that came boiling to the surface. She answered as coolly as she could. "How can you possibly ask me a question with such an obvious answer?"

Sairah walked over and sat down on a large, four-poster bed. Her joy at seeing her daughter was replaced with distress. "I see," she answered. "I can only imagine what you have been told about me." This line of thinking was, however, replaced by Sairah's realization that Blaine was able to find her and penetrate Tevis's defenses allowing her access to the bedroom. She looked at Blaine and asked, "How ever did you get in here?"

"One question at a time, Mother. First of all, no one had to tell me anything about you. What I know of you and your life in Renault I have seen with my own eyes, unfortunately." Blaine answered flatly.

The color drained from Sairah's face. "So, you're a teller," she stated softly.

"I know why you left Renault, Mother, and why you chose to place a binding spell on me, instead of telling me about who I really am."

"So, you understand." Sairah's countenance was one of relief.

"I understand you thought you were doing the right thing for me. I understand you wanted to protect me. However, your choices prevented me from knowing who I am and kept me from my pathway."

"Don't you see, Blaine, I had to protect you. It was a matter of selecting the greater good," Sairah responded.

Blaine could not help but smile to herself as she recalled a line from a television show; she had always had the secret desire to quote the line, with now being the perfect opportunity. " 'There is no greater good, only good.' We use the phrase greater good when we know we are not doing what is right. Your choice was made out of fear and that choice caused us both to veer from are pathways."

Suddenly Blaine's crystal began to give off a strong glow. "Don't waste your energy, Mother," she said as she effortlessly stopped Sairah's attempt to pry into her daughter's thoughts.

Sairah's intentional glare turned to wide-eyed surprise. "You're a spinner as well?"

Ignoring her mother's comments about being a spinner, Blaine continued. "I do understand why you did what you did, but more importantly I need you to understand that you made a terribly misguided decision. That said, I need you to tell me where Tevis keeps the book!"

Now the expression on Sairah's face became one of suspicion. "I asked you a question. I need to know how you were able to get in here. There is no way you could have breached the spells that protect this fortress. I placed many of them myself. They would have prohibited even the strongest spinner to zone jump in here."

Finally addressing Sairah's comment about her being a spinner, Blaine answered, "Yes, I am a spinner but I didn't zone jump in here. I do not rely on human magic. The magic I use is pure ancient. The spells you cast to protect your location here were done with human magic and, therefore, protect only against human magic—quite a loophole as you can see."

Sairah stood up as she asked, "You have full control of ancient magic?"

Blaine nodded.

"I was never taught anything about ancient magic. No one is...I do feel the presence, but it is fleeting so I am unable to wield it."

"No one in Renault is taught ancient magic; however my teacher is in Alatis. Ancient magic does make your human magic stronger; however, human magic is limited to the life force that invokes it. If done incorrectly, human magic can drain the life force of the user, but this is something you are well aware of." Blaine coldly stared at her mother.

"Yes, all too well." Sairah diverted her gaze from Blaine in shame.

"Tevis is having you try to perform spells from the book, isn't he?" Blaine asked accusingly.

Sairah didn't reply to the question. Instead, she changed the subject by asking, "You were able to cross over into Alatis? You were actually allowed entrance by the elves?"

Remembering that Elian had told her that Alatis was believed to be only a myth in Renault, Blaine was surprised at her mother's question. "You are aware of Alatis? You know that it is not just a myth?"

"Yes. Tevis used to talk about it a lot before ... " Sairah sighed deeply before continuing. "This is certainly not the reunion I had envisioned. I have gone over in my mind so many times what I would say to you. Seeing you standing in front of me, however, I understand you are clearly not the teen-aged girl I knew. It feels as if years have passed between us instead of only a few months. You give off all the vibrations of a mature woman. Nonetheless, I need you to realize how much I regret my decisions in the past. I was so young and understood so little then."

As Sairah spoke Blaine no longer saw the strong self-assured woman who had raised her. It saddened her to see her mother so fragile and broken. "It would appear that you still do not understand the consequences of your decisions. You say you have changed yet you still are working with Tevis. Why?" Blaine asked, her patience wearing thin.

Blaine's question cut through the air like a knife. She could see the hurt expression wash across Sairah's face. "To protect you—us—so he will leave us alone once and for all."

Blaine closed her eyes to absorb the horror and sheer foolishness of her mother's reply.

"I did what was necessary to secure our future! I agreed to help Tevis in exchange for our freedom!" Sairah continued trying to defend her decision.

"Our freedom? You made a deal with the devil. Exactly what did you agree to help him do," Blaine demanded. "Did you promise to help him open the gateways?"

"No. I have agreed to help him possess magic," Sairah replied flatly. "That has always been his goal. The opening of the gateway was a ruse to align the people of Renault against the elders. I actually had the ability to open the gateways years ago, but he needed spinners strong enough to execute the spell in the book to believe in his cause so he could manipulate them into helping him."

Blaine stared at her mother in disbelief. "You can't possibly be that naïve. You know the horrible ramifications if Tevis were to possess magic; yet you still agreed to help?" Blaine said raising her voice to her mother.

Sairah's tone became extremely defensive as she replied, "It doesn't matter. All I care about is that he leaves us in peace."

Once again, the selfishness of her mother's decision angered Blaine. Before their arrival in Renault, Tevis did not even know of his granddaughter's existence. Once Sairah had revealed the truth Tevis had used the great love she had for her daughter to manipulate her. However, as Blaine looked deep into her mother's eyes and saw the fear reflected there she could not help but take pity on her.

"Mom, you are not thinking clearly. You have been blinded by your desire to protect us. You have to know in your heart that anyone trying to cast that spell is in danger of losing their life. The magic needed to complete it would be all consuming."

"Of course, I have thought of that; however, Tevis has been gathering powerful spinners over the years, and collectively, I truly believe we have enough magic to successfully cast the spell without inflicting harm on the spinners," Sairah replied confidently.

"We? With you being the essential component," Blaine said.

"Don't you see? If not me, he would eventually find somebody else with the ability to complete the spell. At least we will benefit from his plan. After the spell is successfully cast we can walk away and not look back."

Blaine was outraged. "How can you possibly justify releasing such evil into this universe knowing he will destroy all souls that stand in the way of his quest for power. The darkness in his soul will consume all light."

"I would think you could see there is no other way. Even now he has me in his grasp. I am unable to break the magic that keeps me prisoner in this room. I refuse to regret my decision to help Tevis."

Blaine could tell there was no use trying to convince her mother of the error she was making. She had to stop Tevis before he even attempted to cast the spell. This was the only way she could save her misguided mother. "We can take charge of this situation, plain and simple, before things escalate beyond repair. Please, forget your fear and just tell me where the book is and then you will have your freedom."

Their conversation was interrupted by a knock at the door. "Quick! Hide in the closet," Sairah whispered as she pointed to a door.

Blaine quickly obeyed. As she stood in the darkness of the closet her crystal began glowing. She could vaguely hear the conversation that was going on outside the closet.

"Tevis is ready for you, Sairah." The man's voice sounded familiar.

"Yes, yes. Please give me a minute," Sairah replied.

"No. Lord Tevis's orders were to bring you to him now. The planets are almost in alignment and that incantation must begin prior," came another voice.

Blaine reached for the doorknob, but as she did she felt the closet began to spin. She tried bracing herself by leaning against the wall. Her crystal glowed brighter and began to burn against her chest. A repulsive stench of sulfur filled her nostrils and blinded her senses. She closed her eyes tightly and held her breath in an attempt to stop her urge to vomit. When she opened her eyes again she was no longer in her mother's closet.

She found herself in a darkened cavern. The previous odors were now mixed with that of musty, damp earth. Feeling dizzy as she glanced around, she braced herself against a large rock. To her surprise her hand passed through it. Blaine searched her mind to find an explanation for her present state. It felt like no telling she had ever experienced. It was as if she had no physical body. Then it dawned on her that what she was experiencing was astral projection, which meant that even though she was in this unpleasant location her physical body was still concealed in Sairah's closet. She knew the process was possible, but how could she have ... ? Then she remembered Fayendra's words: "the crystal protects and guides."

The cavern was illuminated by many candles that surrounded what appeared to be an altar made of rocks. She could see that a worn book rested atop a metal box and had been placed on the altar.

Suddenly Blaine heard voices in the distance. The voices got louder as two shadowy figures in hooded robes entered the cavern. "They are bringing her down now, Lord," the taller one informed the smaller figure.

"Good! And the other spinners?"

"They will be with her," the taller figure replied.

"Excellent! Leave me until they are all here."

"Yes, my Lord." The larger figure disappeared from the cavern leaving the shorter one alone. Draped totally in black, he walked over to the altar, picked up one of the nearby candles, and lit the four candles that surrounded the book. He reached down and gently ran his fingers along its edges. Addressing the book, he whispered, "Soon all will be as it should be." He paused a moment. Then as if answering a question, he continued, "Yes, everything is in place. You are right. I, too, believe the spinners will be successful this time." He paused again. It was then that Blaine realized this hooded figure was having a conversation with the book.

"Yes, Master, soon," she heard the hooded man say. He then opened the book carefully as he began chanting quietly.

The taller hooded figure reappeared at the opening of the cavern. "Lord Tevis," the figure stopped to allow Tevis to finish his chanting. He pulled back his hood and said, "We are ready, sir."

So, this is Tevis, Blaine thought. As he turned toward the entrance of the cave an evil smile parted his lips. His attention had been turned toward the entrance of the cavern as six hooded figures entered. Their robes were similar to those Tevis wore, except they were the color of blood.

One of the figures pulled back her hood. Blaine recognized Sairah. Her heart skipped a beat. Sairah spoke as she approached Tevis. "I need you to promise that you will keep your end of the bargain we made. If I help you execute the spell, you will leave my daughter and me in peace forever." Her voice was cold and firm. Her eyes burned with resolve.

"But of course, my dear—just as I promised," came the chilling reply.

Blaine cringed at the sound of his voice. She could hear the deceit and betrayal in his words. Her fears were confirmed. Tevis had no intention of letting her or her mother go free. Blaine was once again struck by the naivety of her mother. *How could she believe his empty promises? I have to stop this,* she thought to herself. She knew she could do nothing in her present state. She thought that if she were to rejoin her body in the closet she could then return to the cavern and stop Tevis. She closed her eyes in an effort to project herself back into her body. Nothing happened. She realized the crystal had only wanted her to view what she was now witnessing. It knew she may not have been successful in defeating all of these powerful spinners. Once again it was protecting Blaine.

All Blaine could do now was watch helplessly as the ceremony began. Sairah retrieved a velvet satchel from her robe. She reached in and methodically handed each of the cloaked figures an item from the bag. *No doubt, ingredients Sairah had collected to perform the spell.* Blaine's thoughts were interrupted as she noticed Tevis summoning the taller cloaked man to his side. The figure drew back his hood as Tevis spoke. It was General Mitchell, Blaine's father. "Assemble your strongest, most able-bodied soldiers at the Druid Circle. I will join you there after the ceremony is complete."

After exchanging a soulful look with Sairah, General Mitchell answered obediently, "Yes, sir."

Annoyed by his sons exchange with Sairah, Tevis shouted, "Now! Mitchell!"

General Mitchell responded to his father's impatience. He turned and left the cavern.

Tevis then walked over and stood directly in front of Sairah. "It seems my foolish son still has feelings for you," Tevis said as he placed a finger under Sairah's chin and lifted her head until her eyes met his. He has no idea how easily you were able to seduce him. He was bewitched by your beauty just as we had planned. He actually believes you loved him and has no idea we manipulated him in hopes of mixing his elfin blood with that of my strongest spinner." Sairah instinctively stepped away, breaking Tevis's hold on her.

Letting out an evil laugh, Tevis continued, "I thought your betrayal of me had destroyed that plan. Now on your return I found it actually worked! Of course, I haven't let anyone know, especially Mitchell, that the spinner he has so desperately sought these last few months is actually his daughter."

Blaine watched in angst as Tevis motioned for Sairah to begin the ceremony. She walked over to the altar and picked up the book. Tevis had walked to the center of the circle of spinners and now stood there as Sairah began chanting a spell that she was reading from the book. She then passed around a stone bowl. Each spinner placed the ingredient Sairah had given them earlier into the bowl. They had joined the chanting. When the bowl was returned to Sairah she drew a crude knife from her belt and dipped it into the bowl. The cavern became silent. Sairah said a few words over the bowl; its contents began to bubble and hiss. Sairah continued the ceremony by approaching Tevis, and taking his right hand into hers she drew the blade across his palm. Blood flowed freely from the open wound. Sairah placed the bowl under Tevis's hand and filled it with the crimson liquid. Releasing her hold on Tevis, she stirred the potion using the blade of the knife. The contents of the bowl began glowing vibrantly.

Sairah anointed Tevis's forehead with the mixture. She then passed the bowl around the circle of spinners. Blaine was completely repulsed as she watched each spinner drink from the bowl. The last spinner handed the bowl back to Sairah. She placed it back on the altar. As she began chanting the same words over and over the spinners took hands and joined in the chanting.

Tevis remained motionless in the center of the circle with his eyes closed. Suddenly the ground began to rumble; the candle flames growing in intensity and chasing away every shadow. For the first time Blaine could see Tevis's face clearly. He had curly black hair, which was streaked with silver. Had Blaine passed him in the streets not knowing anything of his black, cruel soul, she would have thought him almost attractive. He appeared to be a man in his thirty's who bore no signs of his actual age, which spanned hundreds of years.

As the chanting grew louder a piercing crackle rang through the air. A brilliant burst of light shot from Sairah's hands, which were now spread open wide. The light passed through each spinner and then entered Tevis.

Sairah's hypnotic chant rang in Blaine's ears, dulling her senses. The chanting came to an abrupt halt as one of the spinners let out an agonizing scream. Blaine watched in horror as the life force was drained from the spinner who had screamed in pain. The process moved from one spinner to the next; the cavern filled with their horrific screams. Blaine looked away as she mentally addressed the spinners. *"Run! Don't let this horrible fate befall you,"* as if her words could make a difference and stop what she was witnessing.

The cavern finally fell silent as the last spinner crumbled lifelessly to the ground. Blaine looked back to where just moments ago the spinners had stood. Now all their life force was gone. Sairah lay sobbing next to the altar. "What have you done?" Sairah stammered refusing to look at Tevis. "You said the spell would drain a small amount of magic from each spinner for you to keep as your own. You have killed them all!"

"You have become weak, Sairah! Those spinners pledged their undying loyalty to me. It was a privilege for them to die in my service!" Tevis exclaimed.

"You are truly the monster the elders tried to warn me about," Sairah gasped. "You got what you wanted. Now leave! I cannot stand the sight of you!" She screamed as she rose to her feet.

"Oh, my dear, I am afraid that is not possible." Tevis's evil laugh echoed through the cavern.

"Evialiano!" Sairah's voice rang throughout the cavern. As she spoke this word a blast of red light flashed from her hand and launched itself toward Tevis. The attack was deflected as Tevis extended his arms forward, murmuring an unidentifiable word.

The ceremony had left Sairah drained, and this last execution of magic caused Sairah to drop to her knees.

"Foolish girl!" Tevis hissed. "Now that I, too, possess magic I am no longer so vulnerable. I may be new at this, but the years I have spent studying magic will now serve me well. It won't take me long to master my new gift."

By now the extreme draining of Sairah's life force had caused her to slip into unconsciousness. She lay motionless on the floor of the cavern. Tevis walked over to her. Bending down, he picked her up effortlessly and threw her over his shoulder. He turned and exited the cavern. Blaine held her breath as she realized he had not retrieved the book. Her heart sank when he paused at the mouth of the cavern and turned toward the altar. She was sure he was going back to get the book. Instead, to her surprise and relief he simply addressed the book saying, "Yes, I will be back shortly." He paused a moment then continued as if answering another question. "Yes. Yes, I understand, Master. I will not fail again to capture the Bringer of Light." Blaine watched in awe as she saw fear wash across Tevis's face. "Yes, Master, I do know what the consequences will be if I fail again." With these words he turned abruptly and left the cavern.

CHAPTER 29

Suddenly catapulted back into her body, Blaine found herself once again in the darkness of her mother's closet. She collected her bearings, listening for any sounds coming from her mother's bedroom. Hearing none, she cautiously opened the door and stepped out into the room.

The room was poorly lit but she was able to find her way to the bed. She sat down trying to sort through the many emotions and thoughts triggered by what she had just witnessed. She was overwhelmed with sadness by her mother's part in the execution of Tevis's malevolent plan. Sairah had been so easily manipulated. She had been blinded by her own fears, and now people were dead because of her selfishness. Blaine let out a heavy sigh.

Her thought process continued. Blaine was sure that what had just occurred was not a telling. She was meant to experience the events as they happened. What she did not know, however, is how to address the situation. She rested her elbows in her lap and covered her eyes. "What do I do now?" she said aloud.

"Let what is in your heart guide you, Blaine." The sound of Kern's voice cleared her mind as warmth washed over her, chasing away the sadness. Her mother's choices had led Sairah down a very dark pathway. Now, Blaine would have to deal with Tevis and his magic due to those choices. Had Sairah chosen differently, things would not have escalated as they did. "Should have—would have," Blaine once again spoke out loud. It didn't matter. Sairah's pathway was her own and Blaine could not undo what had been done.

The first order of the business was clear; she had to retrieve the book. Shaking her head lightly to bring more clarity, Blaine focused on picturing the cavern where the book lay unguarded. In an instant Blaine found herself—body and all—back in the cavern. With very few candles burning, the once-lit cavern gave way to darkness. Acclimating to the cavern's environs, Blaine climbed out from behind the rocks, making her way to the altar.

In the dim light Blaine could see the bodies of the spinners Tevis had sacrificed to gain magic lying on the floor of the cavern. Blaine shuddered trying hard not to look at them as she approached the alter where the book lay. Reaching to pick up the ominous object, she remembered Maorga's words: "Everyone who ever touched the book was driven mad." She hesitated, subconsciously taking a step backward. *It's just a book*, she told herself. *A book filled with evil but still just a book.*

Blaine stared at the book for a minute as if waiting to hear it talk. It had, after all, evidently talked to Tevis. Her attention was then drawn to the hinged metal box upon which the book rested. Stepping forward Blaine reached out and touched the box. *This must be what sheltered the book all the years it was in Tevis's possession,* she concluded mentally. She decided she would simply pick up the book and place it as quickly as possible in its protective box. The book, however, had other plans. As she picked it up the sound of multiple screams filled her head. They hissed and swirled about her as they repeated over and over, "Bringer of

Light." Blaine dropped the book. It hit the ground with a thud followed by an unnerving silence.

Blaine wanted to flee the cavern like a child running from a haunted house, but she knew that was not an option. She took a deep breath and then reached over and picked up the metal box. Not taking her eyes off of the book, she fumbled with it until she found a recessed button that, when pressed, opened the lid. The metal box was lined with a heavy, dark colored fabric.

Blaine's task was interrupted as she realized that the cavern had grown considerably brighter. For an instant Blaine was fearful that someone with a lantern had entered. She, however, was relieved when she realized that the light was coming from her crystal. It was glowing, but somehow the light it emitted was different from the other times. Her relief was short-lived as once again she heard the hissing voices call her name. The fear it created reached her very soul.

"Open the book, Blaine!" The voice hissed again. Once again multiple voices filled her head as they demanded her to open the book.

Blaine's attention had been focused on the voices so she hadn't noticed that the crystal had surrounded her with light in an effort to insulate her from the evil. Then the light arced forming a bolt that struck the book. This got Blaine's attention. She focused all her energy on the crystal. As she did the light from the crystal became blindingly bright as another bolt shot out and struck the book for a second time, silencing the voices.

Blaine moved instinctively and swiftly. Picking up the metal box she kneeled next to the book. Being careful not to touch the book again, she used the box to maneuver it back into the metal container. She slammed the lid closed and latched it in place. Then as if guided by some unknown force she held her hand over the box. A flash pulsed from her and completely surrounded the box in a violet light. When the light faded Blaine knew the evil in the box had been sealed inside and that the universe was safe for now.

Clutching the box and holding it to her chest, Blaine took several steps away from the altar. She stumbled as her foot became entangled in the robe of one of the spinners. She looked down at the lifeless body and an uncontrollable anger began to rage deep in her soul. Now that she had possession of the box, there was one more task to complete.

CHAPTER 30

She closed her eyes trying to picture her mother's face. Just as she was about to focus on the image that appeared in her mind it disappeared. Elian's image became crystal clear in her thoughts. When she opened her eyes, she found herself standing in the middle of what appeared to be a campsite surrounded by soldiers. Startled by her sudden appearance, several men rushed forward pushing Blaine face down to the ground. She prepared to defend herself just as she heard Elian's voice ordering her attackers to stand down. Confused, Blaine looked up to see a figure kneeling at her side. "Blaine!" The figure whispered softly. "Are you all right?"

She looked around while wiping the dirt away from her mouth. "Yes. I'm fine," she answered. Blaine looked into Elian's eyes. It felt like it had been years since they had seen each other. She threw herself against him, hugging him tightly.

"Well, well, well, looks as if we have a surprise guest." Blaine recognized Armel's voice immediately. He was standing next to them, offering his hand. Relaxing her hold on Elian, Blaine gave Armel a quick smile. Taking his hand, Blaine rose to her feet.

They exchanged a quick embrace. "Sorry for the rude greeting," Armel continued. "We just don't get too many visitors popping into the middle of our camp unannounced and undetected by our spinners. Neat trick!"

"Yes, very impressive, Blaine. It seems your time with Fayendra was productive. Zone jumping is a very difficult maneuver, but you have obviously mastered the skill," Elian commented dryly.

"Yeah, I suppose, but it wasn't a zone jump. That's why your spinners were unable to protect your campsite," Blaine answered trying to explain something even she herself didn't understand completely. "There is so much I have to tell you!" Blaine said, her excitement at seeing Elian reflected in her voice and in her smile. Elian returned a reserved smile. Sensing the extreme change in his attitude toward her, she asked, "What's wrong?" Elian looked away not responding. Blaine's heart dropped.

In an effort to hide the extreme emotion she was feeling Blaine diverted her attention to her surroundings. A small group of men now encircled them. Blaine realized they were the forces Elian and Armel had gathered to face Tevis. *Tevis!* Blaine became alarmed. "The book!" Blaine exclaimed as she dropped to her knees in a desperate effort to recover the prize possession she had retrieved only minutes earlier. She was relieved as she spied the box lying in the dirt in front of her. She reached down and picked up the box that housed a world of evil. As she did so it became clear to her that now she alone was responsible for keeping this destructive force out of the reach of the those that would attempt to use it for their own gain.

Elian gave her a questioning look as he said, "Come, we can better talk over here." The surrounding warriors parted, allowing Elian to pass. Blaine followed him clutching the book tightly as she walked. He entered a small cave. She could hear him telling everyone to go about their way. Blaine entered behind Elian thinking to herself, *Great—another cave.*

A small fire burned in the middle of the cave, encircled by tree stumps. Elian sat down and motioned for Blaine to be seated across from him. Neither spoke. Blaine's heart ached. This was certainly not the reunion she had hoped for. Elian seemed so distant. He was not the same man she had left back on Alatis. Finally, Blaine could no longer stand the silence. "You seem distant," Blaine said timidly.

Elian took a moment before answering. He seemed to be searching for the words to respond to her comment. "I just wasn't expecting you to come back to Renault."

"You knew I had to retrieve the book. We discussed this—my pathway!" Blaine responded quietly. "Are you not happy to see me?" Blaine questioned still feeling hurt and puzzled by his reaction to her being there.

"I understand it's your pathway. I assume that the box you are holding so tightly contains the book, so your task here is completed." Elian's words were cold and emotionless.

"What's happened to you?" Blaine demanded as she jumped to her feet. Hoping for a response that didn't come, Blaine continued. "Surely you realize my task is not complete. I have no other choice than to deal with Tevis. He now possesses magic and I cannot let his evil be unleashed upon this universe. I am the only one strong enough to stop him." Elian once again remained silent. Blaine's patience had run out as she continued. She didn't even try to hide her sarcastic tone. "I was so very happy to see you, but clearly what we shared in the past is no longer valid."

Elian's expression softened. Finally, he gave a response. "Blaine, please sit back down. Of course, I'm happy to see you too. It's just ... " He paused, dropping his gaze to the fire. "I was hoping you could stay in Alatis where you would be safe. Deep in my heart I knew you would come, but I wanted you to be out of harm's way." He looked up at Blaine as he continued. "Even now you could choose to let us handle Tevis."

"I understand there are many choices I could have made. However, I know I am right where I am supposed to be. Everything in my life has led me here. I have never felt surer of anything. Even if it means that I am to lay my life on the line to stop Tevis, then that is what must be done," Blaine stated confidently.

"So that is it? You have chosen to do all in your power to stop Tevis." Elian stood up and took a few steps away from the fire as he spoke.

"Yes," Blaine answered simply.

Elian sighed as he turned to look at Blaine. She could tell he was done with this line of conversation. Her knowledge was confirmed as he changed the subject. "So, the ceremony to give magic to Tevis has been completed," Elian stated more than questioned.

"Yes, and it was horrific to watch," Blaine informed Elian.

"You witnessed it?" Elian asked as he seated himself next to Blaine.

"Yeah, I astral-projected into the cavern where it took place. It was almost unbearable to witness such evil and to not be able to stop it."

Elian remained quiet for a moment before he asked quietly, "Would it upset you too much to tell me about the ceremony?"

Blaine thought for a minute then answered, "Actually, I think it might help if I talk about it with you. There were six spinners, Tevis, and my mother present in the cavern." Blaine looked up and almost laughed when she saw Elian scrunch up his face at the mention of Sairah, as if he had just eaten something very sour. "First, my mother read an incantation from the Book of Death. Then each spinner placed something in a bowl. My mother took the bowl over to Tevis and after cutting the palm of his hand she used the bowl to collect the blood that flowed from the wound." Blaine paused and shifted uncomfortably before continuing. "The bowl was passed from spinner to spinner; each drank from it." Tears began to run down Blaine's cheeks as she recounted what happened next. "Tevis drank from the bowl as well." Blaine stopped, unable to put into words the heinous event she witnessed. Turning to Elian she took his hands in hers. After looking deep into his eyes for a moment she then closed her eyes and relived the scene that was burned into her memory.

Elian jumped with surprise as Blaine channeled her memory of the unspeakable events that followed. His face contorted with anguish as he saw all that Blaine had witnessed. Elian stood up and abruptly pulled away from Blaine. "Enough! Please, I've seen enough!"

They both remained silent. Elian paced back and forth in front of Blaine trying to process what he had seen. Finally, he stopped and looked at Blaine. "Do you realize the implications of this successful completion of the spell?"

"Yes," Blaine said dropping her eyes to avoid Elian's intensive stare. "In reality Tevis is now a vampire of the magic."

"Exactly," Elian confirmed. "He must feed or ... "

Blaine interrupted him, "Or he will lose his magic."

"No", Elian contradicted. "It is worse than that. It was a blood ritual—the darkest of dark magic. He must feed or die. He exchanged what was left of his soul for magic."

Blaine didn't respond. Her thoughts had turned to her mother and her part in perpetrating this inconceivable spell. *How could she not have known the depths of evil she had unleashed?* "He spoke to the book," Blaine blurted out.

"What?" Elian asked in astonishment.

Before Blaine could answer, a figure entered the cave. "Sorry to interrupt. Armel informed me of Blaine's arrival," Alderon said apologetically.

Elian nodded, giving Alderon his permission to join the conversation. Alderon took a seat next to Blaine.

Blaine was overcome with guilt as she timidly addressed the elder. "Alderon, I'm so sorry for leaving you without explaining."

"No apologies needed," Alderon interjected before Blaine spoke further. "You did what you had to do. I know how important your task is. It's just that I felt so useless. Elian arrived shortly after your departure and brought me here."

Blaine shot Elian a concerned look. "We feared for his safety. We had reason to believe that there is an informant in the group taking refuge at the volcano," Elian explained.

Blaine nodded in agreement but couldn't help feel concern that Alderon was now a member of the front line of defense against Tevis. She knew he would be the only one with the wisdom and ability to stabilize Renault after the defeat of Tevis. She, however, trusted Elian's judgment that his troops would be able to protect the elder.

Elian turned to Blaine anxious to acquire more information about this latest revelation. "Are you telling me the Book of Death and Tevis had a conversation?"

"I didn't actually hear the book talk to Tevis, but he definitely heard something. It was like being in a room with someone on the phone. I could only hear one end of the conversation. Nonetheless, Tevis did address the book as 'Master.' " Blaine explained.

Elian and Alderon exchanged strange looks. Noticing the exchange, Blaine asked, "Am I missing something?"

Alderon let out a long sigh. "As you know there isn't much history about the Book of Death—mostly folklore passed down from generation to generation. However, when I was younger I came across an old manuscript that I believe originated in Vestia, an enchanted realm." Alderon saw Blaine scowl at the use of the term "enchanted realm." He paused then explained, "An enchanted realm is one in which all the inhabitants possess magic." Seeing Blaine nodded in acknowledgment Alderon continued, "Vestia was during ancient times a world frequently visited by citizens of Renault. Its gateway was sealed long ago, even before the Council of Elders existed. That, however, is another story for another time. The manuscript I read spoke of an evil—an evil that could not be destroyed. This evil was described as extremely strong and merciless. After many attempts the people of Vestia were finally able to trap it in a book. To add extra protection against his evil ever escaping, the book was sealed in a metal box and then secured in a secret enchanted vault whose location was known to only a few."

"So, you believe this may be the same book described in the manuscript," Blaine questioned.

"I have always felt there was the possibility that they were one in the same. However, hearing your account of Tevis's verbal encounter, I am more sure than ever that they are one in the same," Alderon professed.

Blaine leaned over and picked up the box containing the book and offered it to Alderon. Alderon gasped in utter astonishment as he realized what Blaine held in her hands. Seeing Alderon's reaction she said reassuringly, "It's sealed."

"The book ... it's in there?" Alderon stammered as he carefully took the prize offered to him. He ran his fingers over the carvings on the box. Turning the box over and over in his hands, he continued, "I do not recognize the metal of which the box is made. It's black and appears as dense as lead, but it's so very light."

"Placing the book in the box seemed to stop the voices and screaming," Blaine mumbled under her breath.

"I thought you said you didn't hear the book talk to Tevis?" Elian questioned.

Feeling a bit uncomfortable, Blaine answered, "I didn't hear the book speak to Tevis. However, when I picked it up it seemed to shudder in pain and then it called my name. This was followed by many voices calling to me as the Bringer of Light. The voices ordered me to open the book. At that point I dropped the book and used the box to scoop it up and sealed the lid."

Alderon nodded. "This confirms the manuscript's description of how the entity trapped in the book will use any method to find a way to be free of its prison. It must have somehow been aware of the power that the Bringer of Light possesses. It perceived the possession of that power as a way to break free. Obviously, trapping the evil in the book diminished its abilities immensely."

"Maorga mentioned how all who handled the book were driven mad. I guess hearing voices no one else heard would make one appear crazy," Blaine added.

"So, it appears the origin of the book has been explained. How it was freed from its original hiding place, however, remains a mystery," Alderon concluded.

"Ultimately it doesn't matter!" Elian spoke up. "The book is contained. Now we must deal with Tevis."

"I'm afraid having contained the book will not end our dealings with it." Alderon needed Elian to understand how important it was to get the book out of the reach of anyone seeking the power of its evil content. "The book must be hidden with only Blaine knowing its whereabouts. You are right, Elian, about dealing with Tevis." Alderon continued, "He can only retain his magic by draining others of theirs. Without this regeneration he will lose power and die. I believe he only views Blaine as an extremely powerful spinner and is not aware of her gift of ancient magic. There is no telling what the addition of her ancient magic would do for him since it doesn't rely on the draining of life force. He could possibly stabilize his need to constantly feed on the magic of others were he to achieve his goal of possessing her. Either way, he must not be allowed to reach his goal."

Alderon's words made Blaine's heart skip a beat. She had ancient magic and it could add the element of stability making Tevis undefeatable. He was after her but wasn't aware of how her magic could turn the tide in his favor. If he knew, his efforts would be even more intense. She only hoped her mother had not told him about the ancient magic. Once again, the poor judgment of her mother could affect the outcome of the battle. She was sure Tevis would use Sairah to lure Blaine to him.

Blaine's thoughts were interrupted as she heard Alderon say, "It's best for everyone for Blaine to leave Renault with the book. That way he would never be able to obtain her power."

"No!" Blaine exclaimed. She looked from Alderon to Elian, then spoke her words carefully. "I believe Tevis to be calculating and intelligent. I am convinced he chose to draw the life force from his strongest spinners giving him great power. I understand that we have spinners with great ability also." She then turned her gaze to Elian as she continued. "Unfortunately, magic with no conscience is always going to trump a spinner that possesses a good heart."

Elian nodded in agreement. "She speaks the truth, Alderon. If he truly does possess and knows how to wield this newfound power, I believe as you do, that he is an extremely deadly opponent. Blaine, if you stay and confront Tevis," Elian paused and smiled at Blaine knowing she had already made up her mind, "hesitation will be your greatest foe!"

The vision Fayendra had shown her flashed through Blaine's mind. "Yes, I know this to be true," Blaine confirmed.

CHAPTER 31

Their conversation was interrupted by a loud explosion. Leaping to her feet, Blaine secured the box in her backpack and quickly followed Elian and Alderon out of the cave. As they exited the cave they were shocked to see that the ground outside was heavily peppered with burning debris. Several soldiers lay on the ground moaning in pain. Many others tried to take cover against the attack.

Elian pulled Alderon and Blaine into some bushes that were off to the side of the cave entrance. "Stay here!" he demanded. "Blaine keep alert," he further instructed as he darted off toward the chaotic campsite.

Blaine peered intently into the darkness watching figures run to and fro. She detected the sound of hand-to-hand combat. "This is maddening," Blaine whispered to Alderon. "I feel so helpless. I should do something."

"No, there's too much confusion. We need to stay put. Elian will return," Alderon said reassuringly.

Suddenly Blaine's crystal began to glow intensely. Instinctively, Blaine wrapped her arms around Alderon. Closing her eyes tightly, she was able to create a protective bubble around them just as a loud sonic wave spread out across the camp, knocking everyone in its path to the ground. At the same time a bright light rose from the other side of the forest. It was an orb which generated an intense light source. As it hovered above the camp it illuminated the area as if it was midday.

Blaine released her hold on Alderon, the protective bubble that had shielded them from the wave of destruction dissipated. The light from the orb revealed that the campsite was now littered with lifeless bodies. It seemed to Alderon that no one had been spared the wrath of the intense wave that had swept through it. "Is everyone dead?" Alderon whispered.

"No," Blaine answered quietly as she motioned to the far side of the forest where several figures emerged. "*Tevis*," Blaine hissed under her breath.

Tevis was shouting orders. "Find her. I know she was at this camp. I have been kept very well informed of every move made by this so-called army."

"It would seem our secure hiding place was compromised by a spy." Alderon sighed as he spoke.

"They are searching for me," Blaine said locking eyes with Alderon.

"I know. That is why you must leave. Go quickly!" Alderon urged.

"No!" Blaine responded. "This ends now!" Blaine closed her eyes blocking out everything around her as she focused on her breathing. Everything had led up to this crossroad. This was her destiny.

Opening her eyes, she focused on the five figures as they drew closer to her position. She watched as the soldiers and General Mitchell searched among the motionless soldiers. Tevis held Sairah tightly by the arm. Blaine took a deep breath. She then clasped Alderon's hand in hers as she addressed him. "Stay here. All of Renault needs you. You will be the voice of reason that will bring order and prosperity back to this land you love once Tevis has been defeated."

Not giving Alderon a chance to reply she stepped from her protective cover into the lighted campsite. As Blaine took several steps toward Tevis, she felt as though her heart would pound out of her chest. Then standing strong and tall she called out, "I am here!"

"Blaine! No!" Sairah cried as she struggled futilely trying to break free of Tevis's hold on her.

"Enough!" Tevis croaked at Sairah as he tossed her effortlessly to the forest floor. She tried to stand but was quickly knocked to the ground by a jolt of Tevis's magic.

General Mitchell lunged toward Sairah to help, but stopped dead in his tracks by the disapproving look Tevis shot him.

Blaine analyzed their interaction carefully. With one look General Mitchell had gone from a strong war hero, leader of men, to a little boy in desperate need of his father's approval. Blaine also took notice of the dark aura emitted from Tevis when he used his magic on Sairah. The aura seemed to have a life of its own, reaching out as if seeking all that was living.

Kern's voice reverberated in Blaine's head, "The souls of the spinners Tevis consumed."

Blaine's thoughts were interrupted as she heard Tevis let out a sinister cackle. He motioned toward Blaine, looking directly at General Mitchell as he mocked, "This ... this girl ... is the mighty spinner that has eluded you all this time?"

General Mitchell did not meet his father's eyes. Instead, he hung his head in defeat.

As Tevis drew closer to Blaine she saw Mitchell kneel down at her mother's side. When Tevis was about three feet from Blaine he stopped dead in his tracks as he stared wide eyed at Blaine. It seemed to Blaine that for just an instant his expression softened. "Do I remind you of someone?" Blaine questioned. Tevis's expression had once again grown hard and cold as he smirked at Blaine. "Does your son know that you murdered his mother?" Blaine continued her tone reflecting her disdain.

"He knows that sometimes there are hard choices that must be made to serve the greater good. Just like your mother's choices were all for the advancement of the cause," Tevis boasted.

Blaine did not even acknowledge his rationalization with a comment. Instead, she waved her hand and Tevis was immediately thrown to the ground.

He lay motionless for a moment. Then his evil voice filled the air as he slowly rose to his feet. "So that's how it's going to be?" As he waved his hand a fireball shot out and flew toward Blaine. Blaine's crystal glowed brightly and as the fireball entered the crystals glowing light it was extinguished effortlessly. "Perhaps I've underestimated you. I don't believe I've ever seen such a strong protective crystal. A gift from the elves I would imagine. The acquisition of such a special prize could definitely come in handy."

Hoping he had distracted Blaine with conversation, Tevis stamped his foot as he said loudly, "Evata caravens." Suddenly the ground began to rumble and the earth split creating a huge crater that reached out toward her. Blaine nimbly jumped aside as it attempted to swallow her. She landed safely to the left of the gaping ditch but was immediately knocked to the ground as Tevis blasted her with an electrical shock.

She lay motionless staring up at the artificially lit night sky. Tevis was now standing over her. "Not so strong after all," he quipped as he bent down and ripped Blaine's crystal from her neck. Blaine was helpless as jolts of electricity surged through her body.

Reveling in what he considered a victory, Tevis continued. "You see, my dear, though I have only recently gained the gift of magic I have studied and memorized every written word about the craft. With this knowledge I have easily harnessed my new-found talent. You, however, clearly have much to learn." Holding Blaine's crystal in his hand he examined it carefully. "But don't fret. Your generous gift will not go to waste. It makes a superb addition to my other attributes."

He raised his arms toward the sky as he spoke the words, "Savala depatis." Blaine, still unable to move, watched as the dark aura she had noticed before began to engulf her. She was unable to breathe as the aura began siphoning the life energy from her body. Her eyes rolled back in her head. Somewhere in the distance she heard her mother's scream ring through the night air as a blinding light blasted Tevis out of Blaine's blurred vision.

Blaine coughed and gasped as once again air filled her lungs. Sairah had rushed to her daughter's side. Kneeling next to Blaine she stroked Blaine's hair as she told her, "Breathe! My dearest daughter, you have to get up and leave this place immediately." Tears ran down Sairah's cheeks as she pleaded with her daughter. "I'm so sorry Blaine. If I had been as strong as you, I could have prevented all of this. I've been a fool, always putting my desires before anyone else's."

Blaine struggled to speak, "It's okay, Mom. I forgive you. I also need you to forgive yourself." Sairah broke down and began weeping uncontrollably. Blaine took her mother's hand in hers. "I love you, Mom."

"My sweet angel. I love you." Blaine then watched in horror as a bolt of red light suddenly shot through Sairah, dropping her lifeless body next to Blaine.

"Mom!" Blaine cried out in helpless anguish as the reality that she had just lost her mother set in. Somewhere nearby she that she had just lost her mother set in. Somewhere nearby she heard General Mitchell scream in despair.

"Enough!" Tevis's voice rang through the night as he released another blast toward his son. All went silent. Then Blaine could hear Tevis's footsteps as he drew closer to her. "Now let's try this again, this time without the interruption."

Blaine laid there for what seemed like an eternity, feeling lost and defeated, tears streaming down her face as she still clutched to her mother's lifeless hand. Then a peace came over her and she heard Kern's voice. "Blaine, you must find the strength to use the gift that has been bestowed upon you." A renewed sense of resolve filled her body as she propped yourself up on her elbows. She watched as Tevis approached her.

Tevis was only a few feet away when his attention was diverted; a voice called out to him. Tevis turned just as a blinding blast came from the edge of the forest line, striking him down. Blaine stared in the direction of the blast, to see a figure coming into view. Her heart jumped when she recognized Elian. Rising slowly to her knees, she attempted to steady her body as it shuddered from the effects of Tevis's magic.

Tevis quickly recovered from Elian's assault and directed a jolt in Blaine's direction. While attempting to avoid a direct hit, she clumsily lunged out of the way but was knocked back down to the ground despite her efforts. Blaine lay face down on the scorched earth struggling to regain her strength. Her vision was blurred but she could still make out the outline of Tevis as he effortlessly sidestepped a blast from Elian. She could hear Tevis and Elian quip back and forth but her hearing was distorted as if she were in a dream state.

Blaine closed her eyes and drew a deep breath in, *This will NOT end like this*, she demanded to herself. She focused on the universal energy flowing through her and imagined it amplifying like Fayendra had taught her. She could feel the energy restoring her strength. Opening her eyes, she focused on Tevis. He stood smiling sheepishly. Blaine's hearing was restored just as Tevis responded to one of his soldiers. "I have no need for that lonely spinner," Tevis hissed. Then pointing to Blaine he continued, "Her magic is all I'll need for a very long time."

Blaine turned her attention in the direction of the soldier's voice. She was also shocked to see Elian and Alderon being held captive. Elian's complexion was pale and fading; he appeared to be stunned and badly injured.

"What do you want us to do with the prisoners?" The other soldier asked.

"Kill them!" Tevis said as he waved his hand in the air in dismissal.

Blaine watched as both soldiers drew their swords. Panic filled Blaine's soul when she realized what was about to transpire. She drew a deep breath in an effort to focus. As the two soldiers raised their swords Blaine felt her strength slowly returning. The next few seconds seem to play out in slow-motion. She realized that the distance between Alderon and Elian was too great to allow her in her weakened condition to stop both soldiers from completing their tasks with one attack. She would have to send consecutive shock waves. She was sure she could save at least one; her hope was both. She sent a blast to the soldier guarding Alderon followed by a second blast to the soldier over Elian. She watched in horror as the sword held by the second soldier plunged into Elian a split second before her blast struck him down.

"No!" She screamed. Suddenly her body was filled with a new sensation. She had never felt such power. The ground shook and the wind blew furiously as an intense blast shot from Blaine's hand and pulsed through the air engulfing Tevis where he stood.

He held his hand out in front of him in what she thought was an effort to shield himself from Blaine's fury.

Blaine dropped exhausted to one knee. Everything around seem to be spinning out of control. She shut her eyes in an effort to gain equilibrium. When she opened her eyes, she expected to see Tevis lying lifeless in front of her. Instead, he stood there smiling smugly. Then Blaine realized he held her crystal in his hand. He hadn't been trying to shield himself, he had used her crystal to protect himself against her attack.

Tevis began laughing. "Apparently with this crystal, I am unstoppable!" His laughter, however, ended abruptly as a blinding white light from the crystal began to surround him. "What's happening?" Tevis screamed as the light continued to engulf him. Blaine heard Tevis scream in pain. He dropped the crystal, and as it fell freely to the ground it continued to glow with white hot intensity.

Blaine rose to her feet and approached Tevis. Bending down, she picked up the crystal. When she looked again at Tevis she was amazed to see each of the souls that Tevis had stolen from the spinners leave his body and rise into the heavens. Immediately after the souls had departed, Tevis was lifted off the ground. His shrieks of pain had stopped. Experiencing the same feeling of helplessness he had inflicted on so many victims, he stared at Blaine in disbelief. Blaine stared back, emotionless. Then holding the crystal in her hand, she smiled slightly as she channeled Kern as she spoke with authority. "An instrument of good may never be truly wielded by evil. Perhaps in all your studies you skipped that chapter." She heard Tevis scream one last time as the light imploded, reducing him to ashes.

Blaine stood watching as Tevis's ashes fell to the earth. She looked sorrowfully at her mother. General Mitchell, her father, now cradled Sairah's body in his arms, mourning silently. Blaine's heart ached for his and her loss. She then turned her attention to Elian. She rushed to his side and dropped to the ground next to him. Alderon was trying to attend to his wounded friend. The sky no longer reflected Tevis's magic. Dawn was breaking across the horizon.

Blaine held Elian in her arms and began to weep as she whispered, "Please don't die." But even as she spoke she could feel his life's energy slipping away. "Please don't leave me alone, Elian," she begged in between anguished sobs. "I love you," she told him as she kissed him on the lips.

Elian opened his eyes and raised his hand to Blaine's cheek, "I love you, too," he said gently as he exhaled his last breath.

"No, no, no!!" Blaine screamed. "Not this way; not him!" Elian's lifeless hand fell to his side. Blaine sat there cradling Elian in her arms, unable to think as Alderon said a quiet blessing over him. He watched as a familiar blue glow began to surround Blaine and Elian. Alderon stepped away as the two were lifted off the ground—Blaine still holding Elian in her arms. Then in a blink of an eye Blaine and Elian were gone.

CHAPTER 32

Blaine closed her eyes as everything began to blur into a world of colors. Unable to control her grief, she laid her head on Elian and began to sob uncontrollably. After the tears released some of her pain she realized she was still holding Elian but now they both rested on a carpet of purple moss under the canopy of a large tree that was adorned with leaves the colors of fuchsia and teal.

She had no idea what had just happened or where they were. Even though she was confused she remained where she was and laid her head back down on Elian's chest. Although her grief was overwhelming, she somehow took comfort in knowing Kern had transported them to this serene location. Physically and spiritually exhausted, she fell into a deep sleep.

"Blaine. Blaine, you must wake up," a sweet voice cooed. Blaine opened her eyes and took a deep breath. A light breeze danced across her, rustling the leaves above. She sat up and looked down at Elian. He looked peaceful. Tears rolled down her cheeks as she replayed the events of the last few hours in her head. She thought of her mother. She truly knew her mother's life decisions, no matter how misdirected, were made in the great love she had for her daughter. Even though her heart was breaking she also knew the decision to save Alderon was the only thing she could have done.

"Blaine," the voice came again. Startled, Blaine looked around for the source. "Don't be alarmed," whispered the childlike voice. The canopy of leaves shifted gracefully causing Blaine to look up. It seemed as if the tree had moved. Leaping to her feet, Blaine stared in amazement as the trunk of the tree morphed into a beautiful face.

Wide-eyed at what she had just witnessed, Blaine greeted the tree with a feeble "hello."

"I am sorry if I startled you," the voice cooed.

"No, it's fine. I shouldn't be surprised anymore at anything I see in Renault. I just thought I was alone," Blaine responded.

The tree giggled sweetly as it shifted its limbs slightly. "Oh, you are never alone, Blaine, Bringer of Light, and you are no longer in Renault. Kern brought you here to Vestia."

Blaine nodded in acknowledgment. The thought that Kern was still watching over her filled Blaine's heart with joy. *What a wondrous place*, she thought as she spied in the distance a crystal blue lake sparkling in the morning sun. Kern had brought her and Elian to this restful place. *Elian!* A wave of reality hit her as she remembered her loss. She felt all her strength being drained as she dropped to her knees, sobbing.

"Blaine!" The tree once again called out to her.

Blaine wiped her face with her arm in an attempt to compose herself. She looked up at the tree's beautiful face. "I'm sorry," Blaine said, standing as she spoke. "It's just that I feel so lost. I have no idea what I am to do next. I can't just leave Elian here— not like this." A gentle breeze swirled and gathered a bouquet of flowers that encircled Blaine in a fragrant embrace. Blaine took a deep breath and closed her eyes. Her body immediately relaxed and her thoughts cleared. It was then she remembered the book that was still secured to her back. This was her most important responsibility now.

Before she could continue further in this line of thought she was suddenly interrupted by a melodious cry from above. Blaine opened her eyes just as a scarlet bird streaked across the sky. She was mesmerized by its graceful flight as it left streaks of gold trailing behind it.

"Oh my!" the tree exclaimed in awe, "I haven't seen a Phoenix in hundreds of years."

Blaine turned her attention from the magnificent bird that circled about them and directed her gaze upon the tree. "A Phoenix?" Blaine questioned as she realized the bird had now begun to descend. Blaine suddenly felt a warm sensation course through her body. She looked down and saw that her pocket was glowing. She realized her crystal was still where she had hurriedly placed it earlier, and now it was responding to events as they unfolded.

The Phoenix had now landed and approached Blaine until he stood almost nose-to-beak with her. The stare from his golden eyes seem to pierce her very soul. He cocked his head to the right then to the left as he examined her. Blaine stood motionless. She felt very intimidated by this magnificent creature that stood in such close proximity to her. "Hello," Blaine whispered apprehensively. The Phoenix chirped back softly in reply. "Do you speak?" Blaine asked. The majestic bird cocked its head to one side as if trying to discern her words. He then ruffled his feathers revealing their underside. They looked as if they had been dipped in gold. "I guess that is a no." Blaine then turned back to look at Elian laying so still under the enchanted tree that was now so graciously shading him from the warming morning sun.

The Phoenix let out a loud cry that rang through the morning air and reverberated off the surrounding hills. Startled, Blaine jumped as she let out a scream. The Phoenix seem to ignore her as he pushed past her and walked over to Elian. Standing by his side, the Phoenix began to sing a haunting melody that brought tears to Blaine's eyes. The tree swayed in time to the hypnotic song. Tears that sparkled like diamonds streamed from the magnificent bird's eyes and splashed down onto Elian.

Blaine knew that mythology had claimed that the tears of the Phoenix had healing power. She sighed in despair because she knew Elian had died. Healing power was too little, too late.

The Phoenix continued his song for several more minutes. He then let out another loud cry as he took flight like a bolt of lightning and vanished from sight.

Blaine stood there dazed by the events of the last few minutes. "Blaine," the tree called out to her once again.

Snapping out of her trance, Blaine replied, "I'm sorry. I did not mean to be rude. I was just trying to understand what that was all about. Did the Phoenix come to pay his respects to Elian?"

"See for yourself." the tree urged gleefully.

Blaine looked at Elian in disbelief as she saw his eyes twitch slightly. She rushed to his side. Kneeling down, she called his name timidly. Elian opened his eyes slowly. After blinking several times, he replied, "Blaine?" His voice was hoarse and dry.

"I can't believe it—you're alive!" She exclaimed as she took him in her arms. Elian groaned slightly. Blaine released her hold on him. "Oh, I'm sorry. Did I hurt you?" She asked as she surveyed the area where the wound had been. It was now completely healed.

"No, you didn't hurt me. I do, however seem to be a little sore. What happened? I can't recall much at the moment." He then met her eyes as he asked, "Did you tell me you loved me?"

Blaine began to giggle as Elian sat up. She hugged him

tenderly. "I'm not sure you would believe me if I told you," she whispered in his ear. Elian wrapped his arms around her. Blaine closed her eyes as tears of joy ran down her cheeks.

Suddenly movement at the far end of the tree-lined meadow caught her attention. She spied Kern and watched him as he turned and disappeared into the trees. Blaine drew back slightly from Elian.

"What's wrong?" Elian asked.

"I just saw Kern," she replied.

Elian turned and surveyed the area that had caught Blaine's attention. "I do not see anything. Your eyes must be playing tricks on you."

"No, I'm sure it was Kern," Blaine responded quietly.

"If it had been Kern, he would have come over to see us," Elian added.

"Yeah, I guess you're right," Blaine replied not feeling fully convinced. She knew in her heart of hearts that her eyes were not playing tricks on her. She had seen Kern. She then turned her attention back to Elian. Looking into his eyes, she smiled broadly.

"You never answered my question. Did you tell me that you loved me?" Elian teased.

"Seriously?" Blaine mocked. "That's the one thing you want to know—not where are we and how did we get here? Or maybe you might be curious as to why your clothes are bloodstained?"

Elian paused a moment before he responded. "Yes, seriously. That's the one question I want answered!"

They both began laughing as Elian wrapped his arms around Blaine in a warm embrace. "All right, fine. Then since you are clearly not going to answer my first question, I'll go with where are we, how did we get here, and why are my clothes bloodstained. Oh, and is that tree smiling?"

Blaine looked around at the beauty of the magical land

they now occupied and began telling Elian everything that had happened. Blaine then removed the backpack that contain the book and set it in her lap. She knew her life's path still held many challenges. She had been brought to this land for a reason and she knew her involvement with the book was not over. She was beginning to realize the loss of her mother and the battle with Tevis was only one step on her life's pathway. She reached into the backpack and touched the box that housed the book. She then looked at Elian. She was unsure of where her pathway would lead her, but for now she knew she was right where she wanted to be—at the side of the man she loved.

ABOUT THE AUTHOR

KJ Moullen started her life as an adventurer. She always loved the outdoors, whether it was playing king of the hill with her pet goat in southern California, playing hockey on the frozen lakes of the Kenai peninsula of Alaska, or snorkeling and surfing off the shores of Maui. Amongst the breathtaking places she lived, her imagination and love for writing knew no limitations, allowing for a lifetime of plotlines and characters to be created and written about. She now shares her life's adventures with her husband and two children in their home in North Texas.

Have a book idea?
Contact us at:

info@mascotbooks.com | www.mascotbooks.com